MONKEY TAG

MONKEY TAG

PETE FROMM

SCHOLASTIC HARDCOVER

Scholastic Inc.
New York

Library of Congress Cataloging-in-Publication Data

Fromm, Pete, 1958–
    Monkey tag / Pete Fromm.
        p.   cm.
    Summary: When seventh grader Thad suffers a serious injury while playing monkey tag, his twin brother Eli blames God for the accident and becomes convinced that his Catholic upbringing is a fraud.

ISBN 0-590-46525-2

    [1. Accidents—Fiction.   2. Wounds and injuries—Fiction.
    3. Twins—Fiction.   4. Brothers—Fiction.   5. Catholics—Fiction.]
I. Title.
PZ7.F92033Mo   1994
[Fic]—dc20
                                                                93-34593
                                                                      CIP
                                                                       AC

12   11   10   9   8   7   6   5   4   3   2   1   4   5   6   7   8   9/9

Printed in the U.S.A.   37

First Scholastic printing, October 1994

To my mother, Mary Ellen, who showed me how to think and wonder and hope.

The author would like to thank Anne Gale for her generous help in preparing the manuscript.

MONKEY TAG

CHAPTER
ONE

"Monkey tag's more fun anyway," Thad said without lifting his face from the dew-damp October grass. "There's enough of us here for monkey tag."

The sun blanketed the five boys as they waited for enough people to show up for football. Eli, Thad's twin, sat up, ripping out a handful of grass and throwing it into the air. "Where is everybody?" he said. There weren't even any cars on the street bordering the football field. It was like the end of the world, Eli thought, and they were the only survivors; Thad and him, and Max and Sonny. And Roger, too, he guessed, since he was here, but Eli wished Roger'd disappeared with the rest of the world. "It's like we're the last ones alive," he said.

"Nope," Max said. "My dad's alive for sure. And

he's wondering how come I'm not mowing the lawn. 'Got to get one good mowing in before the snow flies,' " he added, sticking his head into his neck to lower his voice like his father's.

Eli laughed. Max was so scrawny you couldn't believe him ever having a voice like that. Eli threw a handful of grass at him. "I think maybe time stopped, you know, like in that one movie, 'cept for that one guy. But we're the guy now."

"Nope," Max said, throwing grass back at Eli. "My dad says this is just Indian Summer. He says it's almost over." When no one said anything else, Max added, "He says this is the hottest October in five years."

"Since we were seven," Sonny said without looking up.

"Since 1965."

Thad rolled his eyes. "Thanks for helping me figure that out," he said. He sat up then. With his brown bangs cut straight across his forehead, he was a nearly identical copy of his brother, Eli. "Come on you guys," he said. "Let's play monkey tag."

Eli glanced at the bleachers flanking the football field. He didn't want to play monkey tag. He leaned forward, stretching his sweatshirt tight, feeling the heat of the sun across his back. He shivered, thinking of being under the bleachers, out of the sun, swinging hand-over-hand through the scaffolding. The steel would be cold. "We can wait a little more," he said. "Maybe time didn't stop."

Thad stood up and tossed Roger's football into the air. "Who wants to go out for a pass?" he said. No one moved and he tossed the ball to Eli. Eli ran his fingertips up and down the rough pigskin and glanced back toward the street, but there were still no cars. With the cool, gentle breeze, and the smell of the grass, it was one of those days that always reminded Eli of apples. But suddenly there was something lurking behind all that. He wished a car would drive by. Or that somebody else would show up — that anybody else would appear to be alive at all. He stood up and tossed the ball to Thad, but Thad threw it right back.

Eli held the ball as Thad broke into a run. Maybe it was just the thought of losing the last warm days of fall. Though you knew you couldn't stop the winter, there were always a few days like this — even at the end of October — that made you think maybe this time it wouldn't come and kill everything. Eli launched the ball, overthrowing his brother by a mile. He could throw harder than anybody.

Sonny got up, ready to cover Eli when Thad passed back. Eli started to walk away from him. "Come on, Max," he said. "You can cover Thad." He ignored Roger, even though it was his ball. Maybe they could get a game going with just the four of them. Eli looked at the bleachers. They seemed darker than he remembered. "Come on, Max," he said again, but Max didn't move.

Thad threw the ball back and, for a few minutes,

Eli hoped a game of catch would be good enough. Sonny even intercepted once and Eli had to tackle him before he scored. They were laughing and Eli tried again to get Max into the game. Then Roger stood up and wanted his ball back.

Eli dodged Sonny's pass rush and threw the ball to Thad, trying to ignore Roger even though he knew it was too late. There was something not right about the day. Why hadn't anybody else shown up? They played the same time every Saturday and people always showed up.

Roger walked after Thad, tucking his shirt over the chubby roll creeping above the top of his jeans. "Those guys aren't coming," he said, cornering Thad. "I'm not wasting a whole Saturday playing catch with you guys. Gimme the ball, Thad."

Thad grinned at him, waved the ball a little, then punted. He was running before Roger could attack.

"Don't kick it!" Roger shouted. "The laces are almost busted." He ran to the group fumbling for the punt, bunching his fists.

He caught Sonny just as he broke from the pack. He knocked him down and tore the ball away as Sonny dodged the punches.

Roger stalked off, inspecting the football's bulging, frazzled laces. He showed Thad his fist as he passed. "I'da killed you if the laces got busted."

Thad grinned and stuck up the middle finger of his right hand, then ran laughing as Roger gave a hopeless charge. Thad slowed to a teasing skip and

Sonny and Eli backed off warily as Roger stomped off toward the street, his ball clamped under his arm. When he was almost to the street Eli shouted, "Jerkface tub-o'-lard!"

"Why do you even hang around with him?" Thad asked Sonny.

"I don't know. He's not so bad all the time."

"He's a jerk," Eli said.

"He thinks he's so neat, just 'cause he's a year older."

"Yeah. An eighth grader. Big deal."

"If he was so neat, he sure wouldn't be playing with us."

"So, what are we gonna do?"

"I wonder why nobody came today."

"Who knows."

Without a ball to toss, Eli stuck his hands in his pockets. "What do you want to do?" he asked, afraid of the answer, but even more afraid someone would guess he was scared to play monkey tag.

Swinging hand-over-hand through the bleacher scaffolding, monkey style, as if it were a giant jungle-gym, was always a little scary. The top of the bleachers was high enough to make your stomach hurt. Eli had played monkey tag tons of times, but now he knew for certain that this was a bad day. He pictured Vince's two front teeth, so bright and big, lying on the gravel beneath the bleachers after Vince had fallen last year. Vince hadn't even been very high up.

5

"Monkey tag," Thad said.

Sonny groaned, but Max said, "There's nothing else to do."

They started to wander toward the visiting team bleachers, but Thad pointed across the field. "Why don't we use those?"

Eli looked over to the towering home team seating, twice as tall as the visitors' side they'd always used before. Slowly they changed directions and started toward them.

"No tag-backs," Max said.

"Yes tag-backs," Eli shouted, not sounding as sure as he'd wanted.

"Anybody can play no tag-backs," Sonny said.

"Well, any tag counts then." They'd all had close calls trying to twist around for a tag-back. The person who'd just made a tag was so close the temptation to flip around and transfer "It" back to him was irresistible. Being able to tag with anything, particularly the feet, made it a little easier, and much safer. Vince had fallen while trying to make a hand tag on a tag-back. He wasn't allowed to play with them anymore.

They agreed to the any-tag rule and ducked into the shade beneath the cracked and peeling wooden seats. They stopped, resting their hands on the slick, tubular steel. Peering through the slatted bars of light and shade they tried to see the top row of seats, but their eyes hadn't adjusted.

"I bet you winter starts tomorrow," Eli said, shivering, but Max yelped, "Not it!" and was off, running down the first aisle, ducking the crossbars at every second row. Thad scrambled up the bars shouting, "Not it," an instant before Sonny and Eli did.

Eli tagged Sonny and broke to his right. He was nearly at the end of the stand when he started up.

Sonny cracked his head ducking too late to avoid a crossbar, missing the vital tag-back. Thad was high and away, with Eli climbing fast. Only Max was still on the ground. Sonny ducked and raced after him.

Max climbed as soon as he saw the pursuit.

"Look out, Max! He's right behind!"

Sonny paused at the shout and saw Thad resting on a crossbar at the highest section of bleacher. Then he closed in, hand-over-hand through the bars, until he tagged the more cautious Max.

Max wheeled, gripping the bar with both hands, and kicked, just nicking Sonny with his tennis shoe. "Got you back," he shrieked, climbing instantly. He was at the center of the stand, in a row where no crossbars interfered, and he flew up the ladderlike scaffold.

Thad scampered through the tangle of bars, coming tantalizingly close to Sonny. Although Sonny was aiming for Max, Thad would get so close that Sonny almost had him several times. By the time he gave up, Max had crossed the entire length of the bleachers and dropped to a safer altitude.

Eli had climbed out of the way and stopped, holding tightly to the bars, watching Thad swing and drop as if there were no ground to hit. He wished he could do that, and he told himself again that he wasn't afraid so much, it was just that maybe time had stopped and they should be out doing something about it — not wasting time playing dumb games. But they were closing in on him and Eli started to move carefully away.

Thad dropped by right in front of Sonny, actually falling, only to catch the bar below him and swing up and away. "Come on, Sonny!" he howled.

Sonny turned and climbed after him, just catching a glimpse of Eli moving the other way, one set of bars over. Sonny twisted, thwacking Eli on the rump, screaming "Got you," even as he raced down the network of piping.

Thad cackled, flipping over and swinging upside down from his knees several levels above Eli. His hair hung straight down and a bit of saliva escaped his mouth and strung along his cheek.

"You're drooling on yourself!" Eli yelled.

Thad let go with his knees, catching the bar below with his hands and swinging to the next set of bars. He swung his left hand as he let go with his right and the race was on.

But Eli knew Thad always went to the top, because everybody got scared up there and slowed down. He angled to cut him off and, even though this was higher than he'd ever been, he knew he wouldn't get scared this time. For once he'd catch Thad at the top, even on the home team bleachers.

Thad didn't look around until he reached the uppermost level. He had worked his way to the highest corner and turned to fly down the high aisle. But Eli was already there, breathing hard, a tight smile on his face.

Thad grinned and flexed his grip on the bar just below the last, grayed, pine seat. He shouted, "Here I am, Eli!" and started to swing hand-over-hand, directly at him, ignoring the screams from Sonny and Max, telling him he was a goner this time.

Eli peeked down the gray bars, crisscrossing and tapering away as they descended into forever. Quickly he glanced back to Thad and swallowed. He began to swing toward him. Ignoring the ground, Eli concentrated on the feel of the clammy steel and on the stomach-pulling lurch of the rise and fall. The distance between him and his brother closed.

Eli swung on, his tongue poking out of the corner of his mouth in concentration, infuriated by Thad's laughing, unable to understand why he didn't try to escape. With only two rows of scaffolding separating them, Eli realized how he'd been tricked.

Thad suddenly gave a tremendous swing, hurtling diagonally through the section, his hand reaching for the bar in the row to the left and one down from Eli.

Eli was caught in mid-swing, the wrong hand out, going too fast, and too far. He twisted dangerously, reaching out for Thad. But the twist was too severe. He felt his wrist roll as far as it would go, peeling his fingers off the bar. He lunged back into his own row, squeaking out a small, "Gotcha," even though he'd missed the tag.

Eli thudded to a halt, hitting his side against the crossbar. He gripped it tightly with both hands, his feet solidly on the bar below him, and fought down the sickening bile taste in his mouth, still too scared to be mad about being tricked. He turned to see if Thad believed he'd been tagged.

Thad was gone.

Eli only saw the last little bit of the fall. He watched his brother tumble down, cartwheeling off almost every bar. He fell straight for a moment, as if lying on his back, then hit a crossbar with his lower back. Thad twisted slowly off, striking one more piece of steel with his head and pancaking onto his back, his arms out to his sides, like the crucifix in their room at home.

After the twirling cracks ended in that last solid *whump*, the silence closed in beneath the bleachers. Eli's white-knuckled grip on the bar before him tightened. He stared at the motes floating in the bands of sunlight angling below the seats. "Thad?" he croaked.

Eli forced his trembling legs to the next rung down, starting the long descent. Sonny and Max began to drop then, reaching Thad before Eli was halfway down.

"Look at his arm," whispered Sonny.

"What!" Eli yelled.

"His arm's broke."

Closer to the ground, Eli descended rapidly.

"There's blood coming out of his mouth," Max said when Eli's feet were at head level.

Eli dropped the rest of the way, his feet hitting the dirt with a slap that lifted a tiny cloud into the air. He glanced at Thad and pictured him kicking up a body-shaped cloud of dust. "Thad?" he said.

"He might be dead," Sonny whispered.

"Shut up!" Eli bellowed, hitting Sonny so hard he fell over himself. He crawled to Thad's head and lifted it up, touching the blood around his mouth. "He's not dead. He just busted up his mouth is all. Like Vince."

Thad's forehead was already swelling, turning a faint blue on the side. Eli touched the bump, leaving traces of blood over it. He thought again of the body-shaped cloud and wondered if that's what Thad's soul would look like rising out of his body.

"I could fill up some balloons at the bubbler," Max said. "He could suck on one the way Vince did when he bit his tongue."

Eli cradled his brother's head. "Yeah, hurry up, Max."

Silence surrounded them after Max left and Eli looked over Thad to Sonny. "Come on, Sonny. Let's get him out of here. We need to get him to the sunlight."

Sonny grabbed an arm and Eli reached for the other. He waved Sonny away. "This one's smashed. Let's get his legs."

As they pulled Thad to the sunlight Sonny said, "You shouldn't've hit me. He could be, you know."

"Could be what?" Eli answered, not listening to a thing beside the scrape of his brother's body over the dirt and paper cups beneath the bleachers. He began to pray vaguely for Thad and for the sunlight.

"Could be dead."

"Don't ever say that!" Eli hissed, but now he knew that time would never stop.

When he felt the sun on his back Eli mumbled, "That's far enough." He looked at his brother lying on the cinder track with the sun stretching calmly over him. "Don't be dead, Thad. Don't be dead," he whispered. "God, don't let him be dead!"

Max crunched across the cinders, dripping wet, pinching three water balloons against his skinny chest. "One broke."

Eli took a balloon and held it to Thad's mouth, letting some of the water trickle through the pinched-off neck. "Drink some, Thad," he murmured. Some of the water went into his mouth and bubbled bloodily back out. Thad started to cough.

"Come on, Thad, like Vince, you know. Squirt it around and spit it out." Eli let a little more water out.

Thad began choking in earnest and his eyelids flickered. He settled down again, the water dribbling across his chin and cheeks, not wearing through the coagulating blood.

"Eli?" Max ventured. "Eli, he's hurt pretty bad."

Eli nodded dumbly, letting the balloon sink to the track where it burst. He pushed Thad away from the muddy, black puddle. "We gotta take him home."

"I don't think we can carry him that far," Sonny said.

"Well, he's not dead!"

"I'm gonna get my mom," Max said. "We live the closest."

"We'll take him there." Eli jumped up. "You guys get that side."

"I'm getting Mom. She'll bring the car." Max was already off and running.

"Max!" Eli yelled, but stopped, knowing his parents would have to find out anyway.

"Let's take him to Max's," he said to Sonny. "We'll pick him up. You get that side."

They lifted Thad as carefully as they could. Eli pinched his head against Thad's to keep it from swinging and they staggered down the track toward the street.

They rested once at the top of the slope, then struggled to the sidewalk and turned toward Max's house. Eli's neck began to cramp, but every time he glimpsed his brother's bloodstained face he knew he couldn't release the pressure. Somehow it was good to have his head against Thad's.

Sonny had the side with the broken arm. Eli

13

watched it, realizing for the first time that he was looking at bone. He began to cry quietly. "He can't be dead, Sonny," he said.

Sonny nodded, blinking back the sweat around his eyes.

"He just can't be," Eli said. "Come on, Thad," he cried. "Why'd you have to fall?"

The Bergs' blue station wagon screeched against the curb and Max's mother ran around the front. Mrs. Berg's hand shot to her mouth when she saw Thad. Eli stared at her, his face tear-streaked and smudged with blood. "He just fell."

"Oh, my Lord," she whispered. She reached around Eli to help support Thad and said, "Let's put him down, boys."

They eased Thad onto the grass. Mrs. Berg bent over Thad and began to mumble to herself. "He seems to be breathing all right. But that arm! He *never* should have been moved."

Eli and Sonny glanced at each other, but Mrs. Berg jumped up. She gripped Eli by both shoulders. "Everything will be all right, Eli. I'm going to the police station. They'll bring an ambulance. You stay right here."

Eli wilted at the mention of the ambulance. He knew they were only for very sick people — and for dead people.

"Eli," Mrs. Berg emphasized, giving him a gentle shake. "He's hurt very badly. Don't let anyone else

take him, and *don't* move him again. He'll be OK,"
she added. "I've got to hurry."

Max lunged out of the passenger door a moment
before the station wagon sped off. He edged over
to where Eli and Sonny stood. "Wow," he whispered, "an ambulance." He bent over Thad. "Do
you think he can hear us? Boy, if he knew he got
to ride in an ambulance!"

"Don't touch him," Eli warned. "Your mom said
we shouldn't have moved him. She said don't let
anyone else move him."

Max stepped back. The three boys looked at each
other. Sonny glanced at Thad. "You made me help
move him," he mumbled.

"Shut up, Sonny," Max whispered.

Eli looked at Max. "Your mom said he'd be all
right."

Max pointed at the side of his own face, at the
edge of his blond crew cut. "You got blood on you,
right here."

Eli rubbed absently at his temple. "She said he'd
be all right," he repeated.

"My mom used to be a nurse," Max said.

"Really?"

Max nodded. "So she should know."

They all turned to the starting wail of the siren
and saw the white and red van wheel around the
corner and begin to accelerate, its lights blinking
and flashing. When it pulled over, two attendants

jumped from the rear with boxes that looked like Eli's father's tackle box.

In minutes Thad was transformed. A splint encased his arm and tubes ran from his nose to an oxygen bottle and another smaller tube ran into his unbroken arm. Before Eli knew it, the men had Thad tied to a board and shut into the ambulance.

Mrs. Berg stood in front of Eli. "I called your parents. They're going right to the hospital. You'll come home with me."

"I'll walk home," Eli said quickly. The ambulance pulled around in a three-cornered turn and the siren started again.

"I guess I better go, too," Sonny said. He climbed over the slope without anyone saying good-bye.

"I'm gonna go, too," Eli said, looking at the flattened grass where the men had worked on Thad.

"You come with us, Eli," Mrs. Berg said. Turning to Max she told him to get into the car.

"I can walk home. Thad and I always walk from here." Eli had stopped crying but the tear tracks were visible on his dirty face. He pushed his brown bangs away from his eyebrows. "I'll just walk," he repeated.

"Now, Eli, your parents left already. The house will be locked. They asked me to bring you home. They'll call as soon as they know."

"Know what?"

"How Thad is."

"You said he'd be all right."

"He will be. But he's hurt and it's going to take time for him to get better."

"I know that. But he's going to get better?"

"I'm sure of it, Eli," she answered. "Come on, let's go home."

Eli studied her face a moment more. "I know where they hide the key," he said. "I'll walk." He held Mrs. Berg's eyes for another instant. "Thanks," he blurted and ran dead away from the street and over the hill that would hide him from everyone. He barely heard her yelling for him over the pounding of his blood in his ears.

CHAPTER
TWO

It wasn't until Eli was weaving through the short patch of trees beyond the football field that he realized he was crying again. In third grade he and Thad had vowed that no matter what happened they would never cry again. Now, four years later, the pact didn't seem very important. He just didn't want to cry. He flung himself down at the edge of the woods to see if Mrs. Berg would circle the fields, looking for him.

He didn't have anything to cry about, he told himself. Thad would be all right. He'd have a cast. Eli glanced at his own arm, imagining how high the cast would go.

They'd both get it for playing on the bleachers, though. That was for sure. Vince's mom had called after Vince fell. Nothing happened except they were told not to play there anymore. Eli knew playing on the higher side wouldn't count as "not playing there anymore."

When there was no sign of Mrs. Berg's station wagon, Eli ran across the street, not slowing until he was nearly halfway home. He stuffed his hands deep in his pockets and kicked his way through the leaf piles. Why had she said, "I'm sure of it," when he asked if Thad'd be all right? Why couldn't she have just said yes? And why shouldn't they have moved him?

Eli cut through the usual alleys, finally walking down the Crazy Lady's driveway and looking across the street at his own house. Even from here the house looked abandoned. Eli turned and walked back up the drive and into the Crazy Lady's empty garage. He climbed the rough wooden ladder through the black hole in the ceiling. He pulled the ladder up behind him and lay down in the dust, inching forward until he was in front of the cracked, grimy window.

Eli drew lines through the dirt on the glass with his fingers and studied the bars the sun cast through them onto the floor and across his legs. He thought of the black hole the ladder led into and how every-thing was like that now. He wondered if Thad would ever come back out of that hole.

He tried to wonder what Thad was doing now, or what was happening to him. But Eli had only been

19

in a hospital once, when some old aunt or someone was sick. That had been a long time ago and he couldn't remember what a hospital was like. He could only picture brightness and strong smells and whispering.

He suddenly remembered that he and Thad had gone to the old lady's funeral right after the visit to the hospital. He relaxed though, realizing he really couldn't remember how soon after the visit the funeral was. And old people die all the time.

Eli looked out the window and though he could see nothing but leafless branches and the neighboring garage, he thought about how his house had looked. It was the same as ever, but somehow different, with everyone who lived there at the hospital now. Except for him. He didn't want to go into that house, but he knew he had to. He was the only one left who could. He thought he knew how that one guy in the movie must've felt. The one who was the last guy left in the world after time had stopped.

Eli turned away from the window and slid the ladder carefully back through the hole. He climbed to the floor without looking back up to the dark opening. He glanced around the garage and tried to wonder if the Crazy Lady ever came back here anymore. He wondered how long it had been since she'd owned a car, and what it had looked like. But Eli couldn't pretend there was anything to think about except Thad, and he slipped through the broken door and retraced his steps down the drive to his house.

At the back door Eli reached for the hidden spare key before he saw that the door was open. He couldn't remember the last time it had been left unlocked. Maybe they were back already.

He closed the door behind him and yelled. When no one answered he leaned back against it. It was a very rare opportunity to have the house to himself. Every Sunday, after he finished his paper route, he would eat breakfast by himself, enjoying being awake and alone in the house while everyone else slept. It only happened once a week — only the Sunday papers came in the morning. After breakfast he'd pad quietly through the still house — so changed in the predawn vacancy.

Sometimes Thad would wake up while Eli dressed for the route and sometimes he would get up, too. Walking along with Eli, Thad would help carry the enormous papers, and they would talk, interrupting themselves at each house while Eli charged up and dropped a paper.

That was good, roaming the deserted streets, never raising their voices above a whisper, even when there was no reason to whisper. But once they were back in the house everything was normal because Thad was up, too. So, even though he liked to do his route with Thad, he never *tried* to wake him, or ask him to go along.

Eli walked through the house quietly, barely realizing he was making an effort to do so. He sat down in his father's mohair chair and crossed his legs like his dad's, one ankle across the other knee. He flipped his foot back and forth like his dad did when irritated. He pulled at his chin and raised his eyebrows. That was how his dad would look when he asked them where they had been playing.

Eli stood up at the thought of his dad. He walked into the kitchen. The table was set for two. The bread and lunch meat were out, but not yet opened. A single, unopened bottle of beer was on the table, sweat rivulets streaking its side. Eli picked up an opener and spun it on the table.

They'd really run out of here, Eli realized. He thought of how his parents teased each other about the bottle of beer they split each week. His father demanded it icy cold, while his mother liked it warmer. They hadn't even put it back in the refrigerator. "Wouldn't a taken two sec's," Eli mumbled. He wiped the water off the bottle and slid it back into its spot in the refrigerator.

He headed down the hallway and looked out the window, glad to be out of the kitchen. Eli stared at the spot where the car should have been and flattened his hand against the window, wriggling it to let the coolness touch the center of his palm. A tiny ring of condensation formed around his fingers, dissolving as soon as he removed his hand. Eli rested his forehead against the glass and closed his eyes, wondering why his stomach should feel upset.

Eli walked through the rest of the house then, through all of the rooms. He stopped at his room. He looked from his own unmade bed to Thad's. Eli didn't think he'd ever heard the house so quiet. He wondered if from now on their room would always be this silent.

The jangle of the phone made Eli jump. He ran out of the room as if he'd been caught at something. When the phone rang again he started down the stairs to the kitchen. He picked the phone up on the fifth ring.

"Eli?" a woman's voice blurted. "Where have you been, Honey? I've been trying for an hour."

Eli held the phone to his face, breathing rapidly.

"Eli? This is Mrs. Berg."

"Oh."

"Your father just called me. He's leaving for your house. They need you at the hospital. Where have you been?"

"What for?" Eli said, sinking onto the bench at the kitchen table. He picked at the wrapping on a roll of sausage. He felt so small he pushed himself against the back of the bench to keep from falling off.

"Thad might need you. Your father will explain."

"OK," Eli said, hanging up the phone, listening to Mrs. Berg's voice growing smaller before snapping off.

Eli continued to sit at the table, his back pressed

uncomfortably against the wooden bench. His hand tingled from pushing against the seat. He rolled the sausage back and forth, back and forth.

He heard the car advance up the drive and stop. Then the back door whooshed open. Eli glanced up as his father strode into the kitchen. He wished he hadn't seen the expression on his father's face before it was hidden with a smile. "Hello, Eli," he said, sliding onto the bench next to him. His father's arm came around his shoulders and Eli knew Thad must have died.

"We've got to hurry," his father started, rocking Eli in the unusual hug.

"How come?" Eli asked, pushing his face into the scratchy wool of his father's Saturday shirt.

"Because Thad may need you."

"Isn't he dead?"

He felt his father pull back, knowing he was looking at him but Eli kept his head down. "No. Of course not," he said.

Eli glanced up at his father and knew it was the truth. He liked his father's face on Saturdays, the day he let the whiskers go.

"He's pretty banged up, Eli," his father said. He slid off the bench, pulling Eli after him. "Let's get upstairs and get your things."

"What things?" Eli asked, having to run as his father took the steps three at a time.

"You get pjs, I'll get a toothbrush. You might have to spend a night at the hospital."

Eli stopped at the top of the stairway, his face blank. "Dad," he said, "Thad fell. I'm fine."

His father turned and almost laughed. "I know that, Eli." He walked back down the hallway and squatted next to Eli.

"Here's the scoop," his father started, smiling and rubbing Eli's tousled brown hair. "Thad has damaged some of the stuff on his insides."

Eli gazed at his father.

"They've had to take out one of his kidneys." He rubbed the small of Eli's back, where the kidneys lie. "Now the other one's fine. You only need one. God gave everybody two just for things like this."

Eli waited, wondering if he was supposed to believe God gave everybody two kidneys just in case they fell off a bleacher.

"He should be fine, but he's hurt badly enough that the load might be too much for the other kidney."

"He wants one of mine?"

"Well, he hasn't exactly asked." His father chuckled.

Eli looked up. He'd never seen his father nervous before.

"He probably won't need it, Eli. But since you two are twins, one of yours would be perfect. If he does need it."

Eli's stomach rolled. "How will they get it?"

"They'd have to operate. But it's simple. You'd do

that for your brother, wouldn't you?" His father patted his back.

Eli nodded dumbly and moved down the hallway like a sleepwalker. "I'll get my pajamas," he mumbled.

"Maybe some slippers, too," his father called.

"OK," Eli answered, although neither he nor Thad had owned a pair in years.

He pulled open two drawers, the right one his, the left Thad's. He took a pair of pajamas for each of them, wadding them into a package he could carry in one hand. Eli tried to feel his kidneys by thinking hard about them. He wondered which one they'd take. Probably the left, he decided, since he was right-handed.

"Come on, Eli," his father called as he thundered down the stairs.

Eli followed in considerably less of a rush. *Why*, he asked himself, *would Thad work any better on one of my kidneys if his own wouldn't do it?* He swung around the landing, holding the banister. He started down, clinging to the railing, his arm jerking with each step, then sliding down another half a foot.

And why, he asked more ominously, *would one of my kidneys work fine without the other if Thad's wouldn't?*

He heard the back door open and his father call again. His feet touched the floor and he cut through the hallway to the back door, ducking under his father's arm as he opened the screen door. All his insides were beginning to hurt.

Eli got into the car through the driver's door and scooted to the opposite side. As his father backed down the driveway, he held up the fistful of pajamas. "I brought some for Thad, too," he said.

His father smiled at him while he shifted to drive.

Eli couldn't smile back. He sank as low as possible, twisting his back into the seat. His kidneys were killing him.

CHAPTER
THREE

In the elevator at the hospital, even with other people, Eli's father put his hand on his shoulder and
Eli was pretty sure Thad must be dead. The elevator
opened on a corridor which they followed to a large
sitting room. Eli's mother sat huddled in a chair. Eli
noticed for what seemed like the first time, the bright
strands of gray scattered through her long, jet-black
hair. She didn't look like she'd been crying. She
looked worse than that. Her smile quavered when
she saw Eli, and he tried to smile in spite of her
appearance.

"Hi, Mom," he said. "How's Thad's kidney?"

She hugged him and Eli stood still, looking over
her shoulder at his father. His dad wasn't smiling
anymore. "You are so alike," he heard his mother

whisper to herself, giving him one more squeeze and letting him go.

"He's left-handed," he said, trying to see her smile again.

She did for an instant. "I know, Eli." She rubbed her face and sighed. She still had an apron on.

"How is he, Mary?" his father asked. He sat next to her and took her hand. They hardly ever did that.

"Let's get a cup of coffee, Sam," his mother said. "You'll stay here a minute, won't you, Eli?"

Eli shrugged. "Can I see Thad? I brought him some pajamas." He held up his bundle.

"They're still operating, dear. We'll be back in a minute."

Eli slumped into a chair when his parents left. Still operating! It seemed like days since he'd watched Thad tumble off all those bars. *Still* operating! He wondered what there could possibly be left to take out.

Eli sat as long as he could, then wandered about the sitting room, glancing at the boring magazines. The Coke machine's change return slot was empty, as was the pay phone's. He looked down the hallway his parents had disappeared into. He wondered how much coffee they made in one hospital.

He wondered where Thad was. The first door he tried was locked. He was trying a second door when he heard his father say, "That's him now." Eli turned, pushing away from the door as if he'd just been leaning on it. A tall, older man dressed in white walked beside his mother and father. His father and mother were still holding hands. She looked worse than ever.

"Can I see him now?" Eli asked.

His father shook his head.

"Well, you do look just like him," the stranger said, sounding unnaturally chipper. No one else said anything.

"Amazingly so," the stranger continued, holding his hand out to Eli. "I'm Dr. Vernon."

Eli looked at the doctor. "We're twins," he said.

"Identical, I see."

"Just close."

"Eli," his mother said, "Dr. Vernon is Thad's doctor."

Eli swallowed and looked more closely at the tall, gray-haired man. "Are you done operating?"

Eli's mother stroked the back of his head.

"He's sleeping now," the doctor answered. "He will be for quite some time."

The doctor led them into his office. He sat on the corner of his desk, facing them. "I'm a bit vague on some of this, Eli," he said. "Perhaps you could fill me in."

"I'm his twin, you see? So my kidney will work best," Eli blurted. "Do you want it?"

The doctor laughed and said that he didn't need it just yet. Eli felt his dad's big hand on his back. His mom made a strange sound, half sob, half chuckle. She smiled at Eli when he looked to see if she was all right.

The doctor started again. "Your brother is awfully sick. All we've heard is that he was playing tag. Is that true?"

Eli nodded, sinking a little into his chair. He hadn't expected this.

"How did he get so banged up? Were you in the street?"

Eli glanced to his side and saw his mother's questioning eyes. He sank lower in his chair.

"Was he hit by a car?" the doctor asked.

Eli kept looking at his mother. He shook his head.

"Well then . . ."

"Were you playing under the bleachers?" His father's voice sounded like a slap. Eli answered, "Yes," and flinched at the touch of his father's hand, but he just continued to rub Eli's back.

"Sometimes it's best not to give this one's imagination too free a rein," he said to the doctor. "Explain it to him, Eli."

Eli looked up and knew the doctor had no idea what his father was talking about. "We — we were, we were kind of playing tag under the bleachers, at the high school. Thad said, 'Let's play on the home field side,' so we did, and they're so high. Then Sonny tagged me and Thad got to the very top and — and, and I never even touched him! I said I did, but I didn't. And when I turned he was just gone."

The words came so fast they were almost impossible to understand. Eli looked to his mother as he started to cry and felt sorrier than he'd ever felt in his life. "He was just gone!"

As he let his mother hold him, Eli heard his father explain monkey tag. He hated himself for crying and when he heard his father wind up by saying that they used to play it as kids, too, he struggled to sit up, his eyes wide, gazing at his father. His father looked back, not smiling, but not mad. Eli thought his father might start crying, too. Eli would leave if he did.

"They'd done it before and a friend got his lip cut or something. His mother called us, quite hysterical. I said yes, yes, and told the boys not to play there again."

Eli watched his father lift his hands helplessly. "It seemed so harmless. Of all the things they could get into." His father's voice regained some of its strength. "I wasn't as firm as I should've been. But I heard that woman wouldn't let her son play with Thad and Eli and I dismissed her as a kook. They're good kids."

Eli smiled through the tail end of his tears. He never heard his father call anyone a kook before. And he was right, Vince's mom was a kook.

The doctor nodded. "Lord knows we can't protect them from everything. I'm not sure we'd like what turned out if we could.

"However," the doctor added, "as I've told your

parents, Eli, we're all going to have to help Thad on this one.

"I'm going to put this as simply as possible," he said. "Thad broke his right arm in two places. That we can fix. He dislocated that same shoulder and sprained his ankle; those should fix themselves. Internally — inside his body — Thad ruptured his spleen, and we've taken that out. He can get along fine without it. And, as I see you already know, he hurt one of his kidneys so badly we had to take it out as well."

Dr. Vernon gave them a small breather before continuing. "His other kidney is undamaged and it seems to be holding on. Only if something unforeseen occurs will we have to call on you."

Eli nodded and, in an aside to the parents, the doctor said, "With the amount of abdominal surgery and the severity of his other injuries, we tend to expect the unforeseen.

"Also, Eli, there's a certain amount of spinal column injury."

Eli felt his mother's hand tighten over his own and he pictured Thad catching the last bar across his back.

"We won't know anything until more extensive testing is done," he continued almost apologetically. "There appears to be some spinal cord damage, but it is not severed."

"Do you understand what this means, Eli?" his father asked.

Eli said he did.

"It means Thad is going to have trouble walking."

Eli turned to his father.

"He won't walk for a long time. He may need braces on his legs. He will need a wheelchair. We're going to do everything we can for him, Eli, but you should know this. You're old enough now. You have to be. Thad," his father swallowed, dipping his head, "Thad may never be able to walk again, not like before."

Eli froze, seeing Thad twist so slowly off that last bar, bent all the wrong way and dropping again to kick up a dust cloud the shape of a crucifix. Everything inside of him shrank away from his father and the room and from everything in the world.

"Eli?" his mother whispered behind him.

"Thad?" he asked. "How come, Thad?"

"No one knows, Eli."

"We don't know yet," the doctor said. "That's the worst that it could be. It may not be anything nearly as serious. Your folks thought you should be prepared for the worst."

"But why Thad? Why couldn't it have been Sonny?"

"Eli!" his mother admonished. "You wouldn't want that to happen to Sonny. Lord knows none of us wanted it to happen at all — to *anyone*." She took a deep breath. "But it has, Eli, and we're going to have to pray very hard, and do as the doctor says, to help Thad get better."

But Eli did wish it had happened to Sonny. Or even, well not Max. Roger. Roger would have been perfect. But he was too fat and chicken to play. Why did it have to happen at all? Especially to Thad. He knew he should wish, or even pray, that it had happened to him and that Thad would be OK. *"There is no greater love than to give your life for your brother,"* or something like that. Eli couldn't quite remember what he'd had to memorize in religion class. Thad was his best friend and his brother but the thought of having all that stuff taken out of his guts and then being a gimpy, old cripple forever was impossible.

He couldn't do it. He would do anything for Thad, but he couldn't wish that. *"There is no greater love . . ."* he began to think again, but shut it out of his head. It was probably a commandment, and a sin even not to think about it.

He wondered if he'd go to hell now, but felt too miserable to care. He forced back a new upsurging of tears. He wouldn't cry anymore. It was probably the only thing he could still control.

"Eli?" his mother whispered, "are you all right?"

"Yes," he answered. "I'm all right." *Thad's gonna be a gimp and I'm gonna go to hell. Everything's fine.* He wanted to laugh, but he couldn't.

Eli jumped out of his chair. "I gotta see Thad," he blurted.

"Hold on, Eli," Dr. Vernon said.

"I gotta see him," Eli repeated loudly.

"Eli, this may sound funny to you, but you're going to be the single most important factor in your brother's recovery."

Eli stared at the doctor, wondering if he was supposed to believe that.

"What Thad's going to need is a friend. Someone who'll never let him down. Someone who won't treat him like a cripple.

"I have every hope that he'll be able to walk again. But he'll have to work very hard, and it will hurt, and he will get discouraged. You can't let that happen, Eli."

Eli glanced at his parents. They were trying to smile at him. "OK," he said.

"Good. This won't be for months, Eli. I just thought you should know now, so you can get ready for it."

Then Eli sprang the trap he'd prepared during the doctor's speech. "You know, when he fell?" he asked. "Well, we were gonna move him, but I said not to. Was that good?"

"Very good, Eli. Where did you learn that?"

"How come you can't move him?" Eli whispered.

"Well, with any spinal injury, movement may cause further damage to the spinal cord."

"And that's what makes you a gimp?"

"Pardon?" the doctor paused. "Well, yes it could. But in this case I'm sure the damage was all done in the fall."

Eli started for the door but the doctor reached for

his arm. Eli hit his hand away. "I gotta go see him. *Now!*"

"Eli!" his father said in his sternest voice as Eli raced through the door.

Eli sprinted down the hallway and leaped down a flight of steps, popping out one floor below at a nurse's station.

"Hello," he said, walking alongside the counter.

The nurse at the typewriter looked up. "Hi."

"I'm looking for my brother, Thad Martin." Eli glanced back at the door he'd come through.

"Is he on this floor?" she asked, reaching for a clipboard.

"I'm not sure. They brought him in this morning. In an ambulance. He looks just like me."

"In an ambulance? Well, he's probably in emergency then." The nurse studied Eli's streaked, dirty face, and the red-rimmed, brown eyes. "Where are your parents?"

"They're in with him now," he said, looking back at the door. "He got operated on. They took out a bunch of stuff."

She set the clipboard back on its hook. "A bunch of stuff, huh?" she said, smiling. "Then he's probably in I.C.U. You probably won't be able to go up there. How old are you?"

Eli swung his gaze from the door. "You see, I gotta give him a kidney in a little while. I just wanna talk to him once. He's my twin."

The nurse reached for a phone.

"What're you doing?"

"I'm going to call and see if your parents are still there, and if they'll allow you in."

"The doctor already said no," Eli admitted. "But he's my twin brother. I just wanna talk to him for a sec'."

"I'm sure he's unconscious."

"I don't care. I just gotta tell him some stuff. Wouldn't you want to talk to somebody before you gave them your kidney?"

"I suppose so," she said. "Get in the elevator and go to the fifth floor. Talk to the nurses right by the elevator."

Eli ran to the elevator and shifted from foot to foot until the door opened. Then he was gone.

He bumped into a nurse when he leapt from the elevator. "Thad Martin?" he asked, pointing in the direction she'd been coming from.

The nurse gasped, clasping her hand to her breast. "My, you gave me a start. You must be his brother."

"Where is he?"

"I'm not . . ."

"Please lady, I'm not gonna do anything except talk to him." As soon as she opened her mouth he cut her off. "And I know he's asleep. That's OK. Dr. Vernon said it'd be all right."

"Follow me. But just for a minute. What's your name?"

Eli was so relieved to be following the wide, white

rump that he didn't hear her question. She repeated it.

"Eli."

"Eli, you must be very quiet and do not touch anything, not a thing. The people here are all very sick."

Eli agreed, following her breathlessly to a strange bed. For a moment, he saw nothing but the elaborate pulley and cable networks, then the monitors and their bouncing lines of light. Finally he saw Thad, or as much of him as was visible. He was tied up in weird angles and was attached to several more tubes than he had been when they put him in the ambulance.

The nurse nodded to him and Eli inched forward. Thad's head was angled toward him, the face swollen, bluish, with tubing coming out of his nose and mouth. His breathing made an ugly, whistling, rasping noise.

He looked again at the nurse and she backed up a step. Eli turned back to Thad slowly, making sure she wasn't watching. He reached out and grazed his fingertip along Thad's forehead. "I'm sorry, Thad." he murmured. Tears clouded his vision.

"I didn't know we shouldn't move you, Thad," he whispered. "I didn't know. Sorry," he gulped again, inhaling deeply. He'd remembered the smell of hospitals perfectly.

Peeking at the nurse, he withdrew his finger from Thad's head. "You can have my kidney," he told his whistling, rasping brother. "You can have anything," he added, wiping away his tears with his thumb. "You can have both my kidneys, Thad. Thad, I didn't mean to make you a gimp." Eli gripped the railing of the bed. "I didn't know, Thad. I didn't know."

Unable to speak or even to think of all the things he should be telling Thad, Eli stood straight again. "I'm gonna make you walk again, Thad," he told him.

The nurse nudged him gently. Eli sniffed and nodded and when she turned to lead him away, Eli slipped his hand out of his pocket and touched his brother's swollen forehead once more.

CHAPTER
FOUR

The next morning Eli's father threw on his light coat and gave Eli a pat. "You sit tight. I'll be back soon. They always make this early mass quick, so none of the old ladies nod off."

Eli smiled at that. His father was not an irreverent man.

"Stick by the phone. We'll burn our way through breakfast when I get back. Say your prayers," he added, suddenly earnest. "Remember Thad in them."

Eli closed the door, wondering if his father really thought he could forget Thad.

He walked back through the house, but it was just an empty house now. In the living room, he climbed over the couch and lay down on the bench radiator behind it. It was the first time he'd ever been allowed to stay home from church without being too sick to appreciate it.

Max was out on Eli's paper route, struggling with the huge Sunday edition. He'd done the route yesterday, too, while Eli and his father had wasted an entire Saturday, puttering around, waiting for the phone call saying that they needed Eli's kidney.

They hadn't let him see Thad again. They said he was still sleeping. Eli asked himself how long a person could sleep, and what it would be like to wake up days later, wondering what in the world had happened to you.

Eli was still wondering about waking to find yourself tied up with those wires and pulleys when he saw Max strolling up the gray street. He shivered, even on the warm tile surface, then got up and went to the door. "Hey, Max," he called.

Max left the wagon on the sidewalk and came into the house. "Does that house with the pillars get one on Sunday?"

"Nope."

"That's why I came up one short."

"Did you skip the one on that corner?"

"Yep."

"Good. Those guys never tip. Not even on Christmas."

"You told me to skip them if I was short. It's kind of fun in the morning. Once you get up."

Eli nodded and they sat down in the kitchen. He

tossed a banana to Max and then peeled one for himself. "I don't even have to go to church today," he announced.

"That'd be great. I went last night." Max took a bite of the banana and stripped the peel back another inch. "You know what? They announced it at church yesterday — about Thad."

Eli wished they hadn't done that. Now everyone would ask about it. "How do you suppose the priests find out about everything so fast?" he asked.

"I think my mom called so they could get everybody praying."

"I wish she wouldn't've."

Max nodded. He finished his banana and tried to fit the peels back together. "Are your mom and dad still sleeping?"

"My mom stayed at the hospital all night. Dad went to church a little while ago, so he could go down and let Mom go to ten o'clock mass. She likes all the singing."

"Did you get in trouble?"

"Nope," Eli answered, and for a moment he remembered wondering if his father might not start to cry. "You know what? My dad used to play it, too."

"Monkey tag?"

Eli nodded. "And, you know what? He called Vince's mom a kook. Right to the doctor."

Max laughed wildly. "Your dad did?"

"Yeah. It was great."

Their giggles died out and Max asked, "How come you don't have to go to church?"

"I gotta wait for a call — from Thad's doctor."

Max laughed. "Why'd the doctor want to talk to you?"

"I might have to go down and give Thad one of my kidneys," Eli replied. They didn't laugh then.

"What'd they do to him?" Max whispered.

"Didn't they tell you in church?"

"No. They just said he needed our prayers."

Eli grimaced, already hating all the questions. And everyone would say they were sorry. What were you supposed to say to that? It wasn't their fault.

"What's wrong with him?"

"He broke his arm," Eli mumbled. "And they took out his kidney, and his, his . . . something else he didn't need anyway."

"His appendix?"

"Nope. And, Max, don't tell anybody, all right?"

"Yeah."

"Promise?"

"OK, Eli. What?"

"He kind of broke his back, too."

Max paled. "I won't tell." He picked up his banana peel and tore the three segments apart. "Is he paralyzed?"

"No!" Eli answered sharply, then backtracked. "Well, they don't think so. They don't really know, I guess." He threw his peel across the kitchen into the sink.

"Can he move at all?"

"He wasn't even awake when I saw him. They said he might not walk very good for a while." Eli slid off the bench and began to pace around the kitchen.

"Wow. What are we gonna do with him, if he can't walk?"

Eli shrugged. "Guess we'll have to carry him around. They said he'd have a wheelchair — push him around, I guess."

"That'd be kind of fun, rolling around all over the place. He won't be able to get up into the Crazy Lady's garage, though. And what about when we have to run?"

Eli shrugged again and turned to Max. "I don't know, Max," he said. "I don't know anything anymore. You'll still play with him though, won't you?"

"Sure. You guys are my best friends."

"I bet Sonny won't."

"Sonny's all right. Roger'll pick on him though."

"I'll kill him if he does," Eli swore. "I don't care how old he is."

"Yeah. I'll help. We could ambush him."

"He better not try it," Eli said.

Max wandered to the door. "Well, you know Thad," he shrugged. "He'll think it'll be neat for a while, riding around in a wheelchair. But he'll get tired of it."

Eli knew what Max meant. Thad would start walking then and things would return to normal. Away from his parents, and especially from that doctor, Eli tended to agree.

Max stepped into the front hall. "I better go. Mom'll start wondering what happened to me."

"You could stay for breakfast. Why don't you, Max? Come on. You know how it is when my dad cooks."

Max laughed a little. "Naw. I gotta go. They'll be eating soon and I gotta be there. They think I'm too skinny."

"You aren't *that* skinny."

"Well, I'll see you. What're you doing later on?"

Eli followed him out to the porch. "I don't know. I gotta stay around all the time in case the phone rings."

"You really gotta give him a kidney?" Max asked.

"Yeah, but you can come over if you want." The sound of the phone ringing cut him short and Eli sprinted into the house.

"Hello?" he gasped.

"Are you all right, Eli?"

"Oh, yeah, Mom. I was out talking to Max. I thought I might've missed you. He did my paper route."

"That's nice of him. Is Dad there?"

"He went to church, so you could go to ten o'clock."

"Are you both coming down then?"

"I don't know. Can I see him?"

"Oh, I don't think so, Eli. He's sleeping all the time."

"Uh-huh. How is he?"

"The same really. Dr. Vernon says he's very strong."

"He is."

"He'll do fine, Eli."

"Yeah."

"Well, honey, I just wanted to see what your plans were. Have Dad give me a call when he gets home."

"OK."

"Thanks, Eli. I love you."

Eli stared at the silent phone before hanging up. He couldn't remember the last time he'd heard her say that. "Poor Mom," he mumbled.

For lack of anything else to do Eli set the table. He put dishes out for himself and both his parents, gazing for a second at Thad's empty spot. He wondered how long he'd be gone.

When the table was set, Eli brought the eggs and link sausages out of the refrigerator and carried them to the stove. His dad always cooked the same thing.

Eli sat in his place tapping his feet. He wished his dad would get here and start cooking and burn something. That was always the funniest. Eli closed his eyes, thinking about it. He wished his dad would come home right now. He didn't want him at early mass. He didn't want Max coming over at six-thirty in the morning. He didn't want his mom calling with nothing to say. He didn't even want her saying she loved him.

47

He wanted everyone upstairs asleep, while he read the comics, waiting for them to wake up and take him to church. He didn't even want to be able to skip church, he realized. And he wanted Thad to stop sleeping all the time and just walk home.

Eli rocked in his seat, his face screwed up as he clamped his eyes shut tighter and tighter. He wanted to have a fight with Thad about letting them get caught at monkey tag and he wanted Thad to kick him over and over again.

By the time Mr. Martin came in Eli had fallen asleep. He didn't wake until his father dropped the spatula. "Thought you were going to sleep through the whole thing," his dad said.

"I didn't, did I, Dad?" Eli asked with such urgency that his father turned from the stove.

"Not yet," he said, holding up the two eggs he palmed.

Eli stared at the dull surface of the eggs. He remembered his father demonstrating the strength of an egg. They were almost impossible to break unless you hit them or pressed at only one point. Eli no longer thought it so remarkable.

"Mom called," he said.

"Any news?"

"She wants you to call. She just wanted to know what we're going to do."

"You didn't tell her, did you?" His father waved his hand around the stove and winked conspiratorially.

Eli shrugged. "I just told her you were at church."

"Well, somebody's got to go early and poke the ladies when they start to snore."

"Yeah," Eli said, but he saw his father's surprised, almost hurt expression. "Oh, Dad. They weren't snoring."

"Just shows you how well I did my job."

Eli smiled thinly and slumped in his chair. None of this was any good without Thad. His dad prattled on and forgot to turn the burner down and the sausage grease began to smoke. He laughed but it wasn't funny. When his father finally slid a plate in front of Eli, he suddenly stopped and stared at his son. "Are you sure your mother didn't have any news about Thad?" he asked.

Eli shook his head. "Aren't you going to call her?"

"Right after breakfast," he answered. "Eat before it gets cold."

They ate in silence. Eli cleared the table, his usual chore, and his father helped him scrape the dishes and load them into the dishwasher. "We're going to have to rearrange these jobs, aren't we?" his father asked.

"I can scrape them," Eli muttered, realizing how Thad was going to make them change everything. "Till Thad gets back."

"All right. Your mother and I can load and finish then."

While his father began to dial the phone, Eli said, "Find out if I can see him yet. And if they know about his kidney. I don't want to sit around in here the rest of my life."

His father kept dialing. When he finished, he turned to Eli and said, "If that's the kind of thing that's going to come out of your mouth, just leave it shut."

Eli stared at his father a moment before stomping out of the room.

CHAPTER
FIVE

Eli lay in bed trying to remember his parents coming into his room late in the night. They'd said Thad was, "pretty much out of the woods." They said they'd check in the morning, but that he ought to plan on going to school. Eli slid out of bed, got dressed, and shuffled downstairs. He hadn't bothered to put on his school clothes — just jeans and a shirt. His father had his work clothes on, a suit and tie.

"Nice try," his father said, pointing at Eli's clothes. "But the doctor called and said the threat to Thad's kidney is pretty much over. The bad news is you'll be going to school."

"Is he getting better already?"

"No, not yet," his mother said. "But it's looking better."

"How about his legs?"

"We'll let you know as soon as the doctors find out, Eli."

"I don't want to go to school," Eli said, shoveling in a huge spoonful of cereal so he wouldn't have to talk again.

"Why not?"

"Just because."

"But Thad doesn't need you to stay home anymore."

"I know. I just don't want to."

"Well, I don't want to go to work," his father said in his standard answer to the standard complaint.

"Did you know they announced it about Thad, at church?" Eli asked, wondering if his mom and dad were aware of how far out of hand this whole thing was getting.

"Why yes, Eli. The priests announced it at all the masses. Wasn't that nice of them?"

"That's all anybody's gonna talk about," he explained. "They'll all be asking me the same stupid questions all day long."

"They're only trying to help," his father said, wiping his mouth and pushing his chair out behind him. "You'll do fine.

"Time for me to go," he announced. "Give me a call, Mary, if anything turns up. See you all tonight."

He was gone before Eli's mom sat at the table

with a new cup of coffee. "Hurry up, Eli. You've still got to change." When the hopeless expression crossed his face she said. "Everything will be all right, Eli, honestly. You can't put it off forever."

Eli walked to school alone. He couldn't bear thinking about what it would be like with everyone looking at him — as if he'd pushed Thad off the bleachers himself. Instead he thought of the church, towering beside the low bricks of the school. His dad told him God gave everybody two kidneys in case they needed a spare. That was fair, he thought. But what about all the prayers they'd said, him and Thad, and his parents? What about all of them? Weren't prayers supposed to stop things like this before they ever happened? Praying every night and all those Sundays in church didn't mean one single thing. It was the biggest cheat Eli had ever imagined.

Two blocks from school he met Max twirling around a stop sign. "Hey, Eli," he shouted.

"Hey, Max," Eli answered. Max fell into step beside him.

"Think we're late?"

"I don't know. I don't care, Max. I might not go at all."

"Mean skip out?!" Max stopped, then hurried to catch up.

"Yeah. Did you ever do it?"

"Of course not. You'd've known before anybody else."

"I wonder how you do it."

Eli and Max were almost at school before they had worked out a plan for playing hooky. Two nuns were standing at the doors, herding in the last hangers-on. "Come on, boys," they called.

"You boys are going to hold up . . ." The large nun stopped when she recognized Eli. "Just a minute, boys," she said.

Eli watched the hands fiddling with the rosary. Anything was better than seeing the rolls of flesh pinched around the edges of the stiff habit. "Eli Martin," she said. Eli snuck a glance to Max. Why'd it have to be Sister Dorine?

"We're all praying very hard for your brother. The Lord is with him."

The Lord sure wasn't with him under the bleachers, Eli thought. He felt like shouting it into her cowled face. But he murmured, "Thank you, Sister." He glanced up at the other nun, Sister Mirin. She smiled at Eli and looked truly sorry. Eli smiled back. He'd had her for second grade and still thought she was the nicest nun who'd ever breathed. She was as nice as Sister Dorine was weird.

"We have to go to class, Sister," Max said. "We're late."

"Yes, children. You may go now."

Eli and Max lunged up the stairs. "Yes, children," Max mimicked. "Boy, that one's a weirdo."

They slipped through the door moments before Mr. Genskow closed it for the morning. As they walked back to their desks, Eli tried to figure out

54

how he could be lucky enough to have the only lay teacher in the school. Glancing at Thad's empty desk Eli knew it would've been a hundred times worse with a nun.

They were told to rise, and they all said the Pledge of Allegiance. They sat again and Sister Victoria came in and led them in prayers. More prayers. They'd been surrounded by prayers forever. For nothing.

After Sister Victoria left, Mr. Genskow told them which books to take out while they waited for the morning announcements. Eli glanced at the loud-speaker next to the clock and realized what was about to happen. He raised his hand like a rocket.

Mr. Genskow signaled for him to come up front. "Have to use the lavatory?" he asked.

Eli nodded and Mr. Genskow followed him into the hallway. "Sorry about Thad, Eli," he said. "Wouldn't worry too much though. He's a tough kid."

The loudspeaker's introductory static echoed out of the door behind him. "Want to stay in there until this is over?"

"Yes, sir."

Straining to hear as he stood at the sinks, Eli could just make out the announcement about Thad. He shook his head and studied his reflections in the two opposing mirrors. He tried to count how many times his head was reflected, but the reflections got too small and close together, always disappearing.

When the announcements were over Eli shuffled back to class.

As he reached for the door Eli realized that he'd avoided the stares at the moment of the announcement but now he had to walk through the entire class. The back door was his only hope of avoiding that, but it was always locked. Eli walked back anyway. If he could get Max to see him through the window in the back door maybe he could sneak up long enough to let him in.

As soon as Eli peeked in the window the back door swung open and Mr. Genskow stood there, waving Eli to his seat even as he held his book up, following along with whoever was reading. Eli slid low in his seat, hardly glancing as Mr. Genskow closed the door. A ripple went through the room, people turning toward Eli, but Mr. Genskow silenced them, asking, "Who's next?

"Emily, would you pick up where Jeff left off, please?"

As Emily's voice tinkled on, Max showed Eli where they were. Eli followed halfheartedly, gazing at Mr. Genskow. No nun in the world would've ever done that.

Eli spent the morning looking at his desk, but Mr. Genskow ran an unusually fast-paced, sternly disciplined class, and no one had much time to gawk. When they broke for lunch the weather was warm enough to allow them to eat outside.

The students who normally stayed for lunch scattered around the blacktop parking lot, falling into their cliques. Eli followed Max as far as the rectory exit. "I have to eat here today," he told Max.

"You're kidding. How come?"

"My mom's gonna be at the hospital all day. And just in case they need my kidney they can call the school to get me."

"So you can't come over?"

"Naw. I'll see you in a while, I guess," Eli said. He sat down and watched Max until he turned the corner. He dug in his jacket pocket for the crumpled paper bag containing his lunch.

The other students strayed to the north end of the lot, where the sun shone brightly. Eli looked at them wishing he could feel the same warmth, but it was safer in the shade — no one would talk to him there. He zipped his windbreaker and, as he unwrapped a peanut butter and jelly, he thought about how, at this angle, the sun could make the black asphalt look silver.

Eli always went home for lunch, so he didn't really know the lunch routine and he hadn't gone to the basement to pick up his milk. The dry sandwich caught in his throat. He swallowed uncomfortably and wished his mom had had some fruit in the house, but she hadn't been shopping since the accident. He tucked the remainder of his sandwich back in his pocket. *What if Thad dies?* He hadn't realized how bad it could be without him.

He wondered what they were feeding Thad. His

dad said they fed him through a tube in his arm. Eli bet he was starving.

Standing up to cram his hands in his pockets, Eli saw a knot of kids approaching. One broke into the lead and called, "Hey, Eli." It was Sonny. "Hey, Eli," he said again as the group came up. They spread into a semicircle around him.

"Hey you guys," Eli answered, eyeing the crowd. Someone asked, "How's your brother?"

"All right, I guess. I haven't seen him in a few days."

"Did he really break his back?"

Eli couldn't tell who said it. "They don't know."

Sonny said, "I told them about it."

Before Eli could turn on him, someone else asked, "Were you guys really playing on the tall ones? Sonny said you were."

"Yeah," Eli answered. He started to walk toward the school.

"Wow. No wonder he broke his back."

Eli whirled. "Maybe he didn't! Maybe he'll be back before any of you guys think. He's already almost better. So why don't you just leave him alone?"

"Sister said we're going to go visit him," Sonny said.

Eli forced a laugh. "You don't know anything, Sonny. Neither does Sister."

"That's what she said," he protested. "The whole class."

"Shows how much you know. *I* can't even visit him yet."

"I thought you said he was almost better."

Eli trembled. "Shut up! You don't know anything. You were just too chicken to play up high is the only reason Thad fell."

"Yeah? Well, I know more than you. You're the one who moved him."

Eli moved toward Sonny. "So did you," he whispered.

"You told me to," he said, and Eli was on him.

Eli fought wildly, never giving Sonny a chance to cover up. Two nuns were there quickly, but it wasn't until Mr. Genskow pulled Eli off Sonny that the fight was broken up.

Eli struggled in Mr. Genskow's grip and screamed at Sonny, telling him never to say that again, threatening to kill him if he said that to anybody. Mr. Genskow jerked him roughly from the crowd that had gathered. At the outside edge he released him and pushed him toward the school. Sonny screamed, "Your brother's gonna be a gimp forever!"

Eli flashed around Mr. Genskow and sprinted through the crowd. He dodged between the nuns and got in one hard punch, knocking the wind out of Sonny before he was again hauled back by Mr. Genskow. He swore at Sonny and spat at him as he lay gasping for breath on the blacktop. Mr. Genskow slapped Eli on the back of the head hard enough to make him see stars. Eli shut up then and let Mr. Genskow haul him to the nurse's office.

Both his hands were scraped and bleeding. The nurse put a stinging antiseptic on them. Eli turned to Mr. Genskow and smiled a tight, thin line.

Mr. Genskow led Eli back to his room and sat down to finish his lunch. "By the looks of those hands, you spent more time beating the pavement than that other kid."

Eli shrugged and pulled his squashed sandwich out of his pocket and began to unwrap it, trying to keep his hands from trembling. It was forbidden to eat anything in the school.

Mr. Genskow watched, waiting until Eli had the sandwich to his mouth. "Stop it," he said. "Since when do you eat in here?"

"You are."

"But you aren't." Mr. Genskow plucked the sandwich from Eli and threw it into the wastepaper basket.

"You're the one who brought me in here," Eli said, hating his quaking voice.

Mr. Genskow's eyes widened. "Oh, you're pretty tough all right," he said. He sat down and looked at Eli again. "Eli, no one should have said what that kid said out there. I'm not saying you were right to hit him, but I understand it.

"I know your brother's hurt and everything's changed. But you're only going to make it worse by

60

being a fool. Have you ever been in a fight here before?"

"No."

"I didn't think so. You're too smart for it. Don't start acting stupid now. You won't believe it, but this will all blow over and whatever your brother's condition is, that will become what's normal. We're all amazingly adaptable that way."

Eli stared at Mr. Genskow. He would have thought his teacher was smarter than to think that any part of this could *ever* be normal.

After school Eli wandered through his paper route in a trance. He walked the extra blocks to the bluff overlooking Lake Michigan and after seeing the mist rising at the horizon, turned to walk home. That white fog, hanging above the water all winter, doing nothing, seemed to Eli to be as substantial as all their prayers. Maybe the mist was their prayers, years and years of them, stalled out there, where they didn't do anyone any good.

The new street lights came on before Eli reached his house and he listened to them crackle, glowing purplish. The lights strengthened slowly, seeming to draw the last bit of daylight out of the sky and into themselves. He watched until they shone their full, fiery white. He thought of God up in heaven someplace, knowing what he was thinking. The darkness was suddenly scary somehow. He began to run, hurrying home through blackened alleys.

He burst into the front hall red-faced and panting. "Is that you, Eli?" he heard his mother call as he snagged a coat hook with his jacket.

"Uh-huh."

"Where on earth have you been? Dinner is all ready. We've been waiting for you."

Eli slid into his place at the table and they said grace. His father again offered the nightly Our Father for Thad. Eli blessed himself, passed his plate for his father to fill, and asked how Thad was doing.

"I've been saving this for you, Eli, for when we're all together," his father said, smiling enormously. "Dr. Vernon has had more doctors come in, specialists, and tomorrow they're going to take Thad out of traction."

"All the cables and stuff?"

"That's it. They believe most of the spinal damage is in the form of severe swelling. It's pinching his spinal cord. That means his paralysis should be only temporary. Only temporary, Eli!"

Eli grinned, watching his father hug his mother, right at the table. They looked so happy he didn't ask the myriad of doubting questions that jumped into his mind. His smile left slowly, and an uneasiness took its place. He ate his dinner and listened to his parents babble on so cheerily.

Eli was beginning to slide off his bench to start clearing the table when his father asked about his hands.

"Fell down when we were playing at lunch," Eli replied and carried his plate to the sink.

"What were you playing?"

"Are you done?" Eli asked his mom, reaching for her plate.

His father grasped his wrist and examined his hand. "Don't lie, Eli. And don't get in fights over this.

"I'll give you this one," he added as Eli retreated to the sink, turned on the water, and began rinsing a plate. "I know the strain this must put on you. But no more. You hear me? You don't gain a thing by fighting."

Eli scrubbed the dishes much cleaner than was necessary.

"Who was it?" his mother asked.

"Just a guy."

"Eli?"

"It was, Mom. Just a dumb guy."

His father started to help put the dishes into the washer.

"Why did you hit him?"

"I don't know." The desperate feeling was growing in him again. "When can I see Thad?" he asked.

"As soon as he's out of intensive care."

"Why, Eli?" his mother persisted. "You two aren't fighters."

"Oh, Mary. It's all right," his father said when Eli threw the dishrag into the sink.

"Cause he said Thad was gonna be a gimp for-ever!" Eli yelled. "That's why! I wish I'd've killed him!"

"Guess he was just a dumb guy," his father mur-mured. He held his hand out for another glass but Eli felt like he'd burst if he just stood there. He left the room, forcing himself not to run. At the door, he heard his mother ask, "Who would have said such a terrible thing?"

Eli crept downstairs when he heard his parents leave for the hospital. He had the house to himself again. He paced a circle through every room on the first floor. It was all ruined. The empty house had lost its precious novelty. Now it was one of the more predominant signs of how messed up everything was. Eli trudged back upstairs, turned off the lights and climbed into bed.

For the first time ever, Eli skipped his prayers. They hadn't done any good. He and Thad had said prayers every night, forever, but he was still in the hospital and Eli had already been separated from him longer than ever before. And it wasn't even half over yet. What in the world was God doing anyway?

CHAPTER
SIX

When Eli finally saw his brother again it had been a week and a day since the accident — eight days since he had seen, or talked to Thad. After an agonizing hour of delay in church, the Martins drove to the hospital and rode the elevator to the neurological floor, stopping at the nurses' station to get the new room number.

Eli checked the numbers of each door as they moved down the hallway. He peeked through the open doors, trying to get an idea of what to expect. The only room not closed off by curtains showed a bed covered with cables and pulleys, but those had been taken off Thad days ago his father had said.

"Here he is," his mother said. Eli followed them

into the darkened room. "He's asleep," his father whispered.

Eli peered about in the gloom, his nose adjusting to the smell as his eyes fought with the change from the painfully bright corridor. He didn't look at the bed until he could see.

He barely caught the gasp that would have given away his shock. Eli's breath quickened and his nostrils flared with each breath. He clamped his mouth shut. Thad's eyes were sunken and dark, a tube in his nose was taped to his face. Little flecks of old glue peeled away around the tape, showing where it had been replaced. It was surprisingly white on the yellow-gray skin.

How in the world had they ever said he was getting better? How could they have lied so easily? Eli glanced at his mother who smiled back reassuringly. *Look at him!* he wanted to scream. Were they blind?

The same old tube dripped away into Thad's forearm. But it was a new forearm — one with all the muscle stripped away, nothing like Thad's old, wiry, strong arm.

A fatter tube ran from beneath the sheets into a jar, which even in the darkness appeared to be full of the most vile drippings Eli had ever imagined. He instantly associated it with the evil smell in the room.

Eli was eventually pulled back to the drawn, sallow face. The brown hair was matted and seemed

66

to have grown much faster than his own. He reached up and touched his hair, threading a lock between his fingers. The sheets were drawn up to Thad's collar bones, with only the IV forearm hanging out from the blankets. Eli stared and stared at the strange face. At least it wasn't making that noise when it breathed.

Nearly half an hour passed and no one said a word. Eli grew used to his silent brother and began to study the room where he lived now. The bed was an automatic model. The back was raised just above horizontal and Eli wondered how far it would go. Craning his neck, he realized he was sitting directly beneath the television. The Packers game would be on soon. He looked back to Thad, but his face looked the same, with no signs of waking. Catching his mother's eye, he asked, "When's he gonna wake up?"

"They give him medication that makes him very groggy. He sleeps most of the time. That's what he needs."

"Can't we wake him up?"

"It's better that he sleeps."

Eli slumped into his chair. "What do you guys do down here all the time?"

His father smiled and his mother answered. "We sit with him like this, Eli. When he wakes up he likes to see one of us here. It makes it a lot less scary."

"Thad's not scared."

"It's so different here, though. It helps if we're here." Mrs. Martin rubbed Eli's leg. "He'll be so glad to see you. He always asks about you."

"Did you tell him I would've come except for the rules?"

"We told him you broke the rules to see him the first day."

"Good."

The talk dropped off when Thad sighed and moved slightly. Eli held his breath, but Thad appeared to have settled back into sleep. "Maybe if we open the curtains a little?" he suggested.

"Just be patient, Eli. He'll be up soon."

Eli waited again.

"Do they have a bathroom in here?" he finally asked.

"Right by the door."

"How long've we been here?"

"Not even an hour, Eli. Keep your shirt on."

Eli turned on the light in the bathroom and squinted. He was facing the mirror. He put on his long face and muttered, "Keep your shirt on, Eli." He broke into a grin and unzipped his pants. He didn't really have to go, but he thought the noise of the toilet flushing might wake Thad.

Checking to make sure the door was ajar, Eli pushed the button and nodded his head at the roar of the powerful toilet. He flipped the lights off and let his eyes get back to the gloom.

Then he heard his parents talking along with another voice. Eli slipped through the door, still half-blind. "Thad, there's somebody here to see you."

"Who?" he heard Thad ask, his voice unmistakable despite the scratchy hoarseness. Then, as Eli fumbled toward the bed he heard Thad ask, "Is it Eli?"

Eli's eyes could almost pierce the gloom. He stood by the bed, staring down at his brother. The death-camp face was the same, but not nearly so frightening with the eyes open. They were still Thad's old eyes. They even smiled a moment before Thad spoke. "Hey, Eli," he croaked.

"Hey, Thad," Eli answered, then stammered, unable to think of anything else to say.

"How are you?" Thad asked. His tongue, thick and dry, poked out in a futile attempt to wet his lips. He shifted his weight with an elbow and grimaced, closing his eyes. He sighed before opening them again.

"I'm all right, I guess," Eli answered.

"Better than me, huh?" Thad fought to smile again.

"You're all right, Thad. Everybody keeps asking about you." He waited but Thad just stared at him, his eyes growing rheumy. "Max wants to see you, when he can."

His father touched his shoulder and Eli jumped. "We're going to let you visit. Only a few minutes though. He'll probably fall asleep. You do most of the talking. He must have had a shot just before we got here."

Both parents leaned over Eli to Thad. His mom kissed Thad as his dad touched his shoulder. "We all love you, Thad," his mom whispered.

Thad smiled. "Thanks, you guys, for coming."

"Eli's going to stay a minute longer."

Thad nodded, mostly with his eyes. He let his head roll on the pillow so he faced Eli again. "What've you been doing?"

"Same stuff. I beat up Sonny Dunleavy on Monday."

Thad raised his eyebrows but didn't say anything.

"Hardly even got in trouble for it, too." The continuing question in Thad's eyes caused Eli to answer, "He was making fun of you. About falling."

Thad twisted his face into a sneer, trying to show his brother that he didn't care what Sonny said. Thad's eyelids were drooping lower.

"Mr. Genskow says he'll help you catch up when you get back. You're going to have a tutor, but I'm saving all the homework and stuff anyway."

"How come?" Thad whispered.

Eli hesitated. He'd never thought of that. In a way it was like having Thad home, by doing the things he would've been doing. "I don't know," he said. "It's pretty neat really. Taking it all home but not having to do it."

Thad nodded.

"I'll bring it with me next time. Then you won't get so far behind." Thad grimaced at that, but Eli didn't notice. He rambled on and on, not noticing that Thad had fallen asleep.

Their parents came into the room and motioned Eli away. His mother kissed Thad and tucked the sheet around his neck.

"Why don't you and I go home, Eli," his father said. "Your mom will stay for a little while longer."

"OK," Eli said, catching a glimpse of the television. "Think he'd want me to turn on the game?"

"I think he'll sleep all the way through it. Your mom's here if he needs anything."

"OK," he whispered. "See you later, Thad," he said, turning back to the bed once more before leaving.

Over the next couple of weeks Eli and his mother fell into a routine of walking to the hospital every evening after Eli finished his paper route. They helped Thad with his meals when he began eating again and, after his father arrived from work, the three would leave Thad to sleep while they went home and had their own dinner. His mother was at the hospital all day, only coming home when she walked back over with Eli to fix dinner and eat.

The dinnertime visit allowed the twins to see each other before Thad received his pain shots. Thad was usually alert and fairly awake. The weekend visits were spookier; there seemed to be no way to predict what Thad would be like.

On Sundays Eli began walking directly to church after his route rather than waiting to go with his parents. He sat in the second-to-the-last pew and watched the drab old ladies dressed in black and gray with their funny veiled hats. He grinned as he thought of his father poking at them to keep them awake. Why did they get up so early anyway? It'd be like Thad getting up that early now, just to spend another day in bed. His grin faded. The priest marched out and Eli shuffled to his feet with the old, rustling women.

None of what the priests did had ever made much sense to Eli, but now, even as he went through the motions of standing and kneeling and sitting, everything was even more confusing. The priest seemed deceitful somehow, chanting away in his robes, saying he could make flesh from bread and blood from wine. Maybe he could do that, but he didn't keep Thad from getting hurt. And he couldn't fix him once he was hurt. Eli watched carefully until the mass was over, but the priest didn't have any answers.

When Eli got home he announced that he would be visiting Thad while they went to church. Though it would be his first solo visit, it went much more smoothly than he'd expected. His parents even dropped him off at the hospital on their way to church.

He slid through the quiet halls anxiously, but there was no one at the entrance station to challenge his underage visit. He made it to Thad's room easily.

"Where's Mom and Dad?" Thad asked.

"At church. I went early."

"The six-thirty one?" Thad asked. "With all the geezers?"

"Yeah, it was weird. Why do you suppose they get up so early?" Eli's heart slowed when he saw Thad raise his bed and look at him with such animation. "No shots today?" he asked, although the answer was obvious.

"Naw. They say I should get out of here by Thanksgiving."

"That's only ten days, Thad! That'll be great!" Eli said, wondering what it would really be like. It would sure change everything all over again.

"Yeah, I'll say. Maybe we could both get up early and go to church without Mom and Dad. Might make it more fun."

"It is. I sat in the very back." Eli took a pull from Thad's water glass, through the elbow straw. "That'd be kind of neat, always drinking through straws."

Thad shrugged. "Was that one really fat one there? The one with the purple dress?" he asked.

"Yeah." Eli flipped the TV on with the remote that hung from a cord on the wall. "It'd be great to have one of these at home." He flipped through the channels. "Yuck, more church."

"It's still early. I always kind of liked that lady."

"The purple one? She smells, Thad!"

"I know. But she gave me a dime once, to put in the collection basket."

"When?"

"That time I went by myself."

"You sat next to her?"

"She sat next to me. I couldn't help it."

"Wow."

"Yeah, I know. But she showed me which page we were using in the missalette. And then, when they made the collection, she gave me the dime. She kind of sings nice, too."

Eli stared in astonishment.

Thad shrugged. "Was Mrs. Thatchet there?"

Eli gave his brother a long look. He had talked to the purple lady! "Yeah, The Hatchet was there," he said absently. "Yesterday Max cut across her yard and she threw a brick at him."

"She did not." Thad laughed, rolling his head back and forth on the pillow. He sighed. "It still hurts sometimes when I laugh."

"She sure did. Ask Max."

"What was she doing with a brick?"

Eli stared at his brother again. Mrs. Thatchet would wait for days for a shot at a kid on her lawn, everybody knew that. "She was putting some in her garden."

"What's she doing in her garden? It's practically winter."

"I don't know. Probably waiting for Max. I don't

know. But she almost hit him. It was The Hatchet, Thad! You know."

"I suppose."

"She hit you with a rake once!"

"Yeah, but we were swording her tulips."

"And you tripped over that stupid white fence!"

Thad laughed a little, too. "Didn't even hurt," he lied. "I wonder if she can even lift a brick anymore."

"She sure can. She's mean enough to lift anything."

"I bet I know why she gets up early," Thad said.

"Why?"

"So she can dig more of those trenches at the edge of the sidewalk that always catch your bike tires."

"Boy, I hate those. Why do they make them?"

"I don't know," Thad said. Then he asked, "Did Father Miller say your mass?"

"Yep. He's not so bad."

"Yeah. He said it the morning I went. I bet the Monsignor makes him do all the early ones 'cause he's the newest."

"Yeah. That Monsignor sure is a crab." Eli paused. "S'pose that's a sin?"

Thad laughed. "No way. It's the truth."

They were silent a moment and Thad rubbed at his belly. "I can't laugh much. I'll probably bust my stitches."

"I thought they already took them out."

"Well, I'll bust right open then. Like a big zipper."

75

"That's sick."

"You want to know something really sick?" Thad asked.

Eli saw he was still smiling. He leaned forward. "What?"

"Guess who came in yesterday?"

"Beats me."

"Guess."

Eli straightened in his chair. "Not the purple lady?"

"The purple lady!" Thad cried. "Of course not, you retard!"

"Well that's good."

"Guess again."

"Come on, Thad. Just tell me."

"You wouldn't get it in a million years."

"I give up already. Who was it?"

"There were two of them."

"Oh come on, Thad," Eli said. "Who?"

"Father Miller, and . . ."

"The Monsignor?" Eli asked, too shocked to laugh.

Thad grinned and nodded his head. "You know what for?"

"Who knows with priests." Eli stopped and his eyes widened. "They didn't give you last rites or anything?"

"No!" Thad answered. "But I guess they did that first night."

Eli stared at his brother. "Wow. Now you got an

extra sacrament. Baptism, confession, first communion, confirmation, last rites. You only got to get married and that one for being a priest." Eli pondered. "I wonder if you can get both of those."

"I don't think you can," Thad answered. "I think I'll settle for those five."

"I only got four."

"Yeah, well, they came in here . . ."

"They didn't say a whole mass in here, did they?" Eli blurted, waving his hand about the tiny room.

"Uh-uh. They got some sort of thing where they can skip everything and just give you communion."

"Well, why don't they do that all the time then?"

"That's what I wondered. But you know what they can't skip?" Thad stuck his thin arm out to Eli. "Confession!"

"You had to do it in here?" Eli whispered. "Right to his face? Their faces? The Monsignor?"

"Worse. They asked me which one! With both of them standing there, right where you are."

Eli glanced around. "Did you pick the Monsignor?"

"Almost. I figured I'd get hit by lightning if I didn't. But then I figured that wouldn't be much worse." Thad motioned toward his legs. "So I kind of pointed at Father Miller."

"Oh, man. What happened?"

"Monsignor gave me one of those looks, like he's trying to turn you into a pile of dust, and muttered 'I'll wait in the hall,' in that stupid voice of his."

"At least he left."

"Yeah. Then Father Miller was really all right. He had to do some of the weird stuff with the sashes and stuff, but he talked pretty normal. Not like a priest, you know."

"He probably hasn't learned enough yet."

"Yeah, that's what I figured, too."

"Then what? You still had to do it? Right to his face?"

"Well, for corn's sake, Eli. What can you do in a hospital? And I got last rites. That takes away everything you ever did, right? I figured they wouldn't put it back on you just 'cause they goofed and you didn't croak."

"Yeah, I guess," Eli said, unconvinced. He was beginning to believe that priests never gave you anything for free.

"And that stuff about what you think being a sin. I don't believe any of that. I mean what else am I gonna do in here, except think? And it doesn't hurt anybody."

"I suppose," Eli said. "So what did you tell him?"

"Well, I started with the 'bless me father stuff,' and when I got to the part about my sins I stopped. I guess I blushed, you know. I couldn't use the standards. How could I have fought with my brother or disobeyed my parents in here. Even a priest wouldn't have believed that."

Eli closed his mouth to swallow. What would you say if you couldn't use those two? "You know what?"

Eli said. "I don't even say the Hail Marys or Our Fathers anymore."

Thad nodded. "Me neither sometimes. But Father Miller tried to help me remember," he said, pausing to let that sink in. "So, finally, I just told him it was impossible to sin when you can't even get out of bed."

"No way!"

"So he started into the bad thoughts thing and asked if there wasn't something I was sorry about. And before I knew it, I told him I was sorry I fell off the bleachers."

"You're kidding!"

"And he just laughed. Said he doubted that was a sin."

"Probably the only thing that isn't somehow."

"I know," Thad exclaimed. "But the best part is that it kind of was, you know. 'Cause we weren't supposed to be there."

"That's right. He must not've known that."

"No kidding. But then he started back on the bad thoughts and I finally said, 'OK, I had some bad thoughts,' just so it'd be over. But, guess what? He asked me what they were."

"No way!"

Thad nodded his head vigorously. "He sure did."

"What'd you say?"

"Nothing!" Thad almost yelled. "What'd you think! Anyway, he started in on the 'you're really talking to God' thing."

"That's another thing," Eli broke in. "God's supposed to know it all anyway. So if you're really talking to Him, why bother? It's just the priests who want to know that stuff."

"Yeah. But it's supposed to show Him that you're really sorry. But I'm not," Thad insisted. "Most of the time you're not even thinking and then something pops into your head and it's a sin. Then what're you supposed to do? Be sorry?"

"I figure it all doesn't work anyway," Eli started, but the thoughts that had taken root after Thad's accident were too raw for Eli to put into words. He still fought not to think of them at all. "I don't think I believe any of it anymore," he said.

"Yeah, maybe," Thad said. "And, you know, nobody cares what we think anyway."

Thad's voice fell to a hush. "You know what? You know that one nurse? The one with the really big . . ."

Eli leaned forward, nodding and glancing back at the door.

"She came in here yesterday morning and I was still almost asleep. But, you know, I had one of those morning ones," Thad's eyes widened. "You know, when you wake up sometimes?"

Eli nodded, but he didn't quite understand the predicament.

"First thing in the morning they give you the bedpan and stuff, so you can go."

"The nurse?" Eli said, the whole horror dawning

on him. "I would've just wet the bed."

"You can't," Thad answered. "And they don't care. She just flipped the covers up and went to put the tube in and . . ."

"She touched it!"

"They always do, Eli. I can't feel to go. But she just smiled and said, 'We're feeling a bit randy aren't we?' What does that mean? Randy?"

Eli was too dazed to care. "I'll look it up," he mumbled.

"So she didn't even care. That can't be a sin. I wasn't thinking about anything, it just happened. So . . ."

"You didn't tell Father Miller!" Eli exclaimed.

"Are you crazy?!" Thad howled, clutching at his abdomen.

Even Eli had to laugh at himself for saying that. They were both still giggling when their parents walked through the door.

"You two seem to be enjoying yourselves," their mother said.

"We were just talking."

"You shouldn't get him so worked up, Eli. Aren't you exhausted, Thad?"

"Not really, but my stomach hurts."

"Too much laughing," his father said. "It's probably doing more good than harm. But Eli and I will head on home and burn some breakfast before you wear out."

"OK," Thad said, the light in his eyes dying out.

He turned to Eli. "We'll see you later, OK? You can come over and watch the Packers if you want."

Eli glanced resentfully at his parents. "OK, Thad. See you later."

His father said good-bye and he and Eli were in the hallway when Eli heard Thad ask their mother if they could all burn a breakfast together sometime when he got home.

CHAPTER
SEVEN

The hope that Thad would be home for Thanksgiving faded when, after four weeks in the hospital, an infection laid him out as hard as the first operation. In the middle of the long weekend Max dropped over, volunteering to help Eli with the Saturday papers and wondering if they had time to visit Thad before they started. They huddled into their coats and started the familiar walk to the hospital, letting the wind off the lake push at their backs as they laid plans for the coming week. After two days off, with two more to go, they couldn't believe they'd have to go back to school on Monday.

"Maybe we'll have a blizzard," Max said. "Maybe it'll snow so much they'll close the school."

"It's only Thanksgiving," Eli said, kicking a frozen lump of dirt in the sidewalk.

"Yeah," Max admitted. "Hey, why don't we go to the bakery and get a filled longjohn for Thad?"

Eli laughed. "Do you remember . . ."

Both boys stumbled along, laughing until the tears came to their eyes, straining to get out bits of the story. Finally Max had to stop. Struggling to get air, he was forced to look away from Eli. "When we had the contest," he said at last.

"Yeah. When I had all that money from the papers."

The boys walked past the hospital and turned the corner to the bakery. "We bought the whole thing of the filled longjohns, with the chocolate on top."

"We were sitting on the old fountain. Remember? Thad says, 'Bet I can eat more of these than you can,' " Max said.

"And you said you could get a whole one in your mouth!"

"Well, I did."

"And all the filling came out your nose!"

"I almost suffocated."

"We ate almost all of them."

"And Thad won, by one and a half. And he barfed all over the fountain, and there wasn't any water in it, and it stayed there all winter!"

They pushed into the bakery still giggling, wiping at their eyes, their faces crimson. "My ribs hurt," Eli said.

After inspecting everything, Eli asked for three longjohns.

"The filled kind," Max added. "With the chocolate tops."

"The custard filling?"

"Yeah," Eli said, lifting his head from his handful of change. "But make it four."

With the white, waxy bag the boys hit the street again, hustling for the hospital. "We can't stay long," Eli said. "We're gonna be late for the route."

They raced the last block, arriving in a heap at the door. After catching their breath they sauntered in and found a waiting elevator. When the doors had whooshed shut, Eli said, "Come on, Max. You gotta do it. He'd laugh so hard his tubes'd fall out."

"You know what that custard feels like? Coming out your nose?" Max made a face imitating it and they were still laughing when they stumbled out of the elevator into the lonely silence of the neurological floor.

They moved toward Thad's room, Eli hiding the pastry in his coat. He wasn't sure if he was allowed to give Thad any non-hospital food.

Dr. Vernon met them one corner before Thad's room.

"Oh, hello, Eli. Going to see Thad?"

Eli looked at Max, grinning. Dr. Vernon always asked the dumbest questions.

"Yes, sir," Max answered.

"It's not a very good time right now, boys."

"We can only stay a minute anyway. I gotta do my route."

"He's just had a pretty powerful shot, Eli. That infection is acting up and it has him pretty low."

"He's all right though, isn't he?" Eli asked, forgetting to worry about how big a bulge the bag made beneath his coat.

"Oh, he's fine. This has been a big setback for him though. Why don't you two come back tomorrow?"

"Well, we gotta go in a minute anyway, Doc. And I brought a book for him, too." Eli pulled a battered copy of *Huck Finn* from his pocket. "It's his favorite."

"OK, boys. But really just a minute. If he's asleep don't wake him." Dr. Vernon tousled Eli's hair as he walked away.

Max and Eli turned the corner. "Boy, I hate when he does that," Eli whispered, smoothing his hair.

"You've still got the longjohns, right?"

"They're in my coat."

Thad's door was closed. In the early days that had been a bad sign, but in the past weeks it just meant he was sleeping or someone had forgotten to leave it open. Eli pushed it open and whispered, "Hey, Thad. You awake?"

"Yeah."

"It's me and Max." They crept in.

"Hi, you guys."

When they sat down, Thad asked Eli to pull the

blinds. "The light's hurting my eyes," he explained.

Eli recognized the danger signs in Thad's heavy eyelids and slack face and drawling speech. And he was licking his lips again. But it had been so long since those days he was determined not to let it ruin the longjohns. If it got bad he knew Max could be talked into putting a whole one in his mouth. That'd cheer up anybody.

Eli held out the copy of *Huck Finn*. "I brought this for you," he said.

Thad said he didn't want it.

"It's your favorite, Thad."

"Nothing's like that for real. If it was real they'd've killed Jim."

Eli stared at his brother. He'd planned on telling Thad that he'd read the book cover to cover, but now he wondered if Thad would want to hear that. Thad might be able to see that he was trying to be both of them at home. He might be able to see that Eli was practicing being Thad, in case he never came back.

Eli moved to the window and closed the blinds. He came back to the bed and set the book on Thad's small table. "Well, I'll leave it here anyway. In case you want it."

"Don't," Thad said. "I don't want it anymore."

"Don't you feel good?"

"Not really. What else are you guys doing?"

"Max is gonna do the route with me."

"Is it Saturday?"

"Sure, Thad. It's the middle of Thanksgiving break. You knew that."

"Hey, Thad. We got something for you. This'll make you feel better." Max giggled. "If you don't puke again."

"Huh?" Thad turned his head on the pillows to look at Max.

"Show him, Eli."

Max's enthusiasm clouded over his doubts and Eli pulled the bag from his coat, holding it up for Thad to see. "We stopped at the bakery," he whispered.

"Are those longjohns?" Thad said, smiling. He reached up and took the bag from Eli. Laying it on his chest he picked at the folds until they came open. "Smells good."

"They're not all for you."

"Yeah. They just got the fountain cleaned from last time."

Both Max and Eli laughed. Thad tried, but his face wrinkled in the wrong direction. "What's it like outside?" he asked.

"It's cold out. No snow." Eli studied his face. "What's the matter, Thad?"

Thad dropped his hands on top of the bag, fluttering them in a tiny, hopeless gesture. Water began to fill his eyes. "Did you guys play football this morning?" he asked.

"Yeah. It's Saturday, Thad." Eli looked over to Max.

"Come on, Thad. Everything's all right. Do you want Max to eat a whole one?" Eli reached for the bag.

Thad clutched at it weakly. "Don't," he said. "You guys can get them anytime." He turned his face to Max as his eyes overflowed and the big tears rolled down his cheeks.

"Did they really clean the fountain?"

"Sure, Thad. You knew that," Max whispered, glancing at Eli. "They did it in the summer."

"I want to do the route, too," Thad said, the tears coming quicker. He reached his bony hand out and clutched at Eli.

Eli stared. "You can, Thad."

"It hurts all the time," Thad whispered, rolling his head against the pillows. He was sweating wildly. "I'm so tired of it hurting."

"What, what hurts, Thad?" Max whispered, rising from his chair. He and Eli stood side by side against Thad's bed.

Thad lifted his head from the pillow and stared at them. His grip on Eli's wrist tightened. "I can't even feel myself, Eli. It's like I don't even have legs!"

Eli nodded. "It's only for a little while."

"But I want to walk!" Thad yelled. "How come *you* can still buy . . ." Thad choked on a sob. "And, and play football?" His head collapsed back to the bed. "At least it should stop hurting. It's not fair," he moaned, crying quietly, the tears coursing down his face.

He was asleep before Max or Eli had even backed away from the bed. "I've never seen Thad like that," Max murmured.

"That's not Thad. It's the drugs," Eli said, hoping it was true. "And the infection. That — that wasn't really Thad. He's just tired."

Eli stepped back from his brother. "We better go, Max."

Max nodded dumbly. "Should we take the food?"

"No. I think he wants them."

"Won't we get in trouble?"

"Who cares," Eli said. He closed the door behind them. "Come on, we're late."

They didn't say good-bye to the nurse who stared at them as they moved to the elevator. She left the station for Thad's room as soon as the boys were gone. The tight-lipped, pale-faced boys were a far cry from the giggly pair that had entered.

CHAPTER
EIGHT

The first real snow fell early enough that people began to talk of a white Christmas. Eli and Max met at the usual corner and carried on the talk as they kicked through the last unshoveled blocks to school. "I bet it'll melt before Christmas," Eli said.

"No way. Dad says we're supposed to get four more inches."

Eli rocketed a snowball into a stop sign. The snow was shocked from the entire length of the pole and they smiled at the crash and rattle. "Bet it melts anyway."

"What a grinch. Four more inches'll mean almost a foot. Then only a week till Christmas. It might get all dirty and tracked up, but it won't melt."

"Maybe. You guys aren't going anyplace this year, are you?"

Max packed his own snowball as Eli narrowly missed an elm tree. "No. But my sisters are going to Florida."

"There's no snow there," Eli said, wondering why anyone would want to go to a place with no snow. He'd like to see an alligator and a pelican, but he'd do it in the summer.

"Yep. How's Thad doing? Is he still coming home?"

"They think so. Friday, if nothing goes wrong."

"What could go wrong?"

Eli looked to see if Max could be kidding. "How about another infection?"

"Can he feel anything in his legs yet?" They waited at the street then dashed through the slush to the school. They maneuvered through the lower-grade kids to the school doors. Eli launched his last snowball and watched it crash anonymously into a knot of second or third graders. "Mortar fire," he said quietly.

"He hasn't felt anything since he fell. They thought he would by now. They did another bunch of tests last week, when they were sure the infection was over. His back isn't broken, and the swelling's gone down some, but not as much as it should've. He'd've been home by now except for all the tests."

"Did he get a wheelchair yet?" They wandered

into Mr. Genskow's class and sat down.

"Yeah," Eli said, looking at Thad's desk. "He doesn't like it as much as you'd think." He stared at the empty desk. "Why don't they just put that stupid desk away?"

"He'll be back soon, Eli. How'd you like it if you came back and they'd swiped your desk?"

"I know he'll be back. They can always get it back out. I just get tired of looking at it all the time."

Sister Victoria came in for the prayers and the class stood. Eli stood with them but he'd stopped even mouthing the words weeks ago, when Thad's new set of neural tests proved nothing.

"I can't wait for Christmas vacation," he whispered to Max.

"What else is new?" Max whispered back and smiled.

The teachers realized little would be accomplished on the last Friday before the two-week break and the seventh and eighth grades were allowed to mingle, working on art projects and skits. Eli and Max pushed their desks together with Thad's to form a table and they stayed in their room, constructing a kid-sized cardboard king for the class nativity scene.

"You get to go home at lunch?" Max asked.

"Yep." Eli snipped at a crown with a pair of blunt-ended scissors.

"And not come back? Boy, I wish I didn't have to come back. What a waste of time. Are you going to the hospital?"

"No. I gotta move some stuff around. They had the TV room set up, but Thad said he wanted to be upstairs with me. Dad's getting one of those stair elevators put in right now."

"You're kidding. One of those things you can ride up and down the stairs? Neat!"

"Yeah, that'll be all right. We built a ramp last weekend. Now I don't have to shovel around all those stupid flagstone steps anymore. The ramp covers them."

"What're you guys making?"

Eli looked up and saw Roger and Sonny standing by the feet of their king. "A manger," he said. "What does it look like?"

"What do you guys want?" Max asked.

"Nothing. We got stuck making sheep. We got four done and decided that was enough."

"A whole flock of four?"

"What's your problem, Eli?" Roger asked.

"Nothing." He cut more notches in the king's crown.

"I hear your brother's coming home today," Roger said.

"Where'd you hear that?"

"Oh, come on, everybody knows it."

"We were thinking about coming over sometime

and saying hi," Sonny said. He smiled when Eli looked up. "If it's all right?"

"Yeah, well, maybe."

"I didn't mean what I said back then," Sonny said. He lowered his eyes and turned away. "Guess four is a pretty little flock. I'm gonna make a few more. C'mon Roger."

Eli watched Sonny leave. Roger called, "I gotta go back to my own class now." To Eli he said, "I'll stop on by sometime to see Thad." Then he slipped out the back door of the classroom.

For a long time neither Eli or Max spoke. "I guess Thad'll have a lot of visitors for a while," Max said.

"Kind of looks that way." Eli put down his scissors and studied the crown. "I don't like those guys."

"Sonny's all right," Max said. "He even visited Thad once."

"He did not!"

"Yes he did. I was there."

"Thad never told me."

"He thought you'd be mad at him. At Sonny, I mean. But Thad doesn't mind him."

"He sure didn't sound like he liked Thad much."

"He was just mad at you for beating him up. I think he feels pretty bad about what he said — about Thad."

"This thing is done," Eli said abruptly, jerking the king off the desks. He leaned the cardboard model against the blackboard with the growing collection of figures. "That's all we have to do."

"Yep." Max leaned back in his chair.

"Let's just get out of here," Eli said.

"It's only eleven."

"Let's go, Max," Eli said. "Everybody's walking all over. We could get out easy. Wait till no one's watching and run."

Max lowered his front chair legs to the floor. "I have to come back this afternoon. You don't."

"Scared?"

"Oh for crying out loud."

"Well?"

"If they miss you, they'll remember two weeks from now. You know nuns. They'll remember two years from now."

"They won't do anything anyway, Max." Eli pushed his chair closer, hushing his voice. "Haven't you noticed that yet? I'm the poor crippled kid's brother. I can do anything."

"Eli!"

"It's the truth. I'm going. Are you?"

Max shook his head.

"Well, why don't you come over tomorrow then. We can ride up the step-elevator and ice the ramp into a slide maybe."

"What about Thad?"

"I don't think he'll be going out for a while. We'll ask." Eli stood by the back door. "Sure you won't come?"

Max said no and Eli glanced at Mr. Genskow's

back. "They won't do anything," he told Max and slipped into the hallway.

Eli got through the doors to the steps and threw himself down them three at a time. He hooked an arm into his coat, ducked below the window level of the first floor doors as he hit the landing, and dropped the last three steps to the side exit. Pausing just long enough to zip his coat, he pushed through the little-used side door and nearly ran over a nun.

"Heavens," she blurted, as she turned to the door. "Oh, it's you, Eli. Hello."

"Hello, Sister," Eli stammered, recognizing Sister Mirin.

"It's snowing again. I just had to come out and look before the children trample it. Isn't it pretty?"

"Yes, Sister."

Sister Mirin smiled at him. "Always so polite," she said. "Your brother's finally coming home today, isn't he?"

"Yes, Sister."

"Are you going home early to help?"

"Yes, Sister," Eli lied. He wished it was any other nun.

"How is he really, Eli? Has he kept his sense of humor? He was always so happy."

"Mostly."

"I'd like to see him. Do you think he'd mind if one of us horrible old nuns came over to see him?"

She smiled so brightly Eli couldn't help but blurt, "You're not one of the old horrible ones."

If anything, Sister Mirin's smile grew. "Why thank you. I'm sure nobody has ever told me that before."

"I'm just leaving early," Eli said suddenly, unable to believe he'd said it. "I couldn't stand it in there anymore."

"I know how you feel, Eli." Sister Mirin turned for one last look at the gently falling snow. "I've remembered him in my prayers. And you, too," she added, seeming to snap out of her reverie. "This must be hard on you as well. Almost worse than for Thad. Well, hurry home. You must be excited to see him." When Eli didn't answer, she added, "And a little nervous."

Eli stared at her smooth face.

"Have a Merry Christmas, Eli. Perhaps I'll see you at Mass. And I'd be happy if you'd say a prayer for me. Good-bye."

The door shut behind her before Eli could move or speak. He turned slowly and ambled down the sidewalk, not bothering to circle around the school as he'd planned. Even she'd been praying for Thad, he thought, and none of it worked. Why would anyone pray for a nun? They had heaven in the bag. And why would a nun want some kid to say a prayer for her? Eli glanced back at the school and church just before they were out of sight. For a few blocks more he could still see the steeple, with its cross on top, where it could look down on the entire city. Eli still couldn't believe the complete failure of all the prayers.

Eli blasted the elevator man's van with a snowball as he approached the driveway and cut in front of it to the ramp that now led to the front door. He kicked off his boots and coat in the front hall before going inside and shouting that he was home. His father and the elevator man looked up.

"You're early. We're about ready to get Thad. Why don't you start moving the rest of his stuff back upstairs and we'll have lunch together when we get home."

"Won't that be nice?" Eli heard his mother call from upstairs. He saw her step onto the landing and swish past the men working there. She was all dressed up, in her green dress and her pearls.

"You're not gonna play bridge today, are you?" Eli asked as she walked past and he caught the scent of her hair spray.

"No, of course not, Eli." She laughed. "I'm just so glad to have Thad home, I thought I'd dress up for the occasion."

"I just thought we'd try to get back to normal," Eli mumbled, not wanting to hurt his mother's feelings, but too overwhelmed to lie.

"We are, Eli. I just thought he'd feel more like it was a welcome home party if I dressed up. You don't have to dress up. In fact, why don't you change before you start moving any of those things."

"OK," Eli replied, starting for the stairs. He stopped at the base and asked, "You're just going to do that today, aren't you, Mom? You're not going

99

to dress up all the time now, are you?"

"No, Eli. Rest assured. I will return to your old slovenly mother tonight if that will make you happy."

"You look nice, Mom," he said. "I just think it'd be better to be like it always was." Eli waited until his mother smiled, then bounded up the steps to his room.

When he came back down his dad was rummaging through the front hall shelf for his gloves. "This shouldn't take long at all, Eli. We called and Thad sounded great. Boy, is he excited to get back into your room."

"Yeah. It'll be nice not having to go to the hospital anymore."

"Won't it though! Ah, here it is," his father said, pushing his hand into the rabbit-lined glove. "Ready, Mary?" he called.

"Sure you don't need me to help?" Eli asked.

"Not at the hospital, Eli. I have a feeling this will be hectic enough. You can finish this stuff and then you and Thad can do whatever he's up to all day."

"Yeah, OK. Say good-bye to the nurses for me," Eli said, wishing he could go once more.

Eli went into the TV room and sized up the few boxes he had to move upstairs. "Take about two sec's," he mumbled, peeking into the boxes. Just clothes. It would take longer to load them into their drawers and to hang them up.

Eli sat down in his father's chair. He remembered when it had been so much fun to have the house to himself. Now it seemed more normal than not. Eli stood up. Thad'd be back any minute and then Eli'd never be alone here again.

He wondered if Thad would ever leave the house again. "Of course he will!" he said out loud. *But why couldn't they fix his legs?* He pulled himself up the stairs only to slide back down the railing after a listless circle of the second floor. He continued to talk to himself.

"His back isn't even broken. So why can't they fix it?" He thought about moving Thad after the accident.

"He's got to walk again!" Eli suddenly swore, coming to an abrupt halt in the kitchen. Once he gets home, Eli thought, away from all the nurses and doctors, they'd be able to figure it out together. Maybe he'd just bust up Thad's wheelchair, then he'd have to walk.

Eli heard the station wagon crunching over the snow in the driveway. His stomach knotted and after a moment of panic, he dashed to the front door and threw it open. "Hey, Thad!" he screamed as he saw his father opening the back door. His mother circled from the back of the station wagon with the glittery wheelchair.

Eli slithered to a halt on the snowy ramp. He'd never really thought of how Thad would look. While his mother squared out the chair and locked it in the open position, Eli watched his father heft Thad out of the back seat, like a sack. But this sack waved violently and yelled, "Hey, Eli, I'm home!"

Eli's throat contracted so tightly that he couldn't squeak out any kind of an answer. Neither could he take his eyes from Thad's legs. His father lifted Thad higher once he was completely free of the car, but one foot snagged on the arm of the chair, turning it, bending the leg like it was rubber.

He heard his mother laugh, actually laugh, as she struggled to catch and reposition the chair. She clutched Thad's ankle and freed his leg, as if it were an unruly branch poking at her in the garden.

"We're not very good at this yet, I'm afraid," Eli heard his father say, catching their mother's laughter. Then Thad laughed, too. "Good thing you guys aren't nurses," he said.

Thad looked back up to Eli after they'd seated him in his chair. "Neat ramp," he called. "Did you help make it?"

"Uh-huh," Eli stammered. "We're gonna paint it in the spring. When it gets warm enough."

"Let me help you up the ramp, Thad," his father said. "I didn't think this weather through. I'll have to nail some tar paper or something down. It's awfully slick with this snow on it."

"Yeah, watch this Thad!" Eli took a step back, got up speed, and slid flat-footed all the way down the ramp. He crashed into Thad at the bottom and wound up straddling the chair, both boys laughing wildly.

Eli was plucked roughly from his brother's lap,

his giggling cut short by surprise.

"Careful, Eli," his father snapped.

"Eli, we've got to be careful," his mother said.

"Oh, you guys. He didn't do anything."

"Yeah, I was just . . ."

"Never mind. Some good, gravelly tar paper is what that ramp needs. Before somebody busts his buttons."

They all chuckled at that, but Eli still felt the rough grip that had hauled him away from his brother.

"I'll run down after lunch and get some."

"Yeah, well, I'll push Thad up," Eli said, taking over the position behind the chair.

"Let me try, Eli," Thad said. "Just catch me if I slip."

"OK."

"Sam, you stay behind them."

Eli glanced over his shoulder, giving his mother what he hoped was a withering look. Thad started to propel himself forward and Eli followed, hands circled around the hard plastic handles, but not actually touching. One wheel spun and Eli pushed the chair back in line with the walkway.

"Sam," their mother said. "Why don't you just carry him in and then put the tar paper down?"

"Oh, Mom," Thad groaned. He was beginning to sweat with the effort. "If you'd just leave it like this, I could lock up the brakes and slide halfway to school every morning."

Eli chuckled and nearly lost his balance but Thad

pushed on. Their mom circled to the front steps and stood at the top of the ramp, waiting. "Why don't you get it now, Sam. You'll be back before lunch. Look at him. He's nearly exhausted."

Thad made it to the landing. "It's fun, Mom," he panted.

"Nobody's going anywhere till after lunch. It'll be fine, Mary."

She pushed Thad into the front hall and helped him out of his coat. "I guess I am being silly. Listen to me, like some new mother." She hugged Thad, who rolled his eyes and winked at Eli. "I'm so glad you're safe and home I don't know what to do with myself."

"How about eating lunch," Thad suggested. "That'll be the best, not having to eat any more hospital junk."

"Coming right up," she answered, hanging up her own coat.

Eli followed Thad into the house in time to hear his mother exclaim, "Oh, Eli, honestly. You didn't move a single thing while we were gone."

"Oh, yeah," Eli answered. "I'll do it. I just got thinking."

"That Eli," their father joked as they filed into the kitchen. "He's turned into quite a thinker while you've been away, Thad."

"He always was, Dad. I thought enough for the rest of my life though, lying around in that stupid bed."

Eli ducked out of the kitchen and carried the boxes upstairs. Why had he said he'd been thinking? "Oh, about what, Eli?" "Oh, you know Mom, same old stuff. Whether Thad'd ever walk again, whether I did it, whether we should break his wheelchair. You know, that kind of stuff."

Eli had only loaded one drawer when the shout came for lunch. At the stairs he looked at the elevator seat and, glancing quickly downstairs, he climbed on, pushing the "Down" button.

"Oh no," he groaned as the chair whirred to life. He hadn't guessed it would be so noisy. No way they'd miss this, he thought, and then he heard his father call, "Eli, get off that thing; it's only for Thad. And it's too slow to be fun anyway. I already tried."

Eli grinned at that, but this thing really was slow, and, caught red-handed, he wanted nothing more than for the ride to be over. His father came out and waited for him before the chair was two-thirds of the way down. "Pretty dull, huh?"

"I'll say. But I thought I'd bring it down for him."

"Awfully considerate of you. Now come on, lunch is ready." His father held out his hand, but Eli clambered out on his own.

"So what've you been thinking about so hard?"

Eli circled around his father. "Nothing," he said. "What's for lunch?"

That night the boys slept in the same room for the first time since the accident. Their parents bustled about for a long time, putting Thad to bed and positioning everything he might need on the old bench radiator at the head of his bed. His father had even found an old hand bell, like the one the nuns used at recess. Rather proudly he gave it a shake and quickly grabbed it. "Well," he stammered, "Maybe only use that if it's a real emergency." His voice boomed in the stunned aftermath of the enormous clanging. "And Eli will be right here."

"I know, Dad. I can still remember sleeping here."

"You're a smart aleck, Thad," his mother said. She bent down and kissed him.

"It's good to have you back," his father said. "You've got everything you'll need?"

"Uh-huh. See you tomorrow."

Their parents retreated to their own room via the bathroom that connected both bedrooms. His father poked back through their door, turning on the bathroom light and shutting off their light. "Almost forgot your prayers," he said. "I'm afraid it's been so busy around here, I've left Eli to fend for himself." With that, he led them through the night's prayers: Our Father; Hail Mary; Glory Be. He intoned the first half while the boys answered the second half by rote. He finished with a "Goodnight, you two," and added, "I'll leave this door open, Thad, once we're done using the bathroom." Then he closed the door, shutting out all but the line of light at the edges.

"You know," Eli whispered, "He hasn't done that since you went to the hospital."

"Prayers? Lucky for you."

Maybe he'd given up on God, too, Eli thought. Until Thad came home. Maybe then he thought he'd better start again. Eli almost laughed at the idea. His father couldn't be thinking the same stuff as he was. Not his dad. But Eli was too amazed by the idea to shake it off. "Wonder why he stopped?" he said.

"Who knows? Did you ever notice the way he always stands with that light on behind him and it's all dark in front of him?"

"Yeah." Eli shifted to his side. He'd have been able to see Thad if there'd been enough light.

"I bet you he does it on purpose. Looks like Moses."

"Yeah. He would if he had one of those big, huge beards."

"Especially when he's mad, you know? When he blasts through there when we're supposed to be asleep."

"Even sounds like Moses then."

"Bet he's wished he had some big stone tablets to lob at us a couple of those times."

Just then, their father's bellow of "Boys!" sent them both into stifled giggles.

"Like the time all the slats in your bed broke," Eli whispered.

"Quiet. We gotta wait till the bathroom light's off."

"You gotta get them to quit leaving the bathroom doors open. We'll never get to do anything like that."

"Yeah. Maybe tomorrow I'll tell them."

"OK," Eli whispered and the boys settled down, waiting for their parents to finish in the bathroom and go to sleep. The day had been a long, exhausting one for Thad though, and by the time it was safe to talk he was almost asleep.

Eli rolled over. "Hey, Thad," he said, "You awake?"

"Uh-huh."

"You know what?"

"Uh-uh."

"If you ever ring that bell without waking me up first, I'll kill you."

Thad chuckled groggily. "I doubt it. You'll probably just wet the bed."

Eli's laugh died out but his smile didn't. He couldn't believe how good it was to have Thad to talk to again before falling asleep.

CHAPTER NINE

The next morning Eli lay awake a long time, just listening to Thad's slow, regular breathing. Finally he crawled from his bed, closed the bathroom door and climbed into Thad's wheelchair. He pushed back and forth tentatively, then began maneuvering. He had the chair going in circles by opposing the spin on the wheels when he first noticed that Thad was awake.

Eli jerked the chair to a stop and rolled up against Thad's bed. "This thing is great," he whispered, catching his breath.

"I suppose. What're you doing up?"

"I figured we could go down and eat before they wake up. We got Raisin Bran *and* Frosted Flakes.

Mom let me pick." Eli grinned and spun the chair again. "What d'you say?"

Thad hefted himself up. "Get out of my chair."

They wrestled Thad into the chair, panting and giggling, telling each other to be quiet. Thad's pajama bottoms twisted around and after a few futile attempts, Eli said, "I can't get them and lift you at the same time. Can't you help?"

Thad pushed up on the chair arms, lifting his rear, and Eli gave a jerk. The chair teetered on one wheel and Eli lunged, slamming it back down and laughing out loud. "Let's leave them till we get downstairs," he whispered.

"I gotta pee."

"You can do it in the downstairs one."

"I gotta use this one." He pointed to the bathroom joining the bedrooms. "That's where Dad put in the bars and stuff."

"You can't use that one," Eli exclaimed.

Thad didn't say anything and Eli thought. "I can help you downstairs. Or just give you a pan or something."

"All right, I guess."

Eli pushed him into the hallway and they inched past their parents' door. Then Thad saw the stairs. "Oh no," he whispered, pointing at the elevator. "That'll wake up the neighbors."

"I forgot about that," Eli said, looking at their parents' door and fighting down his laughter. "Listen, I'll carry you. Then I'll come back and get your chair."

"Maybe we just ought to wait. If you drop me . . ."

Eli lifted Thad from his chair to demonstrate how easy it would be. "You're pretty light now, Thad."

"All right. But don't drop me."

"I won't. Jeez. This'll be great." Eli lifted Thad out of the chair. "Hold onto my neck."

Eli bent dangerously far forward in order to lift Thad's feet off the ground so his legs would swing to where he could grab them. When he had Thad's legs, Eli tottered down the first steps.

By the time they made the landing, Eli was breathing hard. "I got the railing," he said. "You just hold onto my neck."

"OK. My foot's catching in the railing, isn't it?"

"I'll check." Eli realized Thad couldn't tell what happened to his legs if he couldn't see them. He pinched Thad's calf once and got no response, then felt guilty about it. "Ready?"

"Hi-ho, Silver," Thad whispered and slapped Eli on the back.

Eli started down the seventeen steps with his tongue pinched at the corner of his mouth. Thad wasn't nearly as light as he looked. "Tub-o'-lard," he muttered as he stumbled on.

Thad snorted and bounced on Eli's back. "Tired already?"

"Cut it out, Thad!" Eli snapped, much louder than he'd intended. They both heard the noise behind their parents' door.

"Hurry up," Thad whispered.

Eli's tongue was still out as he raced down the remaining steps, no longer caring about the thumping his trembling legs made at each footfall. He hit the bottom at last, lowering Thad till his legs dragged out behind. Then he rolled Thad off his back and onto the carpet. The boys giggled in relief and listened for footsteps. "You've got to get my chair, Eli," Thad said. "I gotta go to the bathroom. Bad."

Eli leapt up the stairs. He was reaching for the wheelchair when he heard the knob on his parents' door rattle. He froze, one hand on the wheelchair's grip.

His father stopped in the doorway, looking at Eli and the chair in sleepy confusion as he fumbled with the belt of his bathrobe. "What're you doing?" he asked, then, before Eli could get out a "nothing," he added, "Where's your brother?"

"Um . . ."

His dad was awake now. He leaped down the hall and glanced into the boys' room. Then he saw the elevator still upstairs. "Did you carry him downstairs?" his father snapped.

Eli still stood frozen. "We wanted breakfast."

"Did you carry him down?" his father asked again, even more sharply.

"Uh-huh. We didn't want to wake . . ."

"Where have your brains gone, Eli?" His father turned for an instant when Eli's mother stepped out of their room. "What's the matter?" she asked. "Where's Thad?"

"Eli carried him downstairs," his father shouted. "Do you have any idea what you could have done if you'd dropped him?"

Eli pulled the wheelchair to himself. "I didn't."

"But, Eli," his mother started.

"We were just trying to have fun," he said. "We were going to eat some cereal. We were gonna do stuff like we always did!" Eli stopped for breath and realized he'd gone too far. He didn't look at his parents. "It's Thad, you guys. Just Thad." He looked up. "Can't we pretend it's just Thad, and that he's not gonna fall apart any sec'?"

Eli turned the chair around and started for the stairs. "Just a minute, Eli."

"I can't," he answered, picking up the surprisingly heavy chair. He tottered for a moment. "Thad's got to go to the bathroom. Right now."

His father caught his arm on the first step. "Just a minute, I said."

Eli turned to his father. "He's got to go to the bathroom."

"I can understand what you've been going through, Eli. For heaven's sake, we'd all like things to get back to normal. But taking stupid risks will only make things worse. I don't want to ever hear of another stunt like this. You two will have plenty of chances to play together without endangering your brother."

Eli stared at his father, too furious to drop his gaze despite the danger. "Thad's got to go . . ."

"Hey," Thad's voice came up the stairs. "I don't know if I can hold this."

Eli spun away but his father grabbed the chair from him and pounded down the steps. Eli turned and stalked to his room. He pushed his mother's hand away as he passed her.

From his bed he heard his father say, "Just leave him alone until he can control that temper of his."

He'd control it all right. He didn't need any of their stupid breakfast anyway. He'd control it so well they wouldn't even know it was there. But it would be. He wouldn't forget how they'd spoiled everything—Thad's first morning back and they'd ruined it.

He'd built his revenge into an impressive crusade spanning years when his door swung open. He glanced up, saw his father, and rolled so his back faced the door.

"Thad would like you to come down for breakfast."

Eli said nothing. He felt the bed sink, sucking him toward where his father sat. He squirmed back to the high side.

"I'm sorry about the way things turned out this morning, Eli. I didn't mean to shout. But I was scared for Thad. Of course you two can play, but for a while we'll all have to be extra careful about his back. You wouldn't want to put him back in the hospital, would you?"

Eli stiffened. " 'Put him *back* in the hospital.' Did you even know it was Thad's idea?" he spat.

"It doesn't matter who wanted to go downstairs. You've — "

"I mean playing tag on the high side," Eli interrupted. "It's not like everything was all my fault."

"What?"

Eli sat up and turned to his father. "Everyone thinks I pushed him off or something. It wasn't my fault!"

"Don't you start yelling at me, Eli."

"Well, nobody else fell, did they?" Eli yelled.

"You get control of yourself right now, young man," his father said, standing up. "No one ever said you were to blame for that."

Eli's snort of disbelief stopped his father.

"Now I know we've given you a lot more leeway during this whole thing, Eli," he said, pointing a finger at his son. "But that is going to end right now, do you understand me? That is going to end. Nobody's ever blamed you for a bit of this."

Eli fought to give a calm, bored expression, focusing on his father's shaking finger rather than his reddening face. There were so many emotions piling up in him that Eli started to tremble. He knew he couldn't answer without his voice disintegrating. He

115

felt an insane urge to smile, even laugh.

"You're part of this family, Eli, and you're going to have to start acting like it. I won't allow you to use your brother's condition as an . . . as an excuse to display your temper, or to stop using your common sense."

Eli tried to say something but his voice cracked. He swallowed and saw his mother come in and stand behind his father. "You don't know all you think . . ." he started, but his voice failed him again. He ducked his head as he felt his face burn, and tears of utter frustration beginning to well up.

"That's enough!" His father shouted both Eli and his mother down when she tried to intervene.

"No one ever blamed you for any of this, Eli. This is God's will, and I can say . . ." Mr. Martin stopped again, his mouth open in mid-sentence. Eli looked at his father with such contempt that Mr. Martin could not continue.

"God didn't have a thing to do with it!" Eli squeaked, furious that his voice sounded so tiny. "I don't even believe in God anymore!"

Eli's sentence was cut off by his father's slap. He stared up at his father's enraged, puzzled face, and refused to cry or to speak. Slowly he backed off the bed and stood with the bed between him and his parents.

His father's lips worked for a moment, but no sound escaped. Mr. Martin turned and walked from the room.

"He didn't mean that, Eli," his mother said. She circled the bed and put an arm around him. She studied his face for a long time but Eli refused to meet her gaze, or to soften to her hug. He stood stiff and straight, staring after his father.

"This isn't much of a homecoming for you and Thad, is it?"

Eli remained motionless, pressing his teeth together, listening to them grind inside his head.

"Eli," his mother said, stroking his hair and cheek. "It was wrong for Dad to shout at you and to hit you. But it was terribly risky for you and Thad to go downstairs by yourselves.

"I'm afraid we've all been so concerned with helping Thad get better that we left you alone too much." She tried to look Eli in the eyes but he turned away. "That was very wrong of us, Eli. I'm sorry. Can you forgive me?"

Eli stared at the door, listening to his teeth.

"Don't you see that Dad and I don't know what to do any more than you do, Eli? This is new to all of us, and I think we're making a lot of mistakes." She began to rock Eli in her hug. "And not knowing what to do makes your father's temper get bad. Like yours does when you're not careful.

"You saw me in that silly dress yesterday, Eli. You were right about that." She smiled hopefully and gave his head a pat. "Thad didn't want me looking . . ." she paused, then remembered, "looking like I was going to bridge club." She gave a tiny laugh.

"Thad just wanted it to be normal." She sighed. "How we all wish it could be that way again.

"But until it is, Eli, we're all going to have to try very hard, and work together." She paused again, tightening her hug. "I would have helped you down with Thad this morning."

Against his will, Eli's anger was losing its white-hot edge. "We just wanted to get up before you guys," he said, his voice grating over his parched throat.

"I'd have gone back to bed if you'd told me what you wanted."

Eli felt the tears of frustration again. How could he tell her that he'd never be able to say, "Thanks, Mom, now go away." The whole thing was about getting up first and being in charge, having the whole house under control, just him and Thad. And knowing that it was impossible to explain, he felt as if he'd explode. He shook his head morosely.

"Now, come on, Eli. Let me help. Tell me what you need and we'll help. It can't be the way it was, not right away, but we can sure try to make it the best we can."

"But it *can* be the same," Eli insisted, wriggling to get free of her embrace.

"But he's still hurt, Eli. He . . ."

"But you don't have to treat him like a — like a — a gimp! Just make it normal now! Then when his legs get better . . ." Eli's voice went wildly out of control and he shivered, longing to hit something — anything — that would let him vent the things locked inside. "Don't you think he'd . . . how'd you like it if you finally got home and everybody acted like, like you were . . . like that?"

Eli finally looked up at his mother. " 'Don't slide on the walk, you might hurt Thad.' 'Don't get up early, you might kill him.' " His eyes wandered as he struggled to say what he needed to say. "And that," he pointed at the radiator. "That stupid bell!" The absurdity of everything tore out of his throat in a half-sob, half-laugh, and he chuckled as his tears came. His mother laughed and hugged him very tightly.

"Maybe you know more about it than any of us, Eli. Maybe you do," she said as she rocked and stroked his back. When his tears stopped, Eli's mother asked if he thought he could go down and have pancakes with Thad. "I'll cook one more batch. Then Dad and I have some errands to run." She moved back a bit to look at him. "Will that be all right, Eli? Will that help at all?"

Eli shrugged. This was always the worst, trying to avoid his dad, wondering how to act even after things were OK again. It was practically impossible to walk around and say, 'Hey, Dad,' after you were yelling at each other a little while before. And why in the world had he said that about God? He'd never even quite thought it to himself. So he had to go and say it right to his dad's face, the same dad who stood in the doorway every night like Moses. How could he have done it?

"Well, let's go," his mother said. "Why don't you get a drink first. It'll make you feel better."

Nothing was going to make him feel better, but Eli turned on the faucet and waited for the water to get cold. He stared into his reflection in the mirror and said, "You just told Moses you didn't believe in Him." He took one last look at himself and made a face: to God, his father, or himself — he wasn't sure. Maybe all three.

CHAPTER
TEN

Eli followed his mother to the kitchen, slid onto his bench at the table, and smiled shyly at Thad. When their mother was out of earshot, Thad whispered, "He's in the basement." Then he gave the old gesture of steam squirting from their father's ears, and Eli nodded that he knew.

Their mother stacked the pancakes in an enormous pile with instructions to eat as much as they could. Then she called good-bye from the back door, saying that they'd both be gone for several hours. The door closed behind them.

"Wow," Thad said.

"No kidding."

"What would they have done if you'd dropped me?"

"I doubt I'd be alive anymore."

"That's for sure. I heard you yelling back at him. Why do you do that? Why don't you just say OK? Or nothing at all?"

Eli shrugged. "Sometimes I can't."

"Yeah. But you only get killed worse whenever you do."

"Sometimes I just can't," he repeated. He reached for a couple more pancakes even though there were two already on his plate.

"What did he get so mad about when he went up to get you?" Thad asked, rolling his chair an inch or two away from the table and setting his fork onto his sticky plate.

Eli poured too much syrup on his pancakes. He grimaced and pushed his pancakes away from the syrup pool. "For taking you down, I guess."

Thad rolled to the sink and put his plate on the counter.

"You don't have to do that. We rearranged the jobs."

"I can do it," Thad said, rolling back to the table.

"Hey, Thad," Eli whispered, "do you believe in God still?" He held his fork halfway to his mouth waiting for Thad's answer.

"Sure, I guess," Thad said. "Are you done with this?" he asked, sliding the butter plate to the edge of the table.

Eli nodded. "But really, do you? I don't."

"Well, not like they tell you about in school. Not

like the nuns and priests talk about."

"I don't believe in any of it, Thad. Not at all."

"Yeah, I know what you mean," Thad said. Eli was at once comforted and disappointed by his twin's matter-of-fact acceptance of the realization that had tortured him for months.

"Sometimes they throw so much junk in," Thad continued, "that it makes it pretty hard to swallow."

"All of it is, Thad!"

"Yeah, most of it. But I think you go to heaven when you're done. Or hell. But not as easy as they say you do."

"I don't. I mean, babies going to limbo, just 'cause they didn't get a bunch of water dribbled on their heads? What a bunch of goofball stuff! Or all those kids going to the public school. They're not Catholic, so they go to hell?"

"I don't think anybody really believes all that stuff."

"But it's in the Bible. And everything else in there is so true that if you don't believe it, you go to hell!"

"Well, it's like a parable then, or something."

"But how can they say which part is true and which part isn't?" Eli asked.

"I don't know. But some of it's got to be true."

"OK," Eli said. "What if you'd died? What if you died and went to heaven? Then, what if I turned out really bad? Like, what if I murdered somebody or something."

Thad cut Eli off before he could get started on his story.

"But, what if I went to hell? Wouldn't you want me to be in heaven with you? And aren't you supposed to get everything you want up there?" Eli paused, and then replied, "But you couldn't! 'Cause I couldn't come up! You see?"

"Well, what do you think happens then?" Thad said.

"What do you mean?"

"When you die?"

"Nothing. You're just dead, that's all. They put you in a grave somewhere and you're dead. But it wouldn't matter, because you're dead. You'd never even know it."

"What about your soul?"

"They made all that up, too, Thad."

"You mean you . . ."

"There's no such thing! You die, just like anything else, like any animal. We're just an animal, remember?"

Suddenly Thad's face grew distant. "You know what, Eli? I haven't told this to anybody." He looked directly at his brother. "When I got hurt, I don't remember anything. I remember going at you, because I was going to dodge, right at the last sec'." Thad paused and swallowed. So did Eli.

"But then I do remember one thing. I looked up for a second. You were there, I remember, and maybe Max. And it was sunny. I tried to say something, but I couldn't. I couldn't even keep my eyes open. But, you know what? I could still see everything. Even with my eyes closed."

Eli stared at his brother, but his face had faded to that faraway place again.

"I thought that I was already dead or something. So I stopped trying to open my eyes."

"Didn't it hurt?"

"Uh-uh." Thad looked at Eli again. "But I kind of wanted to see what it would be like — dying. It was like floating and it didn't hurt at all.

"Then I remember the first time I woke up in the hospital. It took me a long time to figure out what happened and where I was, but then I did, and then I remembered that stuff I just told you. I fell back asleep right away, but I was kind of sad that I wouldn't find out what it was like, because I knew I was alive. But it felt good going to sleep, because it hurt then, and when I fell asleep it didn't, and I figured I might find out anyway." Thad stopped and smiled at Eli. "I'm glad I didn't."

"Yeah, me too," Eli whispered. He stared at his brother a long time before asking, "But you never saw anything? Heaven, or any saints or God or anything?"

Thad shook his head. "No, nothing like that. But I think it was my soul that was looking around the field then."

Eli didn't answer.

"So I figure there must be something. Someplace

for it to go. And, I guess there must be a God, because He runs the place."

Eli took a breath and scanned Thad's body in the wheelchair. "Well, how come He let this happen to you? If He's supposed to be so great, why'd He let you fall? That's why I don't believe any of it!"

Eli interrupted when Thad started saying it had to be for a reason. "A test, like? Like what He did to that one guy?"

"Job? Yeah, I guess, only . . ."

Eli broke in again. "That doesn't make any sense! He's supposed to know everything. So why bother?" Eli was nearly shouting. He stopped to lower his voice. Shaking his arms, he continued, "That's the whole thing, Thad. He knows *everything*! So why would He do anything — anything at all? Especially just messing up some kid's back? It couldn't be a test. He already knows the answers!" Eli stared at Thad, hoping his brother would understand it all better than he did.

"But then how did we get here, Eli?"

"Who cares!" Eli yelled. "What difference does that make? We're here, and when you're dead, you're gone."

"But what if I did die, back then when I almost did? How'd you like it then? Wouldn't you want me to be up in heaven, waiting for you?"

Eli got up quickly. He hadn't thought of that. He carried his plate to the sink and left it there. He'd have to think later. He was tired of thinking about

God at all. Eli wished God would go away, forever.

"Just never mind, OK, Thad?" He took hold of the handles to his brother's chair, turning him away. Pushing him out of the kitchen he said, "What do you want to do? Want to go outside? The snow's good packing." But, he remembered, as the words tumbled out, that Thad couldn't really throw a snowball anymore. "Let's just do something before Mom and Dad get home."

"OK, Eli," Thad said. "But let's stay inside."

CHAPTER ELEVEN

The snow didn't melt before Christmas and shoveling the ramp to a less-than-glassy surface and sprinkling it with salt got to be as bad as shoveling all of the flagstone steps it covered. Thad demanded to be treated as normally as possible, sitting out with Eli while he shoveled and, to Eli's dismay, insisting on going to church although he'd been offered amnesty — and they had to go to church almost every day this time of year.

The more they went to church, the more sullen Eli became. Thad had ruined his revolutionary ideas. Not believing had made everything so easy. He didn't have to figure out why God let it happen, and why a lifetime of prayers had amounted to nothing, or worse than nothing. They should have at least warded off having his brother turned into a cripple.

But his new belief, or disbelief, would not go away. His blind faith was gone, leaving him to see with a disturbing clarity. Eli didn't want this new knowledge. He had to believe like before or not at all.

Kneeling in church on New Year's Day, Thad kept bumping Eli's elbow, pointing out obvious hangover victims. Eli nodded distractedly and lapsed back into thought. Some of the things the priests did seemed so stupid. And how many people in the church really believed that a bunch of wine was actually blood, let alone the blood of somebody who'd died two thousand years ago, even if he had only stayed dead for a few days? Eli couldn't help glancing around. He knew he was asking for trouble having these thoughts in God's own house.

As he walked back from Communion, the starchy host dissolving on his tongue, he continued to pick at Thad's question. Of course he'd want Thad to be in heaven if he'd died. How could Thad even ask that? But what if it was just a wish? What if everybody who died really was just dead? Nobody'd ever know, because when their turn came it'd be the same for them, too.

Eli filed into the pew after his parents. He listened to Thad's wheelchair roll down the aisle and turn to face the altar.

It'd be a harmless lie, he realized, thunderstruck.

129

I'd die and it'd be all over. I'd never even know I'd been tricked. But it would have made the rest of my whole life easier, because I could think that Thad was still around. Just like he moved someplace else, someplace nicer even. Eli's mouth slipped open as the marvelous scheme unraveled before him.

He knelt ramrod stiff, struggling to untangle the collapsing images in his mind. It'd explain everything! It would explain absolutely everything! He peered up at the half dome above the altar; at the towering paintings of the apostles. The paintings followed the curve of the dome, appearing to reach out for Eli. Their once-kind faces seemed full of condemnation.

Eli grew frantic, but there were accusing eyes everywhere. Even the images in the stained-glass windows reached out in violent rainbows of haloed martyrs. He turned in desperate hope to his parents. But both their heads were bowed over their folded hands, their eyes closed. His mother's lips moved slightly as she prayed.

How could he have figured it out while they'd sat there praying? He scanned the church and was ashamed for thinking that he alone, of the entire congregation, could have seen the truth.

Eli shook his head slowly, stunned by his own audacity. And he began to pray. But it came jerkily. He asked to be forgiven, but his pride told him it wasn't wrong to try to figure things out. Then, repentant, he asked to be forgiven for his pride. For the first time in weeks he prayed for Thad. And, although it wasn't in his prayer, another part of his head thought, Prove it that way, fix Thad. Because making him paralyzed doesn't prove a thing. Then Eli begged not to be held accountable for such a thought. He didn't try to think anything like it. He was trying to pray. His prayer, however, turned around until it was more a challenge to God to prove that he, Eli, was wrong.

It wasn't until Thad reached over and tapped Eli's arm that he realized the mass was over. He looked once more at the twelve apostles above his head, then grabbed Thad's chair and raced down the aisle. Using Thad to part the crowd, Eli fought to get outside before he suffocated. Thad laughed as they skidded to a stop next to a snowdrift. "Are you crazy?" he asked. "You almost mowed down that old lady." But his laughing ended when he saw Eli's face. "Are you sick? You're all white."

"No," Eli gasped. He reached down and put a bit of snow in his mouth. When his parents emerged from the huge, open doors, he said, "I wasn't goofing around. I had to get out. I guess I felt sick all of a sudden."

"Are you all right now?"

"I guess. It feels better out here."

"You probably just stayed up too late last night."

"Maybe," Eli said, eager to have any explanation accepted. If they found out what he'd really been thinking, they'd, they'd . . . Eli couldn't even begin to imagine the hurt it would cause his mother, or the rage it would evoke in his father.

God and heaven and everything else all a lie! It couldn't be true, he insisted to himself as he fell in behind his mother, pushing Thad. I'm not that smart, he begged, wishing someone would tell him it was all true and he was wrong. But he couldn't even tell anyone.

Eli feigned illness the last Sunday before the end of the vacation. It was the last of the holiday masses and Eli could not bear it. His resolve withered, however, when his parents returned and Thad rode up to his room and asked him how he felt. He attempted to make his "recovery" gradual, but the telltale signs of healthiness were there.

As their father stood in their doorway that night, dramatically backlit, he paused before beginning the Glory Be. "I can't hear you, Eli," he said.

"OK," Eli muttered, deciding it would be safer to mouth the words that were becoming so senseless.

They finished and instead of saying good night, his father said, "Is everything all right, Eli?"

"Yeah. I feel a lot better." Eli tried to sink further into his mattress.

"Why didn't you come to mass with us?" his father whispered.

Eli froze. "'Cause I didn't feel good."

After a moment his father said, "Good night boys," and closed the door.

When the line of light around the door snapped out, Eli rolled to his side. "It'll be weird," he said, before Thad could ask about church, "both of us going to school together again."

"It'll be great."

"Yeah. Do you think you'll be very far behind?"

"Naw. That tutor was pretty good. Sure was a crab though. Made me do everything even when I was practically asleep."

Eli giggled.

"What's so funny about that?"

"No, not that. I was just thinking." Eli stopped, unsure if Thad would find any humor in it.

"What?"

"Oh, about Mr. Genskow."

"What about him?"

"About how he's going to look hauling you up the stairs."

Thad answered with a chuckle. "I guess he'll look a lot better than Sister Dorine."

"She could probably do it a lot easier."

"Yeah, with just her little finger."

"I wish we didn't even have to go," Eli said, breaking the long, sleepy pause.

"I know what you mean. But I kind of want to. Just to do something like I used to. It'll be fun seeing everybody."

"You saw Max a bunch since you came home."

"Yeah, but just everybody, you know, going to school and . . ."

"I suppose," Eli yawned, rolling over once more. He tried to listen for Thad's breathing to slow but he fell asleep long before his brother.

In the next morning's rush Thad and Eli shared the bathroom while their mother yelled up the stairs for them to hurry. Eli couldn't help wincing when he saw Thad putting on his rubber gloves and unwrapping the suppository. Thad saw his look. "It's pretty gross, isn't it?"

"Oh, sorry."

"No, it is. But they say if I can do it at the same time every day, pretty soon it should start working by itself."

Eli nodded, hurrying through his brushing.

"I hate it, but I'm kind of used to it. It's kind of weird, the stuff you can get used to."

"I guess so. Do you need anything else?" he remembered to ask, stopping in the doorway.

"No, thanks. I should be able to get down fine. Takes this thing about an hour to work anyway."

"OK," Eli said, hesitating a moment, then rushing downstairs.

"How's Thad coming?" his father asked.

"He'll be here in a minute. He's . . ." Eli mumbled and fell silent.

"Working up a poop?" his father said jovially.

"Sam! At breakfast?" his mother said, pretending to be shocked.

"He sure has got the disposition for it. Hasn't he, Eli?"

Eli filled his bowl and didn't answer.

"So matter-of-fact about everything. No embarrassment at all." Then they all heard the elevator kick in. His father grinned. "He sure has the run of this house again."

Eli started to eat. *You won't even know what happy is*, he thought, *till you see him walking again. Then we'll have some dispositions around here*. Eli was surprised at how easygoing Thad had been. He sure wouldn't have been. Not in a million years. Not till he could walk again, and run.

Overriding Thad's protests, their mother drove them to school. They stopped at the usual corner and picked up Max. He climbed in smiling. "Hey, Thad!"

"I was gonna push him, but Mom says she'll drive till everyone shovels their sidewalks," Eli explained.

Mrs. Martin slowed down as they approached the church and pulled into the spot normally reserved for hearses. They all piled out, unloaded Thad, and headed towards the schoolbuilding beside the church. "I'll meet you here at 11:45, Thad," she said.

"I should just eat here, Mom."

"Not right away. You'll be more tired than you think."

"OK."

"See you, Mom," Eli said. He began to push Thad

toward the ramp to the church. Max walked on Thad's left side.

"Have a good morning, boys," their mother called, lingering beside her car. "Be careful, Thad. And stand by him, Eli. Don't be afraid to ask for anything you need."

"OK, Mom. Jeez."

"See you, Mom. Thanks." The boys were soon swallowed by the crowd and kids began to shout, "Hey Thad!" and, "You're back!"

The nuns by the doorstep allowed the throng to center itself around Thad for only a moment. Then they sallied forth, shooing the children to their classes. When the other kids were all inside, Thad, Eli, and Max stood by the door, in front of Sister Dorine and Sister Mirin. Sister Mirin smiled and said, "I was beginning to wonder when you'd stop playing hooky."

Thad laughed and blushed.

Sister Dorine led the boys inside where Mr. Genskow waited to carry Thad up the steps. She murmured that all their prayers had been answered, and, although he knew it wasn't true, Eli smiled and said, "Yes, Sister."

Mr. Genskow conferred with the boys and hoisted Thad onto his back. "Wish we were set up for you, Thad," he explained as he started up the steps. "But in the old days, kids in your shape didn't go to school with the rest of the crowd."

They reached the landing and got settled. After

Thad wheeled himself to his desk Mr. Genskow sat on the corner of his desk and waited for the hubbub to die. "I don't know how many of you noticed," he said, "But Thad's back in school today." Laughter rippled around as heads turned to Thad.

"Now Thad has missed almost three months of school, but I had a long talk with his tutor. It looks as if we're all going to have to watch out for Mr. Martin. I think he may be ahead of us in most of our work."

Thad grinned and the murmur in the room rose. "So," Mr. Genskow continued, "let's get down to work. You can visit with Thad on your own time. Let's not have his return disrupt our schedule." Pausing, he looked over the quieted class. "And finally, although Thad is not one hundred percent at the moment, it's only a temporary situation. Isn't that right, Thad?"

"That's right!" Eli blurted.

"So let's treat him like we did before, all right? He wants to do everything himself and the doctors say that's best, so we have to let him. By the end of the week we'll all be used to his chair and it will probably be hard to remember him without it."

Mr. Genskow stood up. "Enough said. Thad's back and we're glad of that. Now let's get to business." He pulled the text from his desk top and gave the day's assignment. And, when the time came, Thad brought the collected homework up to Mr. Genskow. He simply said, "Thank you," and turned to the next student. Thad rolled back to his seat.

When school broke for lunch, Thad and Eli waited for Mr. Genskow at the top of the stairs. "Tired?" Eli asked.

"Not at all, really," Thad answered. "It was kind of fun."

"Uh-huh. Did you know Mr. Genskow was going to say all that?"

"He called Dad last night and Dad told me."

"Oh."

"It helped, I think. Then they don't think I'm a weirdo or anything. Or some kind of cripple."

"Yeah," Eli began, but Mr. Genskow appeared and they worked their way down the steps. Rolling to the door they saw their mother parked at the curb. "Thanks, Mr. Genskow," Thad said as he held the door for the boys.

"How was it?" their mother asked as she pulled away from the curb, still breathless from loading Thad into the car.

"Fine. Everybody was pretty nice. I'm not behind at all."

"That's great, Thad."

"Everybody was real glad to see him," Eli said.

"Well, I knew they would be." She turned and looked at Thad in the back seat. "Are you awfully tired?"

"I'm fine, Mom."

"A little lunch should fix you right up."

"He said he was fine, Mom," Eli said. He turned

to the window and stared at the dirty snow flashing by.

There was no way he was ever going to forget what Thad was like without that stupid chair. Mr. Genskow had no right to think that anyone would.

CHAPTER TWELVE

Their mother drove Thad and Eli to school for more than a week, but they finally convinced her to let them walk to school. They started by alternating blocks — Thad rolling one, Eli pushing one — until Thad built up enough endurance to wheel himself the whole way. When they started walking home for lunch, it doubled the distance Thad wheeled his chair everyday. Eli told him he was going to have arms like Popeye. Thad said that'd be okay. After school, Eli would start his route, and Thad and their mother would go to the hospital for the endless therapy sessions. Everything quickly settled into a routine, and it was hard to remember when Thad hadn't been able to wheel himself wherever he wanted to go.

But months passed and Eli never got used to the chair.

One evening during the week before Easter vacation, Eli waited for the light around the bathroom door to go out and whispered, "Hey, Thad? When do you suppose you'll start walking again?"

Thad sighed. "Beats me."

"Well, don't you ever wonder?"

"Are you kidding? What do you think I do wonder about?"

"So what do they tell you? Don't you ever ask?"

"They just keep saying they don't know. That I should've started to get feeling back already."

"What about Dr. Vernon?"

"I haven't seen him in a while. Mostly therapists. And Doc Caldwell. He's the back specialist."

"He doesn't know either?"

"Just says it should start soon."

Eli rolled over, trying to see anything in the darkness around him. "Why doesn't it start then?"

"I don't know," Thad said, raising his voice a bit.

"Even after all the tests?"

"Yep."

"Don't you think there must be something we can do?"

Eli could hear Thad push himself up. "Like what?"

"I don't know. There must be something." Eli paused. "Couldn't we like, practice walking or something?"

"Not till I can feel something. They work my muscles every day, so they'll be ready when I can feel them. Do you know how dumb you feel, trying to tell your knee to bend when you don't even know where it is without looking at it?"

"There's got to be something, Thad. They're so slow."

Eli heard Thad drop back down, like there wasn't any hope for anything. "Not till I get feeling," Thad said, then paused. "And guess what, Eli?"

"What?"

"I gotta go for more tests. In Chicago. Next week," he spoke as if it were a death sentence.

Eli sat silent a moment, still trying to see anything in the blackness above his bed. "Next week?"

"On Sunday. Dr. Caldwell set it up with Mom and Dad. They didn't tell me till therapy today."

"Sunday? But that'll . . ." Eli didn't finish. Thad knew. The Easter vacation plans they'd concocted were useless.

"Yeah, I know," Thad admitted. "They set it up so I wouldn't miss school."

"What about vacation? Who cares about school?"

"I know."

"Well, did you tell them that?"

"No. You can't say stuff like that to them."

"Jeez, Thad. You should've this time. How long's it going to take?"

"I don't know. Probably only a few days."

"But we only get one week off." For the first time

that didn't seem like such a long time. "Come on, Thad."

"C'mon, Eli. I've got to go. Maybe this time they'll find out what's wrong. Even Dr. Caldwell says he's hardly ever seen one take so long."

Eli lay motionless. "Did they tell you if I was going? Or is it going to be you and Mom?"

"They didn't say. Do you want to go?"

"I don't know. I got to do my route, but what am I going to do here by myself?"

"Probably wouldn't be anything for you to do in Chicago either. I'll be in the hospital all the time I suppose."

"Max is going to Springfield to see his grandma. Is that near Chicago? Maybe he could come and see you."

"I don't know where it is," Thad answered. "I just hope they can figure it out this time. Eli? What if, what if, you know, what if my back never gets better?"

"What do you mean?"

"Well, what if?"

"They didn't tell you that, did they?"

"No. But they're always saying how weird it is, and that it should already be better. Makes me wonder."

Eli squirmed deeper into his bed. Pulling the blanket tight around his neck. "Do they ever say why it might not be working?"

"They say they don't understand."

Eli's voice dropped below a whisper. "I mean, do they say how it might've got hurt, so it won't fix itself?"

"What do you mean? It got hurt when I fell."

"They never say anything about, about getting moved after you fell?" Eli held his breath.

"No. What do you mean, 'moved'?"

"Never?"

"Uh-uh. What are you talking about?"

Eli breathed again. "Nothing. Just something Max's mom said that day. But she's only a nurse."

"What'd she say?"

"That we shouldn't've moved you," Eli said reluctantly. "But the doctors say it doesn't matter, so . . ." Eli hoped he sounded more convinced than he felt. "I guess we'll see if I can go to Chicago with you," he said. "I could go to that one museum. The one with the U-boat. I'll ask in the morning."

The answer in the morning was no. It was a business trip, their parents said, and there wouldn't be anything for Eli to do. Eli said he didn't care, but the answer didn't change. Eli was still mad when they took Thad and his mother to the train station Sunday afternoon.

After they watched Thad's train roll through the gate, Eli and his father drove home from the station in an uncomfortable silence. Eli cranked his window open as they drove through downtown. He cupped his hand into an airfoil and tried to fly it. Tilting it up would make his whole arm climb. Then he would twist his wrist and his arm would swoop into a dive. On the highway the wind was so fast you had to be careful or it'd throw your whole arm out of control. But they were driving slowly in the city, and Eli was faking it.

Eli'd seen Thad fly his hand on the highway a hundred times. He'd caught him once, rocking back and forth in his seat, eyes intent on his hand as he struggled to regain control of his fighter. He told Eli he'd never even seen the enemy plane. He said it must've come out of the sun.

Thad hadn't done that since the accident though, and now Eli's hand drooped in the too-slow rush of air. *With his engine dead, Eli managed to undo his seat belt and slide back the shattered canopy of his fighter. Despite the oily smoke billowing through the cockpit, Eli radioed that he was bailing out.* He remembered how he'd laughed when Thad had told him how hard he was hit, and he watched his hand flutter down till it hit the side of the car door. It exploded there and as Eli floated down in his parachute he could hear the enemy pilot laughing.

"What are you doing with your hand, Eli?"

Eli glanced at his father, surprised to hear another voice so high above the ground. "Nothing," he said. He pulled his arm back inside the car. He didn't like his father's "I'm trying to be friendly" voice.

"Listen Eli, I'm sorry you couldn't go to Chicago.

But it wouldn't have made any sense. Your mom and I talked about it last night though. How does this sound? She'll give us a call after the tests are through. Then, if I can get off work and you can get someone to do your route, maybe we could drive down and pick them up. It would save them the train ride, and maybe we could get to that museum, too."

"That'd be all right, I guess," Eli said. He hated to give in so easily, but it seemed like a fair plan. "Max is going to be gone, but I suppose Sonny could do my route."

"Great. That leaves me then." He winked at Eli. "I'll be able to sneak away."

Eli looked at the dashboard. "Dad?" he said.

"Mmm?"

"Do you suppose they'll be able to fix him this time?" Eli fought his urge to shudder when his father reached over and stroked his shoulder. That usually meant bad news.

"I don't think they'll be able to fix him right away. But we hope they'll be able to find the problem. If they can find out why he isn't getting his feeling back, then they can start trying to fix it." Mr. Martin glanced away from the road and smiled reassuringly at Eli.

"Well, what if they don't?"

"Don't find out, you mean?" his father asked.

"Yeah."

"We'll have to keep praying, Eli, regardless."

146

"What if he never gets it back?" Eli turned in his seat to look out the window.

"I think he will, Eli. They're almost sure the cord is undamaged, and . . ."

"But what if?"

"I don't think that will happen. We all pray it won't." He paused. "But if he doesn't walk again we'll learn to deal with it. I'm sure we'll have more of a problem accepting that possibility than Thad will."

"But we'll still be walking."

"Don't worry, Eli," his father said, rubbing Eli's shoulder. "I'm sure Thad will walk again. It just seems as if it might be a while. He'll be fine. All we can do, whatever happens, is try to help him however we can, and pray that he recovers."

"Do you think that really does anything?" he whispered, regretting it even as he spoke. That was a question to ask his mom, if he had to ask anyone. She'd listen some, but his dad got so mad so fast it just made things worse. But Eli needed to know right now. He couldn't go on trying to figure everything out by himself. His brain was wearing out.

"Prayer, Eli?"

Eli was so stunned by his father's quiet tone that he chanced a peek at him. His big face stared ahead, eyes flicking at the road. Eli wished his father didn't have to shave for church. "Uh-huh," he said, still looking at the face. He didn't look at all like Moses right then.

Mr. Martin sighed. He turned to his son and gave a shaky, friendly smile. "Sure doesn't seem like it sometimes, does it?"

Eli dropped his eyes from his father's face and stared at the hand that rubbed his shoulder yet again. He'd never seen his father unsure about anything.

"But we can't lose faith, Eli. We can't stop trying. As hard as I try, I can't see why this had to happen. But it has, and it's God's will. It simply has to be. Maybe our faith is being tested. So let's pray and show Him we're strong and that we believe He can help."

"It's not fair," Eli murmured, looking at his father's clean, strong fingers and thinking of God's cruel tests.

"I know it seems like that, Eli. But we don't know even the smallest part of His plan."

Eli heard his father's voice change and knew that the discussion was almost over. As frightened as he was, he wished it would continue. Eli wished his father could know all he knew, without Eli actually having to tell him. He felt his father's fingers under his chin and reluctantly he let his head be lifted.

"As hard as it is to understand, we'll all come through this. Cheer up, Eli. Maybe this time they will find out how to cure him. I'm sure he'll be fine. We'll keep praying and we'll see the prayers work. I know it."

Eli stared into his father's questioning, smiling

face and wished he could believe that, too. Maybe he should tell him what he thought, explain all the reasons he had that proved God was fake. Maybe then his dad could show him he was wrong.

But as Eli studied his father's face and his strong hands curled around the steering wheel, he knew that his father never had such doubts. The moment of confusion had passed from his father's face. Eli slumped in his seat, so that he could barely see over the dashboard. He stuck his hand out the window and said, "Can we drive home the rest of the way on the freeway?"

After his father said yes, Eli closed his eyes and curled his hand into an airfoil. Feeling the press of the acceleration and listening to the engine surge and shift, Eli pulled his fighter into a climb, and waited for the enemy to pounce.

CHAPTER
THIRTEEN

Eli and his father had dinner together that evening and as soon as they'd finished cleaning the dinner dishes, Eli called Sonny, explaining he might need him to do his route later in the week. "But it's not for sure yet," he said.

"Yeah. Thad's in Chicago now. But I won't know for how long till a few days."

"OK," Sonny answered. "I can probably do it. Let me know when. I'll have to go around with you once before you go. It's been a while since I've been on the route."

"OK. Come over any time. Maybe tomorrow or the next day."

"Hey," Sonny said suddenly. "What are you doing tonight?"

"Nothing."

"Roger's coming over. We're gonna go out. Want to come?"

"Where are you going?"

"I don't know. No place, I guess. Just walk around."

Sometimes Eli and Thad would walk at night, talking some, enjoying the anonymity of the dark, but Eli couldn't imagine doing it with Sonny or Roger. "And do what?" he asked.

"Nothing," Sonny said. "What do you do? Sit around with your parents all night?"

"My mom's in Chicago."

"Oh yeah. Well, do you want to come over?"

"I don't know. I'll ask my dad. Hang on."

Eli crawled out of his seat at the kitchen table and walked down the dark hallway to the TV room. "Dad?"

His father looked up from his book. The room was dark, except for the light beside his father's chair.

"Sonny wants to know if I can come over."

"When?"

"Now, I guess."

"Sure, Eli. Be in by nine."

"It's vacation tomorrow, Dad."

"Nine-thirty, then," his father said, lifting his book.

Eli ran back to the kitchen. "I can go," he told Sonny.

"All right. We'll meet you at the school."

Eli was putting his coat on as he re-entered the TV room. "What are you going to do?" his father asked.

"I don't know," Eli answered truthfully. "Roger's already over there."

"Who's Roger?"

"Just a guy."

"Well good, with Thad and Max both gone you'll probably want to get to be friends with Sonny again." His father picked up his book. "Have fun."

Eli looked at his father, circled in the darkness by the small ring of light. His face, in the shadows, looked craggy and tired — or old. Eli walked slowly to the door and called out "See you." He waited for his father to answer before going out. Then he launched himself down the steps and sprinted across the driveway toward the school.

When he was a block away from the school, Eli settled into a walk so he'd be breathing normally when he got there. Soon he could see Sonny and Roger standing under a street light. Sonny was swinging around a pole. Roger's thicker form stood a little to one side, at the edge of the ring of light.

Pushing his hands deep into his pockets, Eli crossed the street, which was almost deserted on a Sunday night. "Hey, you guys," he said as he approached the light. The old street lights had not yet been replaced on this side of town. Eli liked the circles of light linked by stretches of darkness much more than the newer lights' encompassing glare.

As soon as Eli joined them they started walking away from the school. Roger was kicking a rock but lost it as they crossed the street. "What're you guys doing?" Eli asked.

"Nothing," Roger said. "What about you?"

"Nothing. Thad's in Chicago."

"Yeah. Sonny told me."

"Where do you want to go?" Sonny asked.

Roger shrugged.

"Down by the lake?"

"Naw. They got the new lights there." Roger turned up a cross-street. "Let's go this way."

Already this was nothing like Eli's walks with Thad. He could tell Sonny and Roger didn't talk much, even to each other. The hunch of their shoulders and a kind of fake toughness in their few words made Eli feel like they were somehow angry. He walked along quietly — waiting.

Roger stopped in a dark stretch of street and pulled something out of his pocket. A match flared. Eli's heart bumped. They must have firecrackers. Then he smelled the smoke and saw Roger's face as he lit the cigarette. Sonny followed Roger with a second match. "Here," Roger said, bumping Eli's arm.

They were only out here to smoke. For a moment Eli thought of his dad completely alone in their house, with just a single light between him and the darkness. He wondered if his dad ever used to like

153

having the house to himself, the way Eli did before Thad had gotten hurt. Roger bumped Eli's arm again.

"I don't want any," Eli said.

"Did you hear that, Sonny?"

"I told you he wouldn't."

Eli looked to where Sonny's voice came from. At that moment he guessed Sonny was all right.

"What a bunch of babies," Roger said and started to walk on again. Sonny and Eli followed.

"Lay off," Sonny said.

"Yeah, yeah, okay," Roger said, taking a deep drag and flipping his cigarette, half finished, into the street.

Eli had been wondering if he could beat Roger, and he knew Roger was thinking the same about him. Fat wasn't muscle, he thought, almost laughing. Eli wondered if he should say it out loud. Sonny dropped his cigarette as they crossed the next circle of light and he smiled at Eli.

"You guys don't have any firecrackers, do you?" he asked.

"We did," Sonny said. "But we used them all up."

"My sister's boyfriend said he'd get me a bunch of M-80's," Roger said. "But he hasn't yet."

"M-80's. Wow."

"They're equal to a quarter of a stick of dynamite."

"Yeah. I heard that too."

"At least a quarter stick." Roger yawned. "They'll

be great. I'll ask him next time he comes over."

"So what are we gonna do, Roger?" Sonny finally asked.

"Don't worry. We're almost there."

"Where?" Eli asked, matching Roger's whisper.

"Here," Roger answered, pointing at a house with a dark front. "All the front lights are off. That's good."

"How come?"

No one answered. Eli followed Roger and Sonny, tiptoeing down the driveway. When they reached the backyard Roger curled around for a view of the back windows. "Damn," he muttered. He checked the garage. "Empty. Let's go."

They shuffled quietly back up the drive and continued their aimless stroll down the street. Eli whispered, "What was that?"

"Do you know Vicky Dobney?"

"Uh-uh."

"She's a friend of my sister's. In high school. That's where she lives," Roger nodded toward the house.

Eli thought a moment. "So?"

"Her bedroom's on the first floor," Roger said impatiently. "She never closes the shade and she lies around naked all the time. She's got the biggest knockers you've ever seen."

When Eli recovered from his shock he grinned. *Anybody's* would be the biggest he'd ever seen. "Have you seen her, Sonny?"

"Once, for about a second. Then she turned off the light."

"Yeah. He hasn't been there any of the good times. I see her all the time."

"I bet," Eli mumbled in Sonny's ear and Sonny had to bite his sleeve to keep from laughing.

Eli followed for several more blocks. This was dumb. He didn't want to smoke or peek in anybody's windows, although the thought of a naked girl intrigued him more than he wanted to admit — and it was kind of fun teaming up with Sonny again.

"Do you want to do the route with me tomorrow, Sonny?"

"Yeah, sure."

"You got to be there by three-thirty."

"You really have a paper route?" Roger said.

"Yeah, sure."

"What for?"

"To make money."

"Why?"

"What do you mean?" Eli said, realizing he didn't really know why. "In case I need it for something."

"Just take it out of your mom's purse. That's what I do."

Eli rolled his eyes at Sonny when they passed under another light. He had never realized how big a creep Roger really was.

"Well, I gotta go," Eli said.

"You got a curfew?" Roger laughed. "Oh boy."

Eli thought of his dad sitting in the darkness alone. He thought of his mother and Thad in Chicago alone. "Shut up, Roger," he said, not bothering to move away from him.

"What'd you say?"

"I said, *shut up*." He almost added, "What're you gonna do about it?" but Roger was beginning to back down.

"Yeah," Roger spat but then fell silent — for a moment. "Did you guys notice all those grass bags piled on the curbs?"

"Sure," Sonny answered. "Everybody was mowing yesterday."

As he spoke they passed a house with four grass-filled wicker baskets set along the curb. "Those aren't any good," Sonny whispered.

"What do you mean?" But this time, Eli knew what Sonny and Roger were talking about. They used wicker baskets at his house. Sometimes in the morning, especially on Sundays, he saw the grass that had been packed in plastic bags strewn all over the street. The broken bag was always at the end of the grassy trail, and always reminded Eli of the Scarecrow in *The Wizard of Oz*, after the flying monkeys had pulled out his straw.

"You've never done this either, have you?" Roger mocked.

Eli didn't answer.

"Just run at them as fast as you can and kick

them," Sonny explained. "Usually you can kick them a couple of times. Be careful not to get your foot stuck though, or they'll trip you."

Eli licked his lips and nodded. "There," Roger said, pointing across the street. They broke into a run together, Eli a step behind.

There were only two bags and Eli wanted to watch once anyway. He peeled off slightly to the street side as they made their run. He watched as Sonny and Roger's feet crashed into the bags. Gaping holes appeared, spilling thick grass that looked black in the night.

Roger laughed and the three of them raced down the block and quickly turned onto the next street. Eli looked back and saw the two deflated bags lying in the middle of the street, lumpy trails of grass leading back to the curb. He could almost hear the cries of the flying monkeys.

They stopped running. Eli caught his breath and thought of his father mowing the lawn, raking the grass, and hauling it to the curb. Eli and Thad always helped and he knew most people didn't have kids to do that. Remembering the two shattered bags, Eli felt ridiculous. He had an urge to go back and pick up all the grass. But he'd get caught for sure if he did. Sonny and Roger began to giggle and Eli joined in. "Boy, you run slow," he said to Roger.

"I know," he laughed. "Makes it even more fun."

Eli laughed hard at that. It was the first time he'd ever heard Roger admit to anything.

"Here we go," Sonny said, making noise like a shifting car.

They broke into a trot. "Plenty of them this time," Roger panted. His breathing hadn't yet slowed from the last attack. They crossed the strip of lawn between the sidewalk and curb, each running for all they were worth.

Sonny struck first. His bag wasn't quite full and it arced into the street. He followed it, giving a second kick that broke it in half. Each half spun onto the pavement, spewing grass.

Roger kicked his bag, and then, just to Roger's right, Eli selected his own and kicked viciously. He was halfway over the bag when he saw the second stacked behind it. His foot wouldn't come out of the heavy, humid grass and he tumbled onto the remaining bags, rolling away and laughing until he heard the shouting.

"Hey you! Goddarn kids!"

Eli scrambled to his hands and knees. He could hear the pounding of street shoes on pavement.

"Hold it right there!"

Eli was up and running before he even regained his footing. The hard slapping of the shoes didn't fall back. Eli saw Sonny flash through a band of light, already in the next block. Roger turned at the corner. The man was gaining on Eli.

Eli cut a hard left. He wasn't going to make it to the intersection. He flashed across a front yard and up a driveway, praying no fence separated the backyards. He could hear the ragged panting of his pursuer and he cursed himself for not knowing what street he was on.

Eli saw the fence at the same time the dog charged out of its house, a chain clinking on an overhead runner. He squeaked through the open gate an instant before the snarling rush.

Eli stopped in the next yard, gasping against a tree. The angry barking was almost matched by the man's shouting. The man who'd chased him must've known the owner. He began to call his name, asking for the dog to be called off.

Lights flicked on and Eli heard a screen door creak nearby. Fighting to breathe and sneak away at the same time, Eli crept to the nearest dark house and slithered through its driveway to the next street. He circled around street lights and started to zigzag to a safe neighborhood.

When he finally arrived in the alley across from his house, Eli was walking and breathing normally. The stomach-knotting fear had been replaced by a rush Eli had rarely felt. That guy couldn't have been more than a few yards behind him! It couldn't have worked out better if he'd known about the dog and the open gate. It didn't take long for the realization of how close he came to being caught to settle in. Eli had to go to the bathroom all of a sudden. He walked faster, afraid of what would happen if he risked stretching his stride to a run. But the urgency faded and Eli slowed again, wiping the fresh sweat from his forehead.

If that dog had been one second faster! Or the man! The rush swept him up again. He had done it! He'd gotten away! He laughed out loud in the alley. A single light at the end of the alley illuminated a row of garbage cans and the side of the Crazy Lady's garage.

Eli wished he had a watch. He would like to go up in the garage and think about his victory in the safe, musty darkness. But he couldn't risk being late. If he got home early he could answer the inevitable question with, "nothing much," and it would be accepted. If he arrived later than nine-thirty he would have to explain why.

As he walked down the Crazy Lady's driveway the thrill began to fade. He and Thad had always avoided telling their parents what they did — how they filled their idle time. But it had been for no reason — other than to have a secret. Or sometimes, on Eli's part at least, out of fear that their games would seem foolish to their parents. He often wondered what his father would think if he knew about the things Eli thought about. Like deciding there was no God.

"He'd think I was crazy," he said out loud as he crossed the street to his house. "Crazy or straight on my way to hell."

He called "Hi, Dad," as he walked through the

door and he found his dad in the same chair he had left him in, sound asleep.

Eli watched his dad, his mouth as wide open as Thad's would get when he was *really* asleep. He thought about his father mowing the lawn again, before he and Thad had been old enough to help. They would watch cartoons and play, waiting for him to finish so they could all do something. There were times when they would follow him, pretending to help. One week they'd even followed the mower with rakes, after the catcher basket broke.

It was wrong to bust all those bags, and Eli knew it. His father would say "Vandals!" as if it was a swear word. There were few things his father hated more. And, while his stomach sorted out the tightening knots, Eli remembered how he'd felt when he woke to find the pumpkin he'd carved smashed all over their sidewalk. It was the same people, his father always said. They broke grass bags when there weren't pumpkins. And now Eli was one of those same people.

Whatever his father had done as a kid, Eli figured, he hadn't busted grass bags. He wouldn't hate vandals so much if he had. Eli could still feel the ecstatic surge after the terror. His heart began to beat faster just thinking about it. He would probably do it again, he realized. The excitement and the fear and the challenge were too great not to.

Eli was still standing there when suddenly one of his father's eyes opened. His mouth closed slowly.

"Sonny said he'll do the route," Eli said.

His father sat up and rubbed at his face. "That's great." He smiled. "I've been working hard myself, as you can see. What trouble did you guys get into?"

"Nothing."

"Well, if I'm going to sleep it might as well be in bed." His father turned off lights and followed Eli up the stairs. "Don't forget to brush your choppers and say your prayers."

For the first time since Thad had come home his father didn't come in to lead the prayers. Eli couldn't have asked for better timing. He didn't know if he could say them without Thad there to make most of the noise.

The bedroom was different in the darkness, without Thad — like it was back in the hospital days. Eli was surprised to find he'd almost forgotten about those days. They seemed to last forever at the time. He got into bed, rolled onto his back, and folded his arm over his eyes. He hoped Thad would be OK this time.

Thad would be shocked when Eli told him about the things he'd done with Roger and Sonny. But if Thad had a chance to try it, Eli was confident he'd be hooked. Eli wondered if Thad would want to look into that girl's window. He shook his head in the dark. Thad wouldn't want to. That was *too* dirty.

The same familiar shadows blackened the corners of Eli's room, but tonight they seemed darker and more menacing — capable of hiding dangers.

163

Temptation. The word sprang into Eli's head. He rolled onto his side and opened his eyes. If the girl's window wasn't temptation, nothing was. He'd never really thought about it, despite the nuns' constant harping. They'd used the word so much it didn't mean anything anymore. And he'd never had to worry about it. The bad things he did usually just happened.

Eli realized every time he swooped down on a grass bag, it was in defiance of the temptation rules he'd had drilled into him since first grade. But he'd already chosen. The adrenalin screaming through him turned him into a different person, and it was well worth any inconvenience he caused his victims.

Looking at the girl was different though. Eli squirmed into the mattress. Very different. It concerned feelings that were new to him, feelings he preferred not to think of, or pretend weren't there. And Eli had been told since he could remember that these feelings were particularly abominable. They made him feel unclean. Yet, when he allowed himself to admit it, he knew he would've liked to have seen her.

Eli rolled over again, his mind going too fast for sleep. If he had a sister, he sure wouldn't want Roger Dubinski's fat-slob self looking at her when she didn't have any clothes on. Goosebumps rolled down Eli's arms. "What a creep," he mumbled to himself. He wouldn't want Roger looking at her even if she had her clothes on.

There was one other thing in the back of his mind. If he ever got caught breaking grass bags he'd live. It would be tough with his dad, but, Eli thought boldly, I might even be able to explain why. I could at least try. But if I *ever* got caught looking at that girl I'd die. That was for sure. There was no way to get out of that except by dying.

Eli rolled over once more, kicking one of the blankets away. Thad's first night away and he'd already wandered into this mess. He struggled to remember all his thoughts so he could talk them over with Thad. He needed to know what Thad thought, and what he'd do.

Whatever happened, if Thad wanted to do anything after dark, he'd *have* to be able to run. Eli fell asleep smiling, thinking of pushing Thad through the small fence gate at about one hundred miles an hour with the slobbering dog snapping at his heels. It wouldn't work. Not even in Eli's head. Thad had to start walking, and running.

CHAPTER FOURTEEN

Terrifying dreams of slashing Baskerville-like hounds flashed through Eli's nightmares, with even more disturbing pictures of girls looking back at him through brightened windows.

Finally the girls chased him out of his sleep and Eli wiped at the sweat on his face. He climbed out of bed and quickly got dressed. He was anxious to get out of the bedroom. His father wasn't awake yet and Eli slipped down the stairs, leaning on the railing to avoid the squeaky steps. It seemed like years since he'd carried Thad down these steps on his back. He wondered how Thad was. His first test was this morning. Maybe they'd call home tonight. Of course he wouldn't be able to tell Thad anything he needed to because his father would be sitting right beside him — but it'd be good to hear his voice.

"Those tests better work," he said out loud as he walked into the kitchen. He reached for the plates and set the table. His dad would be down any minute he guessed. Eli poured them both a bowl of Frosted Flakes, remembering at the last instant not to pour milk on his dad's.

"Good morning, Eli," his father said an instant before entering the kitchen, knotting his tie.

"Well, goodness. Thank you, Eli. I'm afraid without Mom here to drag me out, I overslept. How long have you been up?"

"Not long."

"I thought you'd sleep in today."

"Thad's the sleepyhead."

"Mmm. Frosted Flakes," his father said, smiling.

"I thought I'd fix your breakfast for you, like Mom."

"Thanks. And I need it this morning." He ate a spoonful of cereal and made a face. "These aren't bad." But that's not what his face said and Eli started to giggle.

"I'm late, I'm late," his father sang after rushing through his cereal. He pushed back his chair, stood up, and put on his suit coat. "My number's on the wall," he said.

"I know."

"All the other numbers you might need are there," his father continued. "Rake the lawn if you find time." His father turned at the car door. Eli had followed him outside. "Don't forget lunch." He winked. "And there is no such thing as a cookie sandwich."

Eli grinned and waited for the car engine's starting roar to quiet. "Can we call Thad tonight?"

"Capital idea!" he boomed in one of his incomprehensible accents. "As soon as I get home." He started down the drive. "You're by yourself. Use your head. See you tonight."

Eli waved and called, "See you."

The horn beeped once and then his father's head and arm poked through the side window. "No knives and no fires," his father called.

Eli turned into the empty garage and carried out the thatching rake. He wondered how his dad could be so much fun sometimes and so mean other times. Eli knew he would never be mean to his kids.

When the raking was done the long day still stretched out before Eli and he started to spade up the garden beds, the worst job of all. His dad would be proud of him for doing it. He'd probably croak when he saw them.

At lunchtime Eli staggered inside and climbed into the shower. He hoped his dad would come home in a good mood, and that they'd call Thad, and that, for once, Thad would have some good news. He wished he could call Thad right now. Then he could talk to him alone. Eli's head was a jumble of vicious dogs and girls and wheelchairs and Moses and bleachers and spaded earth.

He made a sandwich and sat inside for as long

as he could stand it. Then, with a sudden burst of inspiration he ran to the closet and pulled out his baseball mitt and a tennis ball. Outside, Eli hurled the ball as high as he could, camping under the pop fly he'd tricked the batter into hitting. He punched his mitt once, then made the catch, clinching yet another World Series. He was probably the only pitcher alive who consistently won all four games.

Before he'd realized it, Eli was out of his yard, tossing the ball in the air and running after it to make the catch. He wandered down the sunny sidewalks, tossing the ball into his mitt and back out again. When he passed the school he admitted to himself where he was headed.

He stopped tossing the ball as he neared his destination. He crossed the street and, as nonchalantly as possible, Eli peeked into the backyard. The low cyclone fence was there, and the doghouse, but no dog. He'd wanted just one glimpse, to assure himself it didn't have jowls that glowed with saliva or foot-long fangs.

Eli walked on nervously, turning the corner at the end of the block with a sigh of relief. The grass had all been picked up and rebagged. He wondered if the man had done it last night after his neighbor had called off the dog. Eli chuckled, quickly looking around to see if anyone had seen him.

He continued to stroll in what he pretended was another aimless path. It wasn't until he was sure that he couldn't find the girl's house that Eli smiled again. Hurling the ball into the air, Eli gave a whoop. He didn't even know where she lived! Eli started to run, his feet feeling like they were moving on air.

He made it all the way to the alley before he stopped. His ribs ached and he found himself gasping with each breath.

The alley looked so different in the daylight. There were garbage cans stretched over its full length, not just the three he could see beneath the light last night. He passed the can where they'd found the *Playboy* last year, opening it out of curiosity. They'd hidden the magazine in the Crazy Lady's garage, but it had disappeared within a month. No one really minded, though Eli still suspected Sonny. Even a *Playboy* got dull after a month.

Eli popped out of the alley just as Sonny reached the Martins' front door. "Hey," he cried, running across the street.

"You're alive!" Sonny gasped. "How'd you get away? I heard that guy. When I looked around you were still on the ground!"

They met at the bundle of papers on Eli's curb. Eli picked up half the stack and waved Sonny to the other. "We can carry these papers. If you're going to deliver on Wednesday, the papers will be way heavier. You can use my wagon then. It's in the garage."

"Eli!"

Eli started off, but Sonny coaxed the story out of

him. He was overcome with laughter when he tried to explain the dog's role in his getaway. Sonny stopped dead more than once, too stunned to do anything but listen. Then he'd run to catch up.

Eli dropped the first paper behind a screen door. "Everybody on this block, 'cept the third house," he instructed.

"Yeah. I remember that one."

"They put a wire in their hedge. So make sure to step over it. It really got me the first time. It was on Sunday and it was dark and snowing and I was running. Wiped me out. It took fifteen minutes just to get the papers put back together, and then they were all wet and crumpled." Eli stepped over the wire and made his way across the lawn. "They're creeps."

"I'll say."

"You know who's really a creep? Roger."

"Yeah, I know."

"How come you hang out with him?" Eli asked. They turned the corner and Eli explained the paper distribution on Newton Avenue.

"I don't know. He lives right down the block. But he's getting worse. He just started smoking."

Eli realized that Sonny probably didn't have anyone else to hang out with. "You ought to come over here more," he offered. "Let Roger play his own stupid games."

"Yeah, probably."

"Maybe the next time that guy with the booby-trapped hedge mows his lawn we can bomb his bags."

"Or how about every time?"

"Yeah! That'll teach the creep."

They delivered several more papers without speaking. Eli took some of the papers Sonny carried to even the load. "Have you done that a bunch? Going out like that at night?"

"Kind of, I guess. 'Specially since it got warm."

"Yeah. I guess there wouldn't be much to do in winter."

"We throw snowballs at the buses."

"Everybody does that. It doesn't have to be dark."

"Roger busted one of their windows."

"With a snowball?"

"It had a rock in it."

"Must've. Roger throws like a girl."

They were nearly done with the route when Eli asked, "Do you go to that girl's house very much?"

Sonny hesitated. "I guess. We go by there a lot anyway. But there's always something wrong, Roger says. Or else nobody's home, like last night. I think Roger's chicken."

"But you really saw her once?"

"Uh-huh."

"Without any clothes on?"

"She had underwear. And you got to stay out of the light so you're pretty far away."

"Did you ever go by yourself?"

"Nope." Sonny looked to see if Eli was laughing

at him. "It's kinda scary really. And you don't get to see much anyway."

Eli nodded. He couldn't quite ask Sonny if he could find the house by himself. It was so much easier not knowing. "Probably better in pictures anyway. Like in a *Playboy*."

"Yeah. If you can get one. Roger says his dad gets it."

"What a liar." Eli paused. "Did you swipe ours?"

Sonny stared at Eli a moment, but the relief of being off the other subject was so great both boys broke into laughter.

"Come on," Eli panted. "That's the last one. We're done."

"I'm gonna go home from here. Call me when you want me to do your route."

"OK." As the distance between the boys increased Eli shouted, "You can come over tomorrow or some time. If you want."

"OK," Sonny yelled back. "See you."

"Yeah. See you." Eli hurried home. Sonny really wasn't so bad a guy when Roger wasn't around.

CHAPTER
FIFTEEN

Sonny never did do Eli's route that week. Thad came home Thursday afternoon on the train. Their father couldn't get away from work, he said. But the news from Chicago didn't make anyone feel much like touring museums.

When Eli asked his father he told him nothing was sure, yet. He said they'd wait to see what Mom had to say when she got back. The look on his father's face was enough to make Eli spend all day Thursday lying on the couch. He felt sick.

When he finally heard the car pull into the driveway, Eli was afraid to look out the window. He'd conjured up a vision of Thad encased in chrome pulleys and thin cables. When he finally peeked, the taxi was pulling away and Thad was rolling up the ramp, the same as ever. He saw Eli in the window and he started grinning. He waved but Eli was already running for the door.

"How'd it go?" Eli yelled, flinging the screen door open.

Thad lifted his hands. "Those guys don't know anything."

"No kidding," Eli said. He grabbed the front of Thad's chair and spun him in a circle. "Hi, Mom," he called. He ran to help her with the suitcases. "How'd it go?"

"It was long, Eli."

Eli pushed Thad to the door, bumping the chair forward with his thighs. "Come on, Thad. Get out of my way, you big tub."

"Tub, schmub," Thad said, pulling the brake.

"Boys. Let's get inside at least."

Thad released the brake and Eli shot him into the house. "Do you want the suitcases in your room, Mom?"

"Please, Eli."

Eli raced upstairs with the suitcases, then leaped back down the stairs and into the living room. "How's the train ride?" he asked Thad.

"OK. Hard to get around though."

When their mom went upstairs to change, Thad asked, "So what've you been doing?"

"I'll tell you later." Eli indicated their mother's presence with a jerk of his thumb. "Sonny's been over almost every day. He was gonna do my route."

Eli paused. Thad knew why he didn't have to do the route. "But, remember that jerk who put the wire in his hedge that tripped me?"

"Yeah."

"Well, I finally got him back."

"How?"

Eli could barely sit still. "I got to tell you later, really. But I will."

"Just tell me, Eli."

"I can't. Honest. It'll take too long." When Thad seemed to agree, Eli asked, "But what about you? What'd they find out? Dad said, 'We'll wait and see what Mom has to say,' but he said it that way, you know, so I thought they must've cut you in half or something, by accident."

"Felt like they were going to a couple times."

"So?"

"So, nothing." Thad paused, hearing his mother coming down the steps. "They didn't find a thing."

"What do you mean?" Eli blurted. "They didn't find out *any*thing?"

"Not this time, Eli," their mother answered.

"Nothing?" Eli looked at Thad.

Thad shook his head.

"Nothing at all? Not even anything bad?"

"Nope. Same as before. I'm supposed to get feeling back."

"When?" Eli turned to his mother but Thad answered.

"A couple of months ago."

"Well, yeah, but . . ."

"It's good news, really, Eli. They were afraid they'd missed something that was causing the problems. That's what this series was about. But they didn't find any problems."

"But you still can't feel anything. Isn't *that* a problem?"

Thad shook his head again. "Not yet."

"Well, for corn's sake. Now how long's it supposed to be?"

"Anytime," his mother said. "They just can't tell us an exact date."

"Even after all the tests? How many have you had now?"

"About a million."

"Now boys."

"Well, Mom!" Eli shouted. "Why'd he even go?"

"They had to see, Eli."

"But, jeez . . ."

"At least they still think it should come back."

"I saw your mitt out," Thad said, changing the subject as he rolled toward the front door. "C'mon. I'll be the catcher. I can really block the plate in this thing." He beat a fist on the arm of his chair.

Eli half turned to follow.

"Eli," his mother whispered.

Eli shot a glance to her, then turned and saw Thad out on the ramp, holding up his mitt, signaling for him to follow. She was waiting for Thad to leave, he thought. He tried to swallow, but his throat wouldn't work. He could barely breathe.

"We've got to keep our patience, Eli." She stopped until Eli looked at her. "You've been great through all this. Thad is awfully discouraged. Please try to help him. Be cheerful."

"Is that it?" Eli stared hard at her face.

"Can you try?"

"Is that all? You weren't gonna tell me anything else? The doctors really didn't find anything?"

"No, Eli."

"He's the same as ever? He should still get better?"

"Yes. I just wanted to ask you to try to help him through the disappointment. I'm afraid we had our hearts set on a big breakthrough in Chicago."

"OK, Mom. I thought you waited for Thad to leave so you could . . . oh, never mind."

"Thanks, Eli. He needs you to keep treating him like you have been. Like he's going to get better any day."

"How else would I treat him?"

"That's all we can do now," she said as Eli started for the door again. "And keep up our prayers."

Eli spun around. "I'll keep treating him that way 'cause it's true. But all the stupid prayers and the stupid doctors haven't done one stupid thing!"

That night after dinner Eli asked if he and Thad could go out for a while. His parents glanced at each other while Eli shifted his feet. "We're just gonna walk around," he explained, "I mean, what trouble could we get into with Thad in a wheel-chair?" Before he'd finished he knew it was a mistake — nobody had mentioned trouble. But he finished the sentence anyway, adding a bravado he didn't feel.

His father spoke up when their mother began to ask what they would do. "Sure, Eli," he said. "It's kind of nice to be out in the dark, isn't it?"

The bravado was shocked straight out of Eli. He stared at his father a moment before answering, "Yeah, I guess. I just thought Thad might like to get out."

"Don't be too long. Try to make it in before nine. But even if something great comes up, nine is still your time."

"Vacation?"

"Nine-thirty. Going any place special?"

"Uh-uh. I'll go tell Thad." Eli left before that line of questioning could go any further.

As they left Thad asked, "You want to go to the lake?"

"They got the new lights up there."

"Not on the other side of Capitol."

"Oh yeah. Okay."

As they walked along Eli began tossing rocks absently, hardly aiming. When he beaned a new street light they stopped in their tracks. The light flickered and buzzed. The stone had knocked a plastic side piece against the bulb.

"It's melting," Thad whispered.

The plastic bubbled and stretched until a hole appeared. "Let's get out of here!" Eli said, grabbing Thad's chair.

As Eli ran, Thad said, "Why bother, Eli? If anybody sees us they'll know who it is. How many kids go around in wheelchairs?"

"Yeah, I suppose. But if we get away fast enough, they won't see us."

"We can't go fast enough."

"Yeah, I guess."

Neither of them said anything after that, and silence settled over them until Eli began to fill his brother in on the week's goings-on. He skipped the part about the girl's house.

"Roger really said that, about stealing from his own mom?"

"Yeah. That guy's sick."

"He always has been."

"I think Sonny was with him just because he didn't have anybody else to hang out with. I don't think he's done anything with him all week. I think Roger is probably afraid of me."

"He always was afraid of me," Thad said. "At least before I fell. He probably still is. He's a chicken. All you got to do is tell him to get lost a few times and he knows you're not afraid of his big, lard belly. Then he leaves you alone."

"Yeah. I'm pretty sure I could take him now."

"*I* could take him now, Eli! He wouldn't even fight.

Have you ever seen him hit anybody he thought would hit back?"

"He used to hit Max some."

"But only once. Then he'd stop. 'Cause Max didn't care enough to hit him back. But if he started pounding on him, Max would get mad and whip him."

"Max is pretty skinny."

"Doesn't matter. All you'd have to do is sock him once."

"Yeah, maybe. He's a creep for sure."

"Yep." They came to a slight decline and Thad let himself roll. Soon Eli had to jog to keep up. "Mom'd kill me if she saw this," Thad giggled. "I really got going once in Chicago. I thought she was gonna have a heart attack." Thad gripped the arms of the chair and shot across the intersection. The next block was a small hill and Eli caught up with his brother.

"It was kind of mean, I guess," Thad continued. "But it got so boring. Go to the hospital, go to the motel. Mom's great, but she's so careful."

Eli hummed an agreement and Thad suddenly burst out laughing. "That really happened?" he yelled. "That dog stopped that guy from getting you?"

"Yep."

Thad pounded his fists against the wheelchair's arms. "We got to get me out of this thing."

"I know."

"I can't do anything stuck in here."

"We gotta get you walking again! You know that guy who put the wire in? Sonny and I bombed his grass bags the last two nights. Hey, you and I could do it tonight! His house is uphill from ours. The whole way."

"Yeah," Thad started, but then added, "Downer's just after his house. That's a pretty busy street."

"I could run down first and check it out. Make sure there are no cars coming. Then you'd roll while I bomb the bags. You'll be going a hundred by the time we get there."

Thad grinned and turned his chair toward the house. As they moved in for the kill, Eli said, "You know what else, Thad?"

"Huh?"

"Right before we busted the first bags that night, when I went with Sonny and Roger, we went to this girl's house."

"What girl?"

"I don't know. Some friend of Roger's big sister."

"What for?"

"Nothing. Nobody was home." Eli wanted to get that clear before he went on. "But Sonny's been there before, with Roger."

"What for?"

"Well, her bedroom's right there, and, I guess, she like, hangs around in there at night. Without any clothes on."

"And you can see her!"

"I didn't! They didn't even tell me what we went back there for until later. But Sonny has, once."

"Wow!"

"Yeah. But he said it wasn't very good."

"It figures Roger would do something like that," Thad said.

Eli grinned. He knew Thad would say something like that. "Have you ever seen a girl naked?"

"Only in pictures."

"Yeah, me too."

Eli walked beside his brother trying to hide his smile. Thad's tone had answered some of Eli's doubt. Looking in that girl's window was something Roger would do. It was a lot worse than busting bags. Thad wanted to do *that* even from his chair. Eli stifled a relieved giggle. "We're almost there," Eli said. "I'll go check the traffic."

When Eli puffed back up the hill he said, "Should be clear right after the bus." His voice was higher than normal with the adrenaline rush. "We'll really have to go. This'll be the third night in a row. He'll probably be watching."

"Well, jeez, Eli, then . . ."

"That's the bus! Let's go."

Eli jogged along until Thad had built up attack speed. Then he dodged across the street and lined up his target. Choosing the one closest to the street, he ducked his head and swung his leg in a round house, soccer style. His foot struck, but nothing in the bag gave way.

Not quite stifling his howl of pain, Eli stumbled back onto the street. He hopped for several steps holding his kicking foot off the ground. Though his eyes were watering, he could see that there was no pursuit. He started to put his foot down, running as fast as the pain would allow.

Thad had been drawing away since the foiled attack. Eli saw his chair bounce shakily under the corner street light, Thad still trying to add speed by pushing on the wheels. He flashed into the intersection.

Still behind and uphill, Eli could see beyond the hedge that blocked Thad's vision. He started to yell, but it was already too late. He heard the tires screech and ran even faster, trying to ignore his foot.

Eli reached the intersection as the car began to accelerate. Thad was on the other side of the street, still pushing at his wheels. "Thad!" he hissed, but knew his brother wouldn't hear. Thad flew past their house and slowed, finally turning up the Crazy Lady's driveway.

Eli cut across the front yard, his foot hurting more as he slowed and the danger passed. He met Thad in the garage. They couldn't go upstairs, but it was still the safest hiding place.

"What happened?" Thad blurted as Eli fell against a wall.

Eli caught his breath. "Didn't you see that car?"

"No! You said it was clear."

"It was." Eli panted. "He must've turned on after."

"That was close. I couldn't've stopped if I'd wanted to."

"Yeah."

"What happened to you?"

"That guy's gonna die," Eli cursed. He took off his sneaker and gingerly pawed his toes. "He must've put bricks in there."

"That's what you kicked?" Thad started to laugh.

"They feel broken," Eli said. "It's not funny."

"Oh, they are not broken. It's a good thing you didn't fall over."

Eli kept rubbing his toes and Thad asked, "Hey, Eli. Can you smell anything?"

"What do you mean?"

"I can't really tell. But when that car came, I was looking right at the headlights."

"Yeah. That was too close."

"Eli? I think I might've, I might've pooped my pants."

Eli howled, slapping his hand on the floor.

"Hey, I'm serious!" Thad shouted. He glanced to the door. "You gotta check. I can't feel it."

"That was me," Eli barely managed to squeal. "I farted."

"Well, check anyway," Thad said, catching the giggles himself. "I can't go home like this."

By the time Eli had lifted Thad up and patted his bottom, neither of the boys could say a word through their laughter. Eli couldn't even make out his brother's face through the tears in his eyes.

"You're fine," Eli groaned at last. He sat down, and poked at Thad's chair. "But we got to get rid of this thing."

"No kidding," he said. "But, hey, Eli. You know what?"

"What?"

"Well, you know, it almost felt like I pooped or something."

"I checked!" Eli said, chuckling painfully.

"No, I mean, I like . . . no. I guess not really. Never mind." Thad's voice trailed off.

"What, Thad? Did you feel something?"

Thad shook his head. "No, I guess it couldn't've been." He turned his head toward Eli. "It was just your smelly fart."

"Fart, schmart."

Thad started to push himself from the garage. "It's kinda neat being scared. Isn't it?" Eli asked, following him.

"Yep. But we can't do that again. If a car hit me, it better kill me. I'm not going back to the hospital again."

"I know what you mean."

"No, you don't," Thad said. "But somehow we gotta figure out a way to get me out of this stupid chair."

"You get your feeling back. Then we'll be able to get you running pretty fast, I think."

"Yeah. I'm sure not gonna wait for those doctors to do it."

"No kidding."

They crossed the street and headed for the ramp. "You better stop limping before we get inside."

"How come? I just stubbed it on the curb." They grinned at each other as Eli opened the door.

CHAPTER
SIXTEEN

Eli lay in bed listening to his mother rattling pans downstairs. He wondered how he could hear so well in the morning. He never heard his mother fixing dinner. Maybe his ears were rested up. He wondered when Thad would wake up. He still had to get up earlier than Eli to dress. At least he didn't need those suppositories anymore. They were sick.

"Eli!" Thad gasped.

Eli sat up straight. Thad was still lying down. "What?"

Thad didn't answer, but Eli could hear him breathing hard. "What?" he asked again.

"How come you're not out of bed?"

Eli knew that's not what Thad was going to say. He continued to stare at the rigid body under the blankets. He got out of bed on the side closer to Thad.

"What Thad?" he whispered. Thad's face was wrinkled in concentration. "You OK?"

Thad seemed to come a long distance before he said, "Yeah. I'm OK. Boy I was having some wild dreams."

Eli knew that was not the reason Thad had called to him. But then the bathroom door sailed open and his father said, "What? Not dressed yet? Come on boys." He stopped when he saw Eli's face. "Are you all right, Thad?" he asked.

"Yep. Just lazy." Thad sat up and pushed his legs off the bed. "I don't want to go to school."

"I don't want to go to work," his father said. He looked at Eli and Eli shrugged and moved to the dresser. "What do you want to wear today?" he asked.

"Whatever's on top."

Their father watched a moment more, then backed through the bathroom into his own room to finish dressing. Their mom yelled, "You better hurry," from the foot of the stairs.

Thad was the last one down for breakfast and whatever he'd meant to tell Eli was gone.

"You two have got to snap out of it," their mother said. "Vacation has been over for three days now. And you've been slow getting down for every one of them."

The boys ate in silence and rushed to school.

Max had given up on them two days ago, and Eli pushed Thad the rest of the way for speed's sake. When they reached the door Mr. Genskow wasn't waiting for them and Thad said, "Boy, we must be *really* late."

"Do you want me to take you up the stairs?" Eli asked.

"So long as you don't drop me."

Going up was easier than going down and Eli had Thad up the stairs in no time. He made another trip for the chair and they wheeled toward the room. "Think we're in trouble?" he asked.

"Naw, I never get in trouble anymore."

Eli chuckled and opened the door for Thad. An old-lady substitute glared at them and made them excuse themselves to the entire class, and Thad told everyone about the jammed brake on his chair and how they'd fixed it with a stick. Eli's face turned red as he listened to the story.

When they were seated she gave them a written assignment, then perched at her desk, searching for disorder. Eli got caught first. He was trying to tell Max how Thad had made up the whole thing about the brake.

"Young man, are you talking?" Before Eli could answer she said, "Don't lie to me. Or we'll be here for a long, long time."

Eli kept his head down and his pencil moving, ignoring the old woman. He wrote the story for Max.

When it was complete he dropped his pencil and passed the note to Max.

Eli looked forward as he sat up. She stared suspiciously but said nothing. Eli smiled and leaned his head against his forearm on the desk, pretending to write as he watched Max.

As soon as Max turned, pointing to the substitute and giving the crazy sign with his finger, they started to giggle.

"Young man!" Eli heard again. Max's head snapped back over his work and Eli did the same. If he looked up now, at her wrinkled, old prune face, he'd die laughing for sure.

"Young man!" she repeated, more sternly. "Look at me."

Eli heard her fumbling with the seating chart.

"You know very well who I mean," she went on. Eli could almost see her wrinkled finger skimming down the second row to the last seat. He took several deep breaths and lifted his head an instant before she shouted, "Eli Martin!"

Eli suppressed his smile. Took her long enough.

"Eli Martin," she said again, savoring her discovery. "So that's my little troublemaker. Rest assured, Eli Martin, that Mr. Genskow will receive a full report of your conduct. Now don't force me to say your name again today!"

Eli dropped his face back to his paper, glancing

over to Max. His face was purple and Eli had to bite his lip to keep from laughing.

The assignment was ridiculously easy. The work covered what Mr. Genskow had gone over last week and Eli finished early. He kept looking at the clock only to be amazed at how slowly the time passed. But he kept his head down and his pencil up, knowing he was being watched.

"What a cranky old thing," he mumbled, wondering if she was going to make them sit with the stupid paper all morning. He began to doze, but caught his head as it began to tip forward.

"Eli!" Thad said way too loudly.

Eli sank lower in his chair and looked over at his brother in amazement. What in the world was Thad trying to do to him?

Eli stopped caring about the substitute even as she started to shout at him. Thad's face had the same sweaty intentness he'd had in bed this morning. He was staring at his legs.

"What is it, Thad?" Eli said.

"That is enough, Eli Martin!" the substitute said, nearly spitting his name as she arrived at his desk. "You will sit in the hallway until . . ." She grabbed Eli's shoulder from behind.

Eli reached back and brushed away her hand, not hearing what she was saying. "What's the matter, Thad?"

He saw the puzzled expression begin to steal across Thad's face again. "What, Thad?" He leaned so far over to his brother he was almost out of his seat. "Is it your legs? What is it?"

"Mr. Martin!" the substitute bellowed.

Eli turned for an instant, not quite enough to see the old woman. "Just shut up a minute," he snapped. He turned back to Thad and now Thad was looking at him. Eli waited.

But Thad shook his head. "I thought I felt something," he said, sounding a million miles away.

"In your legs?"

Thad pointed, touching his knee. "Right here."

"Can you feel that? Can you feel your hand there?"

Thad rubbed his knee and shook his head. "I guess, I guess I just imagined it. I can't feel anything."

Eli thought Thad might cry. "Well, maybe it's starting. Maybe that's the way."

The door flew open then, the substitute marching back in, pointing her bony finger at Eli, the principal one step behind.

"This one's a kook," Eli whispered to Thad as he stood up. He walked to the front of the room, right by the nearly hysterical woman and out the door. He stopped in the hallway.

The woman raved her accusations as Eli watched her, not even caring to hide the look of amusement on his face. When she stopped for breath, Eli said, "Thad thought he felt something in his legs. I was just asking him about that."

"Did he really?"

"Not now, but he thought he did for a second."

"Go back to your seat, Eli," the principal, Sister Mary Margaret, said before the substitute could say another word.

Eli hurried back but Thad sat rubbing his leg and shaking his head. "I might've fallen asleep and kind of dreamed it. I think that's what happened this morning."

"That's never happened before though, has it?"

"Uh-uh."

They shrugged at each other, Eli trying to smile hopefully.

The substitute entered the class again, alone. She fixed Eli with a glare and said, "Everyone turn in your papers. Right now. Whether you've completed your work or not."

They were given a reading assignment as soon as their papers were on Mr. Genskow's desk. Eli cracked his book with a yawn and winked at Max, spinning his finger around his temple.

Eli was halfway through the assignment when Thad gasped again. This time there was no puzzlement on Thad's face. Now it was pain. Eli jumped out of his seat. "Your legs?"

Thad squeezed back his tears and grinned at his brother. "My feet. They're burning."

"Bad?"

"Kind of," Thad said, biting his lip.

"How about your legs?"

"They tingle. Like they're asleep."

"Maybe they're waking up," Max said, kneeling on his chair.

"Are they coming back?" Eli asked, too excited to think.

Thad shrugged. "I don't know." He turned to Eli with a laugh. "But I'm not imagining this."

Eli jumped up, shouting. "Come on."

"Where?" Thad kept laughing despite the pain.

"Home!" Eli yelled, pushing on Thad's chair. The substitute smiled uncertainly and stepped out of their way as Eli shot down the aisle.

"My legs are burning, Eli. Both of them. All over."

"Real bad?"

"It hurts."

Eli knew it must be pretty bad then. He stopped at the top of the stairs and hauled Thad onto his back. As he manhandled Thad down the steps, he asked, "How are they now?"

"They hurt. But, Eli," Thad added breathlessly, "I can feel them! I can feel where you're holding them!"

"Am I hurting them?"

"Who cares!" Thad howled. "I can feel them, Eli! I can feel my legs!"

They bumped down the last of the steps and Eli started to lay Thad down. Sister Mirin came out of her classroom and ran to the boys. Eli saw her and beamed. "He can feel them!"

"Thank God!" Sister Mirin said. "Is your chair upstairs?"

Eli nodded and held Thad tighter as Sister Mirin

picked up her skirts and took the steps two at a time.

"I can feel them, Eli! All over!" Thad kept repeating. "I can even feel my butt again. Everything!"

Sister Mirin thundered down with the chair. "Here it is."

"I can feel that, Sister," Thad said as they sat him down.

"That's great, Thad! It really is." She patted his leg and laughed. It was a nice sound. Then she said, "Isn't it wonderful when He turns around and does something so good?"

Eli gaped at her but she shook her head and laughed again. "Can you move anything?" she asked suddenly.

They fell silent and Thad's face twisted with his effort. "Uh-uh," he finally gasped. Then he smiled again. "Not yet."

Thad sat there smiling a moment, then said, "Let's go home, Eli." Eli took the handles of his chair and headed for the door. Thad shouted, "Thanks, Sister," and Eli went through the door at a run, nearly dumping Thad on the steps. They both laughed wildly and shot down the ramp in front of the church.

Across the street Thad told Eli he wanted to push himself. "How are they?" Eli asked. "Do they hurt a lot?"

"They hurt. Like they're burning. Kind of itch too."

"You'll be walking! Anytime, I bet," Eli said, practically dancing beside Thad.

"It'll take a while, they said."

"Yeah," Eli laughed. "And they've been right every time."

Thad laughed at that, too.

Eli followed Thad's chair and wondered how long it would take to walk again, or even just for the pain to go away. He wondered if Thad was thinking the same things.

"I'm glad they hurt," Thad said, though not as convincingly as before. "It's great to feel anything. They said it would hurt at first."

Suddenly Eli saw what was coming. They'd get home and their parents would get the doctors and everything would be out of their control again. As soon as they found out he would be a bystander again. So would Thad, practically.

Halfway home Thad asked Eli to push for a little bit. Eli jumped behind the chair, but not before seeing the pain in Thad's face. "Getting worse?"

"Not really. But they're really starting to burn. The same, I guess, but I'm thinking about it more. I'm glad we got out of there." Thad closed his eyes and tipped his head back.

Eli wondered if Thad had thought about the doctors yet. "What do you think Sister Mirin meant when she said it was good to see God do something right?"

"She didn't say that."

"Something like that."

"Who cares?"

"I don't think there is a God, Thad."

"Yeah. I know," Thad said without interest.

Eli looked at Thad. "I haven't prayed for you for months. Since the first few days. 'Cause I knew it wouldn't help."

"That doesn't prove anything," Thad said softly.

"Well, I didn't even go to church on Sunday!" Eli blurted.

Thad opened one eye. "Which Sunday?"

"The last one."

Both of Thad's eyes were open. "Easter Sunday? I thought you went after your route, to the early one."

Eli met Thad's eyes. "I just said I did," he whispered. "But when I walked up to the church I couldn't go in. Not after Good Friday and Holy Saturday and everything. I just couldn't."

"But Easter, Eli. That's a big one. Maybe the biggest."

"They're all the same."

"Wow, Eli. I don't know if I'd do that. We're both . . ."

Eli waved his hand in Thad's face. "Don't you see!"

"See what?"

"That that just proves it! I skip Easter Mass and you get better three days later, and . . ."

"I'm not better, Eli. My legs hurt is all. I don't . . ."

"But practically better. Anyway, you and I said

prayers every day since we could talk. That's about ten years of prayers, at least eight a day, that'd be . . ." Eli calculated. "That'd be a couple of million prayers anyway. And you still fell off the bleachers. So they didn't do any good."

"Yeah, maybe. But . . ."

"But nothing! I stop praying and skip Easter Mass and you get better. What more do you want? It's all a trick! God's got nothing to do with it! There's no such thing as God!"

Eli paused, then continued more quietly. "They made it all up. They made it up so if you'd died I would've thought I'd see you later, in heaven. So I wouldn't be sad. Mom and Dad, too."

"You don't believe in any of it?"

"Uh-uh," Eli said. "I can see why they made it up. I don't think it was a mean trick. But, for crying out loud, Thad, I would've been sad if you'd died, no matter what anybody told me."

"Yeah, me too."

"But you wouldn't have known, Thad. You'd've been dead."

"Yeah, I know."

"So it's not true at all. I'm gonna keep skipping mass."

"When I went with Mom and Dad they were talking about you going early. They were sad, I think, 'cause you didn't go with the family, you know?"

"But it's not true," Eli insisted. Why did everything have to make somebody sad? That was the worst part about it. Even if it was supposed to be a good trick, it always wound up making people sad. That's why he couldn't believe it. Tricks were always like that.

"They'll get suspicious," Thad pointed out, closing his eyes again. "They'll find out pretty fast."

"Maybe I'll just tell them."

"Oh, you will not!" Thad said. "We're just kids, Eli. They won't listen to that from us."

"But it's not true!"

Thad sat up in his chair and waved his arms. "Who cares, Eli? What difference does it make?"

"A lot. If . . ."

"It does not! Not one bit. Not now at least. Can't you just forget about it? I know you don't believe in God. Great. Big deal! But don't go telling Mom and Dad." He twisted around to look at his brother. "My legs are burning. They're getting better, I'm sure of it. Do you think I care why? So, can't we, can't we . . ." Thad ran out of words. "You haven't believed for a long time, you said before. You didn't have to tell them then. Can't you just forget about it? Don't you see how bad it'd be if you told them?"

"I wasn't gonna tell them," Eli admitted quietly.

"Good. Let's just go home." Thad's tone began to change. "You might be right, Eli. I don't know. I don't care! I do know I got to get out of this chair. And I can feel my legs again, Eli. I'm halfway out of here already!" he said, pounding the chair with his fists.

"I'll push," Thad said. Eli let go and Thad waited for him to walk alongside so that they could look at each other.

He smiled when Eli was next to him and then hit him on the arm. "They hurt like crazy," he laughed. Eli grinned back slowly. "They do!" Thad yelled at him. "But, Eli, I can feel them!" He slapped Eli again and cackled. "I can feel my legs!"

When they blasted through the front door of their house Thad screamed, "Hey, Mom!"

"Thad?" they heard her yell from the back of the house. Eli could hear her running. "I just got in. Sister Mary Margaret just called."

When she could see them she slowed. "Is it true, Thad?" she asked breathlessly. She knelt by his chair and took both of his hands in hers. "Is it true?"

"I can feel things, Mom!" Thad yelled, though his mother's face wasn't a foot from his own.

"Both legs? All over?"

Eli was stunned to see her crying.

"Yeah," Thad said, more softly. "I can feel your elbow."

She pulled her elbow off Thad's thigh and petted his leg gingerly. "Thank God, Thad. I knew if we were patient. . . . isn't it wonderful, Eli? Thank God!"

Eli felt alone as he covered up his thoughts and smiled. "They hurt him, Mom," was all he could say.

"Really, Thad? Where?"

"Kind of all over. They sort of burn." When he

saw the pain in her eyes, he added, "But it comes and goes. Like now, I hardly notice it. When I'm not thinking of anything else it seems worse."

"I'll call Dr. Caldwell," she said and she ran to the phone before Thad or Eli could stop her.

Eli took the few steps to the kitchen entrance and watched her stand with the phone pinched against her shoulder. Her back was to him. He thought of Thad first coming back from the hospital. She'd worn the same green dress that day.

Eli glanced down at Thad when he rolled to his side. "What do you think they'll make you do?"

"I'll have to go to the hospital, I guess." His voice was as tired and flattened as Eli's.

"Yeah. Do you think they'll keep you there long?"

"I can't even guess anymore."

Their mother was speaking into the phone, rapidly and happily. Eli and Thad looked at each other without listening to her words. Eli managed a hesitant smile and Thad shrugged. "I kind of thought . . ." Eli began.

"Me too. Guess it's going to take a lot more than just feeling again."

Their mother hung up the phone and Eli heard the swishing of her crinkly green dress and Thad's sigh. He reached out and put his hand over Thad's shoulder for a moment.

"They want us to come down right away," she said. "I'll bring the car out front."

"Tests?" Thad asked.

"A few, I suppose," she shouted on her way out.

Eli went behind Thad's chair and began to wheel him to the ramp. "Now what are they going to test you for?"

"Who knows. I just hope they don't hurt. I get so tired of it hurting."

"Do they hurt a lot now? Your legs?" Eli held Thad at the end of the ramp while his mother backed the car into position.

"No, I guess not." Their mother opened the rear door for Thad and he asked, "Mom? Do I really have to do this?"

"Of course, Thad," she said, smiling. "They'll have to see about it. Whether it's a complete return of feeling and all sorts of things."

"I know it is." Thad answered, allowing himself to be loaded into the car. "I know."

Eli jumped to help a little late. "Can't he just stay here, Mom? He could go to therapy this afternoon and they'd know. Can't he just stay? He's getting better!"

"But his legs hurt, Eli. I'm sure they'll be able to do something for that." She was behind the steering wheel already.

"But he doesn't mind," Eli started, but she was already backing away. "Mom?" he said softly. She said good-bye and shifted again in the street; this time she was moving forward.

The car began to accelerate and he saw Thad in the back seat, waving. Eli lifted his hand in reply.

He could barely see Thad's head above the door. We must've got him in pretty cockeyed, Eli thought. He walked up the ramp when the car turned the corner and drove out of sight.

Instead of going back to school, Eli crawled over the couch and lay down on the radiator, thinking of Thad listing over in the back seat, all the way to the hospital. He wondered why he felt like crying, now that Thad was finally getting better.

The phone rang twice during the afternoon, the second time for a long time. Eli listened, betting on which ring would be the last.

He was still on the radiator when the green newspaper van stopped and his papers were thrown out. Eli hauled himself outside and picked up half the papers. Maybe Thad'd be home when he came back for the second half. But Eli doubted it. They'd be too excited to let him leave the hospital so soon.

He checked inside before picking up the second stack. The house was empty. He delivered the second half much more slowly, giving Thad time, but the house was still empty when he got back.

He started for the radiator again but heard a car pull in. He ran out in time to see it continue up the drive. For a heart-stopping instant Eli thought Thad must be better, not needing the ramp or the wheelchair. Then he recognized the car as his dad's. He walked up the driveway, hands in his pockets.

They met at the open garage door. His father ran to him and shook him by the shoulders. "How's this for great news!" he blurted. "It's about time, wouldn't you say?"

"Sure is."

"Well, where is he? Are they still at the hospital?"

"Uh-huh. Since we got home this morning."

His father pushed Eli toward the garage. "Well, let's break him out. Come on, get in. What are you waiting for? Let's get him before those doctors take all the credit."

Eli was getting into the car as fast as he could. When he looked at his father they were both laughing.

Near the hospital Eli gave a shout. "That's them," he cried. He turned around in his seat and saw their other car going home. "It is! I saw Mom."

"OK. Hold on." His dad flipped into a quick U-turn and caught his mom at the intersection. They pulled over and Eli was out of the car before it was in park.

"Hey, Thad," he yelled, skidding to a stop on the grass parkway. But his jaw dropped and he stared at his mother as she stood up on the car's opposite side. Thad wasn't in the car.

"He's not staying is he, Mom?"

"Just tonight, Eli. Calm down."

Eli kicked the car door. "He can't, Mom."

"They're just going to observe him, Eli. All the news is wonderful. It looks like a full recovery of sensation. It shouldn't even be very painful after a day or two."

"But he hates it there." Eli looked to his mother and then his father. "Let's break him out. He hates it. Can't we just observe him at home? Then tell the doctors what we observed?"

"It's hardly going to be like he's staying there, Eli. He doesn't mind at all."

Eli kicked at the new grass and shook his head. They should never have come home with the news about Thad's legs.

"Let's go home and drop off your car," his mother said to his father. "Then we'll pick up some boiled ham and a loaf of bakery bread and we'll all come back to Thad's room and eat." She laughed easily. "I had to promise him no more hospital food."

"I thought he didn't mind at all," Eli mumbled as he and his father returned to the car. He stood beside the door and said, "Dad, I'm going to go to the hospital. I'll see you there."

"But, Eli."

Eli was already running away from the car. "I'll see you there." he repeated. "It's not like I don't know the way."

That night Eli lay alone in his room again, hating the silence. It was just like Chicago and the old hospital days. "But, he's out tomorrow," he said aloud. "They said he'd even make school in the afternoon." He fell asleep, bracing himself for the battle he'd wage if they lied to him again.

*　*　*

Eli went to school by himself the next morning, brusquely fielding the endless, repetitive questions. Only Max hadn't asked where Thad was. He'd watched Eli approach alone and said, "Is he coming tomorrow?" and Eli had shaken his head and said, "This afternoon."

As Eli walked home for lunch he was afraid Thad wouldn't be home and, despite the victorious battles he'd imagined, he knew he'd be helpless to do anything. They could hold him in the hospital forever and all he'd be able to do was visit.

The closer to home Eli drew, the slower he walked. Thad had to be home. Eli broke into a run, imagining that Thad would be there, waiting for him.

Thad was home. He sat at the kitchen table, eating a sandwich. "You're late," he mumbled, stuffing crumbs into his mouth with the back of his index finger.

Eli grinned. "Did they let you go or did you break out?"

"Broke out."

"Oh, Thad, you did not," their mother said.

"Made a run for it," Thad said. "Skipped home."

Eli took another look to make sure. Thad was still in his wheelchair. "So, are you coming to school this afternoon?" Eli held his breath until Thad answered, "Uh-huh."

Eli's breath escaped in a long, low rush. He'd wait then, to ask about Thad's back. He wasn't going to make the same mistake again. He wasn't going to let his parents or the doctors know Thad's condition anymore. Not when it only landed his brother back in the hospital.

CHAPTER
SEVENTEEN

Thad's long, slow relearning of the walking process swept the Martins into summer before they realized it. School ended in the same tired way, as if its last day would never come. Thad's milestones were exciting, but the pace at which they were attained was appalling. When he was first able to raise his leg without help, Eli thought walking would be imminent. But the next hurdle was a series of leg exercises using weights and bungee cords, and that took forever. Eli could hardly believe it — it was the middle of June, school had been out for two weeks, and Thad didn't even have braces yet.

It rained every day those first two weeks, but when the weather finally broke, Eli and Thad walked and rolled down the steamy streets in silence. Thad worked one leg absently against the surgical tubing loop his father had rigged to his chair. "Where do you want to go?" he asked.

"We're heading to the river. Want to go to Hubbard Park?"

Thad said that'd be fine and they lapsed back into silence. At the park Thad rolled wildly down the bluff walks, clattering around the curves when Eli gave the "all clear." The park was so vacant Eli gave up watching the walks for Thad. He strolled to the river's edge, occasionally picking up a round, flat stone and skipping it out across the water. It wasn't a good day though; five was the most skips he could get.

At last Eli found the perfect stone. He crouched and rotated his body once in practice, then hurled the stone. Eli rose from his crouch as it touched down, still pancake flat. It rose so little it was impossible to tell, except by the rings of water, that it had ever skipped.

When it touched again, in exactly the same way, Eli began to smile. The third time, Thad whooped, then it hit a fourth, a fifth, and a sixth time. Then the skips became uncountable. The stone curved to the right and slowed, its tail dragging. Thad whooped again as the stone settled in and sank.

"Good one!" he yelled. "About time, too."

Eli gave Thad's chair a shove. "I don't see you skipping any."

"I can't from here. The chair gets in the way."

Eli looked away from Thad then. He tossed the next stone he'd selected, not skipping, just a throw. He threw the next at its ring of ripples. "Suppose it's true?"

"That you can't land two in the same place? I don't know. I suppose with you it is."

Eli picked a mud clod from the garden and threw it into the ground beside Thad. It exploded and Thad laughed, pushing hard on his wheels. Eli kept lobbing the dirtballs, watching Thad turn and twist as the dirt showered around him. Eli could hear him laughing, trying to make tank noises.

The clod that connected with Thad didn't burst as well. His leg was not as hard as the ground. Eli saw a little dirt fly back into the air from Thad's lap. The laughing halted abruptly and the wheelchair lost momentum and finally tipped over.

Eli ran up to Thad but when he saw his brother's eye peek open he slowed. "Did that even hit you?"

Thad rolled and moaned, then sat up quickly, pretending to spray Eli with machine gun fire. Eli jumped back and hurled his last dirtball into the ground immediately in front of Thad. Thad sprawled back for a moment then said, "Wait a minute, I got you."

"You did not. I blew you up."

"You just blasted my tread," Thad answered, rubbing his thigh. "I climbed out of the turret and blasted you."

"With a machine gun?"

"Yeah."

"I'm a tank, too. A machine gun wouldn't do anything."

"You're a tank, too?"

"Yep."

Thad sprawled backward, throwing his arms to the sides. Then he peeked at Eli and began to laugh.

Eli dropped to the ground next to Thad, pushing the downed chair with his feet. "This grass is still wet."

"Yeah, I know." Neither of them made a move to get up.

Thad began bending his legs slowly. Eli watched his blue jeans hang from the thin supports of his brother's legs. "How are they?" Eli asked.

"Fine, except where the tank bomb landed. Kind of makes you wonder if paralysis is such a bad thing."

"I bet." Eli said, rolling over to look at the river and let the sun dry the dampness from his back.

"I'm gonna get fitted for braces next week," Thad said.

"Really?" Eli sat up. "You never said anything."

"I couldn't before. Mom or Dad were always around."

"Don't they know?"

"Sure they do. But you know how they get if I talk about anything. 'Oh, Thad, now don't get your hopes up.' "

"Yeah. How long till you get to wear them?"

"They have to fit them and make them. Then I should get them. I don't think it'll take very long."

"Wow. Then you'll be walking again." Eli kicked at the wheelchair. "And we can dump this thing."

"They keep saying it's going to take a long time still. The braces are just the next step."

"That's just more of the 'don't get your hopes up' stuff."

"Yeah, maybe. But I'll still need the chair a while."

"Don't you hate it?"

"It's OK. I'm sure sick of it though."

"Don't you just wish you could take it up to the top of the hill and let it roll all the way down into the river?"

"When I'm done, maybe."

"Or maybe keep it until we can drive and then run over it."

"Naw. I don't want it around till we can drive."

Eli sat up when the lawn mower started on top of the hill. "You know, I was just thinking. This is a lot like that day."

"That was in the fall."

"I know. But with the grass and that mower." Eli paused and shook his head. "That was practically a year ago."

"A whole school year," Thad answered. "Seems longer."

"Seems like it's been forever," Eli said. "Don't you wish we'd never even gone to play football that day?"

"Or that those other guys had shown up. Then

we would've played football, not tag."

"Or if we'd played on the other side, maybe . . ."

"Or if only I'd gotten tagged, or just didn't slip."

Eli was surprised to hear Thad's voice catch. He'd been daydreaming more than listening. Eli turned his face to the river, away from Thad.

"I still lie awake a lot at night," Thad continued. "I just start thinking. 'If only they'd come. If only it'd rained. If only I'd caught that bar.'" Thad swallowed. "Drives me nuts sometimes. A hundred things could've happened and I wouldn't've fallen. But none did. Makes me feel like crying sometimes."

Eli tried to hold one of the sun spots dancing on the river's surface. No matter how hard he concentrated the one he watched would wink out and flash back on a little to one side or the other. "How come you never said anything?" he asked. The sun spot leapt away.

"It was always when you were asleep."

Eli closed his eyes, but the spots stayed in his head. "You should've woke me up."

"There's nothing anybody could do."

Eli listened to Thad pull himself across the ground and he opened his eyes in time to see one of Thad's legs pushing against the grass as Thad righted his chair.

"You just get thinking is all," Thad said. "You know — what if. So it was better that you were asleep. It's just thinking." Thad paused, then added, "You know, sometimes I wish I couldn't think anymore. I don't like thinking anymore."

Eli stood and turned his back to the glittery reflections on the river. He'd never heard anything so lonely in his life. He watched Thad manhandle the chair around, his legs trying to help, and he hated himself for sleeping and not knowing that his brother felt so alone.

"Hang on, Thad," he said, pulling Thad's chair away. "Let's try it once. Let's try it once without the stinking chair."

Thad's face came alive and Eli tried to lift him up. Stiff-legged, Thad began to straighten. "Bend your legs," Eli grunted, stepping backwards. Thad slid after him.

"I can't this way. Ease up."

Eli let Thad down. "Can you just stand up?"

Thad strained, then shook his head. "Lift," he said, still pushing with his legs.

Eli pulled hard and Thad tumbled into him. He giggled. "Jeez, Eli. Not like that. Try going straight up. Don't jerk like that. I haven't stood up in a year. This'll take a while."

Eli giggled a little, too. He placed his hands under Thad's arms, around his rib cage. Although the muscle from Thad's shoulder down the back of his ribs stuck out hard as rock Eli could feel all of Thad's ribs. He slid his fingers into the depressions between his brother's ribs.

"OK," Thad said, taking a deep breath. "Slow. And try to go straight up."

214

Eli lifted until Thad was just a head below him. He could see Thad's face turning purple and he felt the unsteadiness. "Hang on," he grunted, squatting and giving one more slow shove.

They stood face to face. Eli's tongue was out, but Thad's entire face was twisted with effort. He squinted at his twin and, when Eli did not release his grip, he forced a tiny smile. "Boy!" he exclaimed, "you don't know how good it is not to be looking up your nose."

Eli started to relax his grip, but Thad clutched at his arms. Eli let Thad hold on but didn't hold on any tighter. "Come on, Thad," he whispered. "Let's walk." And Eli moved one leg backwards. Thad's eyes widened and Eli stepped back.

Thad collapsed immediately. His grip on Eli saved a crash, but he slid down his arms and let go, sitting in a crazy heap.

"That was pretty good," Eli said. His tone was so false and disappointed that they both began to laugh.

"Guys *without* legs could've stayed up longer."

"Those braces'll help," Eli said. "You'll probably just need them for a week. Maybe less. Till you get used to taking steps again or something."

Thad stared at Eli, a smile quivering on the corner of his mouth. "Well," Eli protested, "your legs seemed pretty strong."

Thad didn't say anything. He finally laughed and

asked for his chair. Eli got it and Thad clambered in. "Tired?"

Thad shook his head.

"Hurt?"

"A little, I guess. Probably pretty easy to pull a muscle or something like that. They're always talking about pulling something at therapy."

"Think you did?"

"Naw. I'm not that gimpy."

"Probably just a tank bomb."

"Yeah." Thad laughed. "That's about exactly where it is."

The boys started to move away from the river, out of the park. "I didn't mean to hit you," Eli said. "With the bomb."

"Yeah. Sure. Hey, Eli," he said, laughing again. "Did you ever notice how hairy the inside of Dad's nose is?" They left the park laughing, dissecting the migration of their father's hair from the top of his head down to his nose and ears.

Just before they reached the main street, Eli cut across to the bottom of the steep, vine-covered slope. He jerked a thumb toward the slope's top. "You've never been in there, have you?"

"Uh-uh," Thad answered. A tall, wire fence ran along the top, crowned with three strands of outward sloping barbed wire.

"It's the abandoned bus depot. It's really neat inside."

"When have you ever been in there?"

"With Sonny a few times. Max has come sometimes. We all came once with Roger."

"When?"

"Sometimes when you're at therapy." He glanced at Thad. "I would've brought you, but there's no way for you to get in."

"What do you do? Climb the fence?"

"No. Come on. I'll show you." They turned and descended most of the hill they had just pushed up. Eli pointed and they cut down an overgrown path. "It clears some up here," Eli explained. He got behind Thad and pulled and lifted him through the worst of the brush.

Eli continued to push when they broke into the clear alongside the fence. He stopped at the edge of a full sheet of battered gray plywood stuck underneath the fence. A jagged line of scrapes along the board's surface showed how it had been moved back and forth.

"There's a hole under the fence here. Under the board. We try moving the board the same way every time, so it doesn't splinter up. Roger says cops are always here arresting kids."

"They wouldn't arrest a kid for coming in here."

"I know." Eli pulled the board away to show Thad the narrow ditch. "Roger can barely squeeze under. He always rips his pants on the bottom of the fence." Eli smiled, "We have wars in here. And we shoot out all the old windows. There aren't any left except the ones with wire inside them, and they don't bust."

"What do you shoot them with?" Thad whispered.

"BB guns. Max and Sonny both have rifles. You got to pump them. But Roger has a pistol with CO_2. You just got to cock it once. He can't hit anything."

"That'd be great. I could get through that hole easy."

"Yeah, I know. But not your chair."

"Couldn't we dig it big enough? It wouldn't take much. Not if we collapsed the chair."

"I never even thought of that. I always thought of rolling you through. Jeez." Eli dropped onto his knees and started to scratch at the dirt. "It's pretty packed."

Thad slipped from his chair and pulled himself to the hole's edge. "Get a couple sticks." Thad looked up with his old mischievous grin and Eli ran. Maybe, he thought, as he selected two good diggers, things really were going back to the old days.

They scraped at the dirt and soon had the chair collapsed, testing it for fit. Eli drove his stick in and pried at a stone. The chair pushed through and Eli followed after it. "Here," he said. "I'll push it back, you pull."

"What for? Just get it out of the way and I'll come over."

Eli looked along the fence line. "In the middle of the day? If anybody catches us you can't really run away."

"Oh, nobody's gonna catch us. Come on, set up the chair."

Eli did as Thad said and Thad was under the fence and in his chair. "Run to the main door," Eli said. "Nobody can see you inside."

"Nobody can see you anyway. There's too many bushes."

"There's a place up there," Eli pointed. "Cars can pull in and look down. You see them once in a while."

"All right. Let's go."

"I'll push. We gotta run and there's all kinds of broken stuff everywhere." Before Thad could protest, Eli was pushing him across the cracked, faded asphalt at a dead run. The chair bounced over the weed-choked cracks and bits of brick and wood.

They stopped inside the gaping loading door and caught their breath in the cool, shaded interior. Broken glass was everywhere. Nearly three stories above their heads light flowed dustily through the unbroken, wired glass of the enormous skylights. "Wow," Thad whispered. Talking made the old bus bay seem even larger, and emptier.

"I know," Eli said. "It's pretty neat." They began to move forward slowly. Eli stepped around the rubble on the floor, but Thad couldn't help but roll over much of it. The grating and crunching echoed around them.

Eli stopped at the base of an iron ladder. "Look up the tube," he whispered. The ladder went up to the roof and was encased the entire way with a basket of iron. "So you can't fall off," Eli explained.

Thad lowered his head. "Makes you dizzy."

"I know. Especially when you're halfway up. It looks like that up or down. I just look at the wall. It's a great place to shoot from. Good ambush and you can see everything."

"You shoot at each other?"

"Yeah. It's fun. Till you get hit. I wear two of everything, jeans and sweatshirts." Eli paused. "Remember when Dad couldn't find his safety glasses that one Saturday?"

"Uh-huh."

"I had them. I came down before the route with Max."

"Wow. He was mad."

"I know. But I couldn't give them to him then."

"What'd you do?"

"Used them. We had a war." He pointed to the furthest skylight. "See that hole? Sonny was lying on the skylight waiting to pick off me and Max through the hole."

"He was lying on the glass!"

"Yeah. You can run on it."

Thad shuddered.

"You can't hit anything that far away," Eli continued. "Max kept shooting at him though." Eli pointed to an old office, missing all its windows. "We were in there. I crawled out the back way and went up the outside ladder, while he and Max were shooting it out."

Eli started to giggle. "It was so perfect. The ladder

curls over the roof and I peeked up and I'm looking right at Sonny's butt. He even had his legs spread. I aimed a little high, so I wouldn't hit him in the nuts, and let him have it. Then I ducked back.

"Max said Sonny jumped clean off the window and he dropped his gun right down the hole." Eli struggled for breath. "But I was below the roof, going down the ladder like crazy. So he didn't even know who'd blasted him." Eli howled. "And boy, if he hadn't dropped his gun he could've beaned me a hundred times right on the head just by shooting down the ladder."

When the laughter died, Thad eyeballed the distance from the skylight to the floor. "What happened to his gun?"

Eli grinned and crooked his finger, motioning for Thad to follow. They went into the office that Eli and Max had used for cover that day and through a skinny door to a toilet. The floor was buried a foot deep in rubble from a collapsed ceiling. Eli lifted a broken plank while Thad watched from the door.

"This was a toilet," Eli explained as he worked. He threw the top of a toilet tank onto the rubble pile and emerged with a rifle and a pistol. "We hide them in the old tank. It's too hard to take them home all the time. But Max does, he sticks it in his pant's leg every time. He can hardly walk with it, but he says his dad would notice if it was gone."

Eli handed Thad the rifle. "The wood broke when Sonny dropped it, but it still shoots." Thad fingered the thick silver tape holding the stock together. "We could have a little war right now, but we ran out of BBs last time." Eli shrugged. "I didn't know we'd be coming here today."

Thad handed Eli the rifle, reached for the pistol, and aimed through the old windows to Sonny's place on the skylight. "How come you never told me anything about this place?"

"I don't know."

"'Cause I couldn't get in?" Thad handed back the pistol.

"I guess, yeah. But, you know, since you couldn't do it, I thought, you know . . ."

Thad looked away from Eli.

"You know, Thad. You couldn't run away or anything."

"Yeah. You could've told me about it though."

"I was going to."

"When?" Thad rolled away from the bathroom door, letting Eli out. They continued into the main room.

"As soon as you could come. I told you about it today."

"I think it'd be all right. Nobody's gonna find us in here. I can hide if we have to."

"OK. I just kind of thought, you know, after that time we tried to bust those grass bags. I thought we'd wait till you could walk." Thad turned to him and Eli tried a smile. "I didn't think it'd take this long."

"Me neither," Thad said. "But let's get some BBs and Max and Sonny sometime."

"We only have three guns."

"When there's four of us we can be a team. We could cover for each other and stuff."

"Yeah," Eli said, listening to the crunching of Thad's wheels, knowing he could never sneak up on anybody.

"You know," Eli said, "The way that sun comes through, with the rays and stuff, you know what this place reminds me of?"

"What?"

"An old church. Like one of those old bombed-out ones in the movies, during the war."

"It's tall enough."

"Yeah. And it echoes the right way. Like St. Robert's does when it's empty, like when you're early for confession."

Thad agreed.

"And it seems kind of dead in here, you know. All still and dusty and not lived in anymore. You know?"

"It kinda does."

"That's the way church is for me all the time now, Thad. Like nobody lives there anymore."

"Yeah. I know." Thad stopped wheeling at the edge of the old bus barn doors. The boys hesitated in the shadows, looking out at the painful light on the bleached, broken pavement.

"You know?" Eli whispered hopefully. "Do you

feel that way too? Do you think I'm right, Thad? Do you think . . ."

Thad rolled his chair abruptly into the light. "I don't know, Eli. I don't think at all. I don't want to. I told you, I don't like to think anymore."

"But . . ."

"Run," Thad hissed, slapping his wheels to pick up speed. "There's a car up there!"

Eli sprinted with Thad, pushing him when he caught up. "We should've ducked back. It takes too long to get the chair out."

"Just hurry."

Eli screeched to a halt and Thad threw himself out of the chair and slithered through the hole. "Come on, come on!" he whispered, slapping his hand on the dirt, waiting for the chair.

"It's stuck," Eli said, then, "never mind," as the chair collapsed and he shoved it toward Thad. Thad pulled it to himself and Eli was close behind.

His chair was squared in seconds and as Thad climbed in Eli chanced a peek at the turnout on the hill. "Hey. There's nobody up there." He looked down at Thad. "There's no car."

"Maybe they're coming down. Let's get out of here."

Eli allowed himself to be hurried along, though the tingle of fear had died. When they reached the street they started up the hill, trying to look nonchalant. No cars came.

"What'd you ever do with Dad's safety glasses?"

Thad said when he caught his breath.

"Stuffed them in all the sawdust in the drawer under his saw bench. I left most of the strap sticking out."

"Did he find them?"

Eli started to push Thad up the last bit of hill. "Uh-huh. They were back on their hook a couple days later."

"Oh."

Eli watched Thad fiddle with the arms of his chair as the lapse in conversation grew longer. "Hey, Thad," he said. "There never was a car up there."

"Look at me," Thad interrupted immediately. "And this chair. How're we gonna explain this to Mom?"

Eli was silent.

"I mean the whole side of the chair is covered with dirt. That doesn't usually happen on a walk."

"We can stop at that one gas station. They have a hose. We could spray the chair off. It'd dry by the time we got home." Eli stopped at Thad's sigh of relief. Eli figured the sigh was more to change the subject than for anything else. Eli watched his brother pushing his own chair now, but he did not ask him about the car, or God, again.

CHAPTER
EIGHTEEN

Thad's leg braces were fitted and constructed in the next week but, once again, they failed to produce the profound changes Eli had counted on. Thad still used his wheelchair for all his transportation. In fact, Eli didn't even see the fabled braces for more than a week after Thad said he would be using them. But every afternoon Eli hurried through his route and waited on the front porch for Thad to come home. He wanted to be there when Thad walked up the ramp. But the frustration in his brother's face would show Eli that he was still struggling with the braces during the hated afternoon sessions at the hospital.

When the braces finally came home Thad refused to wear them. From his seat on the porch Eli saw the black anger in Thad's face and then glanced at their mother, carrying the awkward metal and leather braces up the ramp behind Thad and his wheelchair.

Thad wheeled by without saying a word, letting the screen door slam behind him. Eli jumped at the rattly bang. His mother followed Thad in, but reached out and ran her hand along Eli's head as she passed. Eli heard the gentle click the screen made behind her and he looked down the painted ramp to the station wagon. Then his eye traveled up the green, evening-still street, finally glancing at the sun, just touching the elms' leafy archway.

Eli stood up and followed them in. They were back from the hospital a little early. Eli picked up a brace and flexed the joint.

Thad ignored Eli as he studied the new braces. Eli stood up and worked the joint. Fingering a buckle he asked, "What's this one for?" He waited, then turned to Thad. "What's this one for, Thad?"

"Just to hold it on," Thad finally grunted.

Eli put the brace down. "They're kind of heavy," he mumbled. "Didn't they work right again?"

"Those things are so dumb!" Thad burst out.

"Now, Thad," their mother quieted.

Thad turned to Eli and mouthed, "Now, Thad."

Eli smiled uncertainly. "Sore again?" he asked.

Thad's smile faded and he shook his head. "Naw."

Eli touched a brace. "Why don't you show me how they work?"

"They don't."

"How they're *supposed* to work." When Thad refused to answer, Eli leaned farther forward. He glanced at their mother, then whispered, "We can't figure how to get you walking without them."

"I know that. But I just can't get them to work. If I didn't have those bars to hold on to I'd fall all the time."

"Well, what do you do with them?" Eli persisted.

"I'll show you tomorrow, Eli."

"Sure," Eli said.

"I *will*. But not now. Take them up to the room, will you? I can't stand looking at them."

Thad finally got the feel of his braces but they continued to be a hated reminder of the sluggish pace of his recovery. Their father installed a hook on the wall at the head of Thad's bed and the braces hung there. Eli woke every morning looking at them while sleep ebbed away. He couldn't imagine what Thad must think, having them over his head like that every night. Eli finally asked Thad as they waited for the light around the bathroom door to go out. Then Eli crawled from his bed and took the braces down and threw them into the closet.

"Thanks," Thad said. "They were giving me bad dreams."

"Yeah. But you're getting better with them. You went all over the house yesterday."

"But still not steps."

"Let's start practicing ourselves," Eli said, rolling over to turn his back to the closet.

"Yeah. Those guys do everything so slow. And Mom and Dad!"

"Shh," Eli warned. "I know. We'll start tomorrow.

Eli and Thad began to practice regularly, Eli spotting for Thad while he crutched around a vacant lot or a quiet stretch of sidewalk. But Thad's humor did not return until the morning he woke while Eli was dressing for his Sunday route. He blinked in the gray light and asked, "Mind if I help?"

"Not if you feel like it," Eli said. "Hurry up. I'll get the wagon."

Eli dragged the wagon out front and loaded the massive papers. He sat on the top of the stack, looking around the quiet, damp street. There were faint pink clouds over the lake and the sky was paling, showing itself mostly blue. Eli looked at the front door of his house and waited. Then he hopped off the wagon and went in looking for Thad.

He found him standing at the top of the stairs. "What's the matter," Eli mouthed, glancing at their parents' door. Then he realized Thad was leaning against the railing, his crutches tucked into his armpits.

"That elevator's too noisy."

"Are you going to do the whole route without your chair?"

Thad nodded. "But I haven't gone down steps yet."

"Do you want me to carry you again?"

"We could. But I think I've got it figured out. Stand behind me while I go down, so you can catch me if you have to."

"Behind you?"

"I think if I try to go forward I'd tip over when I move my crutches."

Thad turned around at the top of the steps. "Ready?"

"Sure." Eli held his hands against his brother's ribs.

Thad shuffled his left foot backwards and it hung in space above the first step. His forearms tightened as he transferred his weight to the crutches and he lowered his foot a step.

When both feet were down, he brought one crutch over and leaned against it to bring the other down. When his feet and both crutches were together again, Thad sighed. "I knew that'd work!" he said. "But they'd never let me try."

They rested a moment on the landing and Thad said, "You probably don't even have to stay there, Eli." He edged to the next step. "I haven't come close to falling."

"Yeah," Eli whispered, but he stayed where he was.

When they reached the bottom Eli caught a

glimpse of the concentration on Thad's face. "Tired?"

"Not bad. My muscles'll relax in a sec'." Thad fought to control his breathing.

"You sure you don't want your chair?"

Eli was surprised by the betrayed look that flashed across his brother's face. "I can do it," he insisted, barely remembering to keep his voice low.

"OK, Thad. Let's get out of here before we wake them up."

Out on the sidewalk Thad thumped along beside Eli. The wagon had to be dragged through the grass, making it hard for Eli to pull, but Thad continued to walk by his side, using the whole sidewalk.

"You're really getting good on those things," Eli said.

"Yeah," Thad grunted. A moment later he turned to Eli and grinned. "I'm getting really close, Eli. I can feel it. There was so long when there was nothing I could do." Thad took a curb in one giant stride. "But now I can do it myself. I'm so sick of waiting, Eli. I can't stand it. If we keep practicing, I'll be better so fast!"

"I know. That's what I always said."

"Did you see me on the steps? How I can bend my knees now and how much weight they'll take? I can't wait anymore."

"Maybe you don't have to."

"That's it! I'm so close! All we got to do is practice."

"We will, Thad."

"Yeah. But we can't tell anyone. They're all still going so slow — 'Be patient, Thad. You've waited this long, Thad.' " Thad put a wiggle into his rear that was so reminiscent of Thad's therapist that Eli burst out laughing.

While Eli raced from his wagon to the front doors, Thad waited on the sidewalk. Soon they reached the corner in the center of the route and Eli parked the wagon. He counted out twelve papers. "This'll do this side," he grunted, lifting the load. He teetered a moment, pinching the papers to his chest, then started up the block.

Thad stayed on the sidewalk while Eli stumbled along the lawns, dropping papers on the porches, but when Eli crossed the next driveway, Thad was waiting at the front door. Eli went through the balancing act of dropping the huge paper, then started to the next house. "You know," he said, as Thad walked beside him, "the only good thing about these papers is that the stacks get small fast." Farther on he was able to sling the papers under one arm, tilting crazily with the weight of the load.

Eli dropped one more paper then stopped and looked at Thad. He looked back down their double trail, dark green in the silvery wet of the grass. "Wow. I didn't even notice, Thad. How was it? You've never been off the pavement before, have you?" Eli whooped. "You even went through that guy's hedge."

Thad grinned back at Eli. "Piece of cake."

Eli whooped again and Thad moved on. Eli caught him at the next driveway. "This is great, Thad!"

"I told you. I'm almost there."

Eli dropped his last paper. "Now we go back to the wagon, get another load and do the other side of the block." He looked at Thad as they hit the sidewalk. "I usually run."

A smile flickered across Thad's face. His crutches ate up an extra foot of sidewalk on his next stride and he swung his braced legs wildly after them. Before they were even solidly on the ground, the crutches were whistling forward again.

Eli trotted until he was even with Thad. He imitated a car engine racing and shifting. Thad grinned "I'm already in high gear."

Eli guffawed and glanced down the street. The wagon was just coming into sight. "OK," he said, starting to slap his feet onto the pavement, slowing down. "Walk from here."

Thad continued to pull away. "Hey, Thad," Eli called. "You gotta walk the rest of the way." Thad raced on. "Thad! Otherwise you're all tired when you start the next part."

Eli watched Thad running and shook his head. He started jogging. "Thad," he called once more. "Thad, you kook."

They met at the wagon. Thad hung low in his crutches, breathing hard and sweating. Even his open mouth looked tired. "That was great," Eli said.

When Thad didn't answer, didn't even look at him, Eli asked, "Are you all right?"

Thad nodded his head vigorously and clamped his mouth shut, lifting his body to look at Eli. "Whew," he exclaimed, grinning again. "They work me out at therapy, but nothing fast like that. I could hardly breathe." He stared up the block and saw what he had done. "I did it though, Eli. All the way to the wagon." He laughed. "I ran a whole block!"

Eli counted out the next block's load and hefted them from the wagon. They started up the next block. "You know," Thad said, "if we got one of those front and back paperboy bags, I could carry a bunch of those for you."

Eli dumped the first paper. "Not running you couldn't," he said. "That thing'd get swinging and massacre you."

Thad chuckled. Soon he was laughing wildly. "This is great," he yelled. "This is great! I haven't done the route in a year. And I get away from Mom and Dad and everybody!" He grinned at Eli. "What a bunch of lazybones," he shouted, looking up and down the street. "Get up! I'm running down your streets. Get up!"

"Thad!" Eli hissed, trying to sound serious. Thad laughed again. "Come on, Thad! You'll wake everybody up. They'll *kill* us." Eli started to hurry, trying to get away from the yelling.

Thad picked up his pace, too. "I can't run much in the grass. It's too slippery."

"Well, shut up then," Eli said. "'Cause I'll be a hundred blocks from here when Mr. Banazynski comes out this door looking for the kid who woke him up."

When Eli dropped the last paper, he turned and ran back down the shallow hill they'd climbed. "I wasn't ready!" he heard Thad shout. He only yelled, "Tough," in reply, but he slowed to Thad's speed and curved back to the sidewalk.

He heard Thad's panting and the *thwock, swush*, of his crutches, followed by his feet smacking the pavement. Eli slowed at the end of the block and Thad flashed by him and yelled, "Chicken!"

"You're gonna kill yourself," Eli said when he reached the wagon. But after one look at his brother's heaving chest and sunken shoulders, Eli began to take more papers from the wagon.

Thad wasn't recovered when Eli was ready to move on. He turned the papers he was holding crosswise to the stack so he wouldn't lose count and sat on top of them. "I'm pooped," he lied.

"No, you're not."

"Well, at least we don't run anymore."

"Why not?" Thad eyed him suspiciously.

"'Cause that's the only part where you're coming back downhill. You remember. I only have to carry papers this last block and then we use the wagon for the rest."

"All right," Thad said at last. "If that's how you usually do it by yourself."

"Hey, Thad," Eli said, "I'm gonna help you. I'm not Mom or Dad. I've been trying to go faster the whole time."

"They help a lot. It's just that they're so slow."

Thad walked with Eli across the lawns for the entire block, and they headed back together down the center of the street's crowned pavement. "It's kind of fun walking right down the middle, isn't it?"

"Yeah. There hasn't been a car since we've been out."

"And you can hear one for a mile if it comes."

Eli's constant chatter faltered as he glanced back at Thad. He walked awkwardly — like his crutches were limping. His head was low, and Eli saw him biting his lip. Eli didn't know what to say. He slowed down. "Hear that?" he asked.

"That bird?"

"Yeah. It's a mourning dove. Listen to this." Eli pursed his lips and gave out the first long call, rising at the end, following it in time with the three doleful coos. He looked at the sky expectantly, then flashed a grin when the dove answered with the same call.

"That's pretty neat. Is he really answering you?"

Eli repeated the call. As the last note dwindled, the dove's call came from down the street.

"Where'd you learn that?"

"Just out here. They hoot around like that every morning. Especially when it's nice like this."

Another dove called from across the block. Thad

shivered as he reached the wagon. "No wonder they call them 'mourning.' "

"Huh?" Eli picked up the red Flyer's handle and turned it around while Thad sat on the last stack of papers.

"They sound sad enough for the whole world."

"Oh," Eli said. "Mourning like sad. I thought it was morning, like right now, because that's when you always hear them." Eli towed the wagon slowly, trying to make it roll quietly and smoothly. The farther he could tow his brother the better.

"No way," Thad answered, his voice tired, almost dreamy. "It's the sad mourning. Listen to them."

Before Eli could answer, Thad said, "Hey, wait a minute. Let me off. You'll bust my butt if you drop me down that curb."

They crossed the street side by side, Eli pulling the wagon, Thad with his new, strange limp. "You can ride if you want," Eli said, heading to the first house with a paper, trying as hard as he could to sound disinterested.

"I can walk."

"I know that," Eli said, dropping the paper.

"You know, I was even thinking that if we got a rope or something I could pull the wagon. Then you'd just have to run back and forth. It'd make the route go twice as fast."

"That'd work great," Eli said, doubting it.

They rounded the corner on the last block and

delivered the last paper. As they approached the short brick wall at the end of the boulevard, Eli asked, "What's the matter, Thad?" His voice took on a pleading he hadn't planned.

"What do you mean?"

Eli almost laughed at that old dodge. They'd used it a hundred times on their parents — "What do you mean?" — as they scrambled for explanations while their parents rephrased the questions. But the time for thinking had gotten so short, just long enough for their parents to answer, "You know what I mean," that they'd fallen out of the habit.

"You know what I mean," Eli said, imitating his father's voice. But Thad didn't smile. Eli said, "You look like you're limping in a hundred places." He let the empty wagon coast into the wall. He jumped on top of the wall and sat swinging his legs.

Thad leaned against the bricks next to Eli's leg. "Don't tell, all right?"

"Thad!"

Thad ducked his head in apology and lifted his hands to Eli, revealing the rows of burst, oozing blisters.

CHAPTER NINETEEN

Thad held his hands carefully in his lap as he rode in the wagon. "How're we gonna hide them from Mom and Dad?" Eli asked.

"I don't know."

"We gotta do something. I'm dead if they find out."

"*You're* dead? I'm the one."

Eli walked down the center of the street, pulling Thad behind him. "They'll kill me for letting you do it."

"I'm the one who . . ."

"It doesn't matter!" Eli insisted. "Jeez, Thad, you think they tell you to go slow? I'm the one who's always getting it. 'You've got to help Thad, Eli. Don't do anything foolish, Eli. Thad's very disappointed,

Eli, you've got to help. He's impatient now, Eli, you've got to help him go slow.' " Eli's voice grew more and more bitter.

"This wasn't foolish," Thad muttered.

"For crying out loud, Thad! Do you think I don't know that? But that's not what they're gonna think when they see your hands. They never saw you running down those streets."

"Maybe I could watch TV all day or something. So they don't see me walk."

Eli said, "Yeah, that might work," but he doubted it. The rest of the way home the wagon's creaky rattle was all that filled the bright, empty street.

Eli turned the corner at their driveway and pulled the wagon into the garage. He helped Thad up the back steps and into the kitchen, then ran upstairs to get the wheelchair. Their parents' door was still closed and Eli walked past it to his room. He pushed Thad's chair out and wheeled it to the stairs.

Eli couldn't believe how wrong things had gone. When he and Thad were halfway home he'd pictured their parents finding the chair and the elevator both upstairs — and Thad gone. But after seeing Thad's hands, Eli doubted that anything could get much worse.

Eli collapsed the wheelchair and put it on the elevator seat. He pushed the button hardly thinking about the racket it made. Without looking to see if his parents' bedroom door opened or not, Eli trudged down the steps beside the elevator.

When he wheeled the chair into the kitchen he saw Thad slumped on the bench, staring at his palms. They were beginning to dry, and he could no longer open them completely. He hid them beneath the table when he saw Eli.

"Did you wake them up?" Thad asked.

"I don't know. How're your hands?"

"Pretty bad." Thad brought out his hands and turned them slowly, palms up. Eli whistled. "We better wash them, I guess."

"No way."

"That's what Mom'd do. But we can't let her do it."

"But," Thad sighed.

"It sure will hurt."

"Yeah, no kidding."

Eli helped Thad into his chair and wheeled him to the sink. "Do you want me to do it?" Eli asked. He took the dish soap from the cabinet beneath the sink.

"I will, I guess. Just put a few drops in this one." He held a palm up to Eli without looking.

The soap came out fast when Eli squeezed. A pinkish puddle crept over the angry red in the hollow of Thad's palm. "Sting?"

Thad sighed. "I'll let you know." Eli hadn't heard Thad sound so tired since the hospital days.

Eli waited, watching the top of Thad's head. "The soap's in there," he finally whispered.

"Why don't you go ahead. Do you mind?"

"Uh-uh. But let me know if it hurts."

"It hurts."

"I mean," Eli started, but Thad knew what he meant.

With the very tip of his index finger, Eli smudged the pink soap over his palm, barely touching Thad's hand. Then, holding his breath, he started rubbing his finger tip against the blistered skin in miniature circles.

Thad's hand jumped but Eli held his wrist firmly. He pressed Thad's forearm against the counter top, watching the muscles tighten, drawing the skin around them. Eli saw the scars where the bone had stuck out when he'd carried Thad to the sidewalk after the fall, but he kept up the tiny circling with his finger, pressing the stinging soap into the torn hand. With the faucet dribbling an unsteady stream, he rinsed Thad's hand. Holding it up for a closer look, he said, "It looks a lot better, Thad."

Thad nodded and surrendered his other hand. He stared at the clean one in his lap.

As Eli took the other wrist and reached for the soap, he realized that Thad was weeping. He paused, letting the soap bottle rest in the sink. "Does it hurt that much?"

"No," Thad said, sighing rather than sobbing.

"Do you want me to do this one too?"

"Yeah."

Eli started to lift the soap, but didn't squirt it out. "Well, what's the matter?"

242

"Nothing," Thad said, but continued without pause. "I just get so tired of everything going wrong, you know. Nothing happens without it hurting. This is the first time I walked without holding on to those two stupid rails at therapy." A ghost of a sob escaped and Thad gulped. "The first time in nine months. But the only thing that happens is my hands get ripped up. Now I can't even use crutches anymore." Thad took a deep, catching breath. "I'll be so glad when it stops hurting."

"Me too," Eli said, staring at the torn spots on Thad's hands.

Thad wiped at his eyes and nose with the back of his clean thumb. Suddenly he chuckled weakly. "Do you remember," he said as Eli pushed in the sides of the bottle and the soap slid out into Thad's hand. Thad caught his breath. "Do you remember when we made that sacred pact?" He sneered the word sacred. "About never crying again?"

Eli mumbled that he did.

"Boy," Thad laughed, even as his hand jerked away from Eli's finger. "If we only knew what was coming. I mean — if we only knew." Thad's voice faded out as he clenched his teeth.

"I know." Eli pushed the soap around Thad's hand. "I probably broke it first. That day you fell. It was practically the only thing I could do all day."

"Cry?" Thad gasped, and Eli backed off the area he'd been circling. "Uh-huh," he answered.

"You? How come?"

Eli shrugged but Thad was still looking down. "I don't know. It was just all so bad. And dumb. And for no reason. I thought you were gonna die."

Eli turned the faucet on again, playing with the flow until it just dribbled. He rinsed his brother's hand carefully, holding it even after all the soap had been washed away. "It was pretty dumb, I guess. The pact, I mean."

"How stupid can you get?" Thad said, sitting up straight and drawing his hand out of Eli's and resting it palm-up in his lap.

"Yeah, I guess. But we could probably do it now — I don't mean make another dumb pact," he added hastily. "But I don't think we'll ever have to cry again. Things couldn't ever get this bad again, you know." When Thad lifted his watery eyes to his brother, full of doubt, Eli said, "You're just crying now 'cause you're worn out. You got up early and walked farther than you ever did in . . ." Eli caught himself just before he said in your life. "Since you fell. And you ran and your hands are all burned up, that's all. They'll get better fast." Eli paused and shook his head. "And, I just know it'll never be this bad again. You're almost better and nothing will ever be this bad again."

Thad wagged his head in an unconvinced "maybe." They sat back at the table and Eli gave Thad the comics and fixed cereal.

"You know," Thad said after a long silence, "Mom

and Dad are gonna find out. They're going to see these." He lifted his hands a few inches from the table.

"Just don't walk today. And eat like this." Eli held his spoon, cupping his hand toward himself, but he didn't have much hope himself. "We can do it, Thad."

Thad dropped his hands onto the table. "We got to go to church in an hour, Eli. I can't walk."

"Tell them you're sick. They've been letting you stay home from church for practically anything."

"They're just saying I can stay home. I think they know I'm going to go before they ever say it'd be all right if I didn't."

"Well, just go in your chair. That wouldn't be too weird. Tell them your leg is sore. That'd even be the truth." Eli knew he was grasping at straws and Thad wasn't helping at all. He saw him shaking his head and his anger flared. "Why do you even go to church? Talk about stupid!"

Thad waited a minute. "Do you still skip — those days you tell us you went after the route?"

"Yeah."

"Really?"

Eli eyed him. He sounded like their dad. "Yeah."

"Do you still think it's so dumb?"

"Of course. Why wouldn't I?"

"I don't know. I don't. You know, I pray every time I try to walk."

"Must be the world's fastest Glory Be's!" Eli flinched at his own cruelty. He wasn't even sure why he was mad.

But Thad chuckled a little. "Yeah, I guess. But I don't say 'prayers' much anymore. I just asked Him to let me walk."

"Seems like He drops everything."

Thad shrugged. "I take some steps," he said, looking at his cereal bowl and toying with the few soggy flakes.

Eli snorted. "Can't you see it doesn't make any difference?"

"I guess so." Thad shrugged again. "But it helps *me*. You know? Just when I start, saying, 'God, please let me walk!' makes it seem more possible. I did a lot of that when I was still in the hospital."

Eli stared at him. "But it's all so . . ." He struggled for a word he couldn't find. "Dumb — or something. I can't believe anybody believes in any of that stuff."

"I want to, I guess. I know what you think." Thad paused. "It kind of reminds me of that doubting-Thomas story."

"What does?"

"You know, 'cause you haven't seen, you don't believe."

Eli almost jumped out of his chair. "I've seen plenty! Look at you! There's no way God would do that to anyone!"

Eli saw he'd hurt Thad. But now he didn't care.

"Yeah, but it makes me feel better, believing He might help."

"But why would He wipe you out and then help fix you?"

"I don't know."

"I just don't know how you can believe it."

Thad waited, then said, "I think it'd be too sad not to. How could you ask . . ." Thad grew confused. "Just makes it easier to hope, I guess."

"But . . ."

"And I don't think everybody else is wrong. I don't think I'm smart enough to figure out something like that all by myself. I don't even like thinking anymore."

"So you think I . . ."

"I don't think anything, Eli! Maybe you're smart enough to figure it out. You're always thinking about stuff. Maybe you have to. I just don't want to! I don't want to be smarter than Mom and Dad. I don't want to be smarter than anybody."

Eli didn't say anything. He didn't think he was smarter than his parents. Not yet. He knew he was still a kid. But he also knew they were wrong about this. Everyone who believed was.

He was startled by his mother's cheery hello. "What have you two been arguing about?" she asked.

"Arguing?" Thad asked. Eli's face burned.

"Arguing," she said back. "I could hear you upstairs."

247

"Nothing," they said in unison. Thad added, "We were just talking."

She moved around the kitchen lightly and Eli knew she wasn't going to pursue it. She didn't really care what they'd been talking about. Nobody did. Her perfume left faint trails in the room. "You two better change into your church clothes. We'll be leaving as soon as this coffee is ready to brew."

Eli pulled Thad away from the table and rolled him toward the steps. He hadn't thought of it before, but Thad needed his hands to do much of anything with his chair.

"Did you help with the route this morning, Thad?"

They were at the kitchen door and Eli kept going, as if he hadn't heard, but Thad answered, "Uh-huh. It was fun. I haven't done the route in a long time."

Eli hesitated at the door, staring down at his brother.

"That's nice," their mother said. "Did you walk a lot?"

"With the crutches," Thad corrected. He refused to call that walking. "Yeah, too much."

"Too much?"

Eli couldn't believe his ears.

"Yeah. I'm tired. Even my hands are sore."

"Well, take it easy today. I'm glad you two got out, but just remember not to try to do so much. You might hurt yourself."

"I know, Mom."

Eli collected his wits. When Thad crawled into

the elevator Eli considered chewing him out but Thad's answers had worked. They'd gotten away with doing the route because they hadn't really lied.

"You better pray your hands get better before they see them," he said as the elevator whirred up.

Thad grinned. "I already have."

Thad and Eli weren't found out until after the mass, when they were helping Thad into the car. Their mother held his hand to balance him and felt Thad flinch. When she saw his hands she looked as if they were her own. "Oh, Thad," she said very quietly, and got into the front seat of the wagon. She didn't mention it again until they got home and sat down to breakfast.

"Did you wash them well?" she asked.

Thad started to ask, "Wash what?" but saw it would not be appreciated. "Uh-huh," he answered. "Eli did."

"That was good of you, Eli. It would be horrible to get them infected now. They looked very clean."

"What looked clean?" their father asked, letting his newspaper sag.

"Thad helped Eli on the route this morning," their mother explained. "He used his crutches until his hands blistered."

"Let's see." He held his hand out for Thad's.

"It's just some blisters."

His father's hand stayed where it was.

Thad inched his hand out and turned it over. His

dad let out a long whistle. "I don't suppose you'll do that again." He turned to his wife and said, "We'd better wrap those up, Mary. You know what kinds of things he'll get them into."

When nothing else was said other than a few "you have to be more careful next times," Eli began to breathe a little easier again. He chanced a glance at Thad who looked very confident, even a little smug.

"The route went better than ever," Thad said, and Eli cringed again. He started to try to ask for the sports page, but Thad went on. "My legs didn't even get sore. And my arms got tireder than my legs. I'll be walking before you know it."

"Those paws will set you back a bit," Mr. Martin said.

Thad shrugged. "Maybe. But it was neat going around again standing up. I got excited, I guess."

Their father sighed. "We know, Thad. But really, you have to pay attention when your body says you've done enough, like the doctors said. Then you wouldn't have to wait for your hands to get better before you could walk again."

Eli excused himself and slid off the bench. He crept to the living room and crawled over the couch to lie on the radiator. He couldn't understand why his parents hadn't even gotten mad. Thad didn't tell them that he'd run, or that he'd gone down the stairs by himself, but they were about the only things he hadn't told them.

"Jeez," Eli mumbled. When he carried Thad downstairs, way back when, he'd practically gotten killed for it. And Thad didn't even get hurt or anything! Now he comes home with his hands looking like he'd scraped them over cement, and nobody does *anything*.

Eli settled his elbows on the radiator so the tiled top wasn't digging into them. Then he put his chin into his hands and closed his eyes. He'd never be able to figure his parents out. Not in a million years. He didn't even know what Thad was going to do anymore.

CHAPTER
TWENTY

Thad came home from his next therapy session with a pair of fingerless gloves with padded palms. "They're bike racer gloves," he told Eli excitedly. "I can push the wheels of my chair now, no problem. Look." Thad shot back and forth several feet. "See? I use mostly the back part." He pointed to the hard back edge of his hand. "Doesn't even hurt."

Eli looked at the gloves. "It's already almost August, Thad. Why'd they wait so long to give them to you?"

Thad just shrugged.

Their father attached a pair of hooks on either side of Thad's chair so that until his hands healed the crutches rode with him, sticking out like shotguns. On the days Thad didn't have therapy he'd roll along with Eli on his route, spinning his chair to "shoot down" passing cars.

The first time Thad tried the Sunday route again, nearly three weeks after he'd gotten the blisters, they'd just started out when they saw a thin, blond figure running toward them. "That looks like Max," Thad said, slapping his wheels for speed. They met at the corner, and Thad yelled, "Hey, Max. How was your vacation?"

"Good. We went to Michigan again. Caught a ton of fish. I don't ever want to eat another fish again."

They all laughed and Max pushed the wagon while Eli pulled. "We got in about midnight," he said. "My folks don't even know I'm gone." Then Max looked at Thad and said, "Hey. What's with the chair? Why aren't you using your crutches?"

"I haven't used them for a while."

"Why not?"

Thad wrestled the chair over a curb. "Right after you left, me and Eli went nuts. I ran the whole route on my crutches."

"Wow. So how come you can't now?"

"Jeez, Max," Eli said, picking up a paper.

"Well?"

"I got a ton of blisters on my hands. I couldn't hold my crutches for a while so I got these gloves." He took one off and gave it to Max.

"Your hands are almost all better," Eli said. "Let me see. You could use crutches with those, couldn't you?"

"Yeah. Easy."

"So why aren't you?"

"Well, in therapy they said I pulled something. In the back of my leg," he said, lifting and pointing.

"You never told me that."

"Yeah. But it's so dumb. It doesn't even hurt anymore."

"Yeah?"

"They say it takes time to heal and that I should take it easy." Thad stopped, interrupted by Eli's snort. "I still walk in therapy, between the bars, but they're just super careful."

"Super slow is more like it," Eli said.

"I was just seeing if all the waiting really works."

"Haven't you figured that out yet?" Eli asked, then turned to Max. "You should have seen him that day. He ran the whole way down from Lake Drive to Stowell. Twice!"

"You still had braces though. Didn't you?" Max looked at Thad.

"Yeah. But he won't even need those before long."

"Don't worry, Eli," Thad said. "I'm not getting like the doctors. I'm going to use crutches again today. As soon as we get to the middle corner."

When they reached that corner, Eli parked the wagon and Thad was up on his crutches in a second. He thumped along the lawns with Eli and Max for the first two blocks, but no one ran back to the wagon. When Max asked how his leg was Thad said it was fine. "Feels just like it used to. I'm not getting sore at all. I thought my arms might get a little tired, but nope."

Thad crutched the entire route. When they were back at the wagon, he peeled off one glove and checked his palm. "They're fine," he said. "You want to take my chair, Max?"

Max leapt into the chair and Thad said, "It's not as fun as it looks."

"I can't wait to get rid of it," Eli said.

"Me, too."

They slowed down for Max. "How do you make it go so fast?"

Thad smiled. "Give it a few months."

Eli wiped at the sweat on his forehead. "It's going to be a hot one today."

"We'll be sweating a ton by this afternoon," Max agreed.

"What do you want to do?" Eli asked.

When no one answered, Eli said, "Hey, maybe we could go swimming! Isn't that supposed to be all right for your legs? We haven't been to the beach all summer. The lake's gotta be warm by now."

"Yeah! They say it's even good for my legs. Takes all the weight off them or something."

"What're you doing today, Max?" Thad asked.

"Are you kidding? We've been gone three weeks: weed the garden; mow the lawn; air the tents; clean the car. My dad hadn't finished listing it all before I went to bed."

"What about going to the beach?"

"Once I go home I'll be stuck there the rest of my life."

"So don't go home. Stay with us." When Max started to protest, Eli said, "You could be home by lunchtime. Holy cow, that's enough time to do jobs. It's Sunday. You're not even supposed to work on Sundays."

"My dad says he likes mowing the lawn. And he says whatever you like isn't work."

"So he can mow it."

Max shook his head. "He says I like mowing the lawn, too."

"Well, you can mow it after lunch."

"Naw. I really don't think it'll work. We'll spend all morning going to church and having breakfast and stuff."

"Yeah, so you won't get anything done anyway!"

"Yeah, but it's not . . ."

"Go to church with us," Eli said. "We can all go early! Right now. We can get our swim suits. We'll leave a note for Mom and Dad and maybe they'll even meet us at the beach."

Thad eyed his brother. "We can't take our suits to church."

"And I don't have one with me," Max said.

"We got one from last year that's too small. It'll fit you." Turning to Thad, he said, "We can ditch them in the bushes, with our towels, by the side entrance." Eli smiled reassuringly. "What do you say?"

"Well, I don't know," Max said. "How'm I gonna tell my folks? If I don't, they'll have every policeman in the state looking for me before we *get* to church."

Eli was only stumped for a second. "We can put it in the note. We'll tell our mom to call your mom when she's awake!"

"You got an old suit?"

"Uh-huh."

"And it won't fall down to my knees when I dive in?"

Eli laughed, shaking his head. He knew Max was hooked. "What do you think, Thad?"

His brother still eyed Eli curiously. "Sounds all right to me," he answered finally. His hair fell in his eyes from the dip and swing of the crutches' rhythm. He shook it back. "Are you really planning on going to church?"

"Sure." Eli turned the wagon into their driveway. "You guys wait here. I'll dump the wagon and get suits and towels." He jogged up the driveway, the wagon clattering behind him.

When he came out Eli had the towels and suits rolled under his arm. With his other arm he had three oranges pinched against his chest. "Here, you guys," he said, offering the oranges.

"We can't eat those, Eli. Church is in fifteen minutes."

"Oh, come on. That couldn't make any difference."

But they both shook their heads.

"Well, I just thought, since we didn't eat any breakfast."

"We can ditch them and have them after," Thad said.

Eli held one out to Max but Max shook his head. "I'll wait till after."

Eli dropped the towels in Max's lap in the wheelchair. "Are you going to walk the whole way?"

"Part of it at least," Thad answered.

As Max rolled along, Eli dropped two of the oranges into the chair's saddlebag. He held the third for a long time, turning it over and over, finally digging his thumb into the top. Juice spurted out and the bright smell drifted along with them. Eli looked at Max and Thad. "Oh, for corn's sake," he muttered at last. He dropped the orange into the saddlebag.

"That's gonna get sticky," Max said, but Eli paid no attention.

When they were halfway to the church, Thad traded places with Max. "Tired?" Eli asked.

"Naw. My one hand's starting to warm up. I'll use the chair for a little while. But I'll be on crutches at the beach. I don't think that chair'd even work in the sand."

"Yeah," Max said. "Hey, didn't you say you walked without your crutches in therapy?"

"A tiny bit."

"Well, wouldn't sand be about the best stuff to fall down in? If you had to?"

"Yeah!" Eli said. "You said your leg's better. Me and Max could help you. I bet you could walk a lot at the beach."

"We can sure try," Thad answered, catching some of the enthusiasm. "But I bet sand'll be hard to get through. And it'll be hard on my braces."

"Oh, jeez, Thad."

"I'm going to do it," Thad answered, staring at Eli.

They stared at each other until Max asked, "Hey, Thad? Do you think you could do it without your braces at all? Then they wouldn't get in the sand."

Eli stared at Max, but when Thad didn't answer right away, he turned to him. Thad started to shake his head very slowly. "I don't think so, Max," he said. "Not unless it goes real good with the braces on."

"You think it might?" Eli said.

"I don't know. But the sand'll be easy to fall into."

"Wow. Just think if you could, Thad!" Eli said, prancing sideways along the sidewalk. "Just think. You'd be walking again, without crutches or any-thing!"

Thad smiled. "Let's see how it goes with the braces first."

"He's been walking a ton in therapy," Eli told Max. "They say he's doing great."

"That's between the two bars though," Thad said. "And you got a guy hanging all over you in case you even start to list a little. It gets too easy, you know?" he said. "Sometimes I wish they'd just let me fall down. Right on my head."

Max giggled, but Eli said, "Why in the world . . ."

"Oh, I don't know. I guess not really. But you know, you walk back and forth between those two stupid, smooth bars — you should see them, they're like glass from all the gimps clutching them for so long. And you do your dumb exercises and nothing ever happens. At least, if you fell maybe . . . I don't know, maybe it'd feel more like you were getting someplace."

"Well, cripes," Max said, "We can take you to the beach and you can fall as much as you want. You can fall so much you'll wind up in China."

They all laughed a little and fell into silence. Eli had his head down, watching his own feet. He heard the wheels of Thad's chair clicking over the sidewalk cracks and the soft contact between his gloves and the wheels. Max thumped and swished in the crutches — nothing near Thad's rhythmical gait. He heard Max take a few skipping steps without the crutches, to catch up. Eli jumped ahead of the group and turned around, stopping everyone. "Hey!"

Thad looked down. "I knew you were going to do this."

"Let's go to the beach, right now," he pleaded. "C'mon, Thad. There won't be anyone there yet. You could practice walking all over and nobody'd sit around watching you."

"There won't be anybody there after church either.

It's not even seven o'clock." He started to wheel around his brother but Eli stepped in front of him.

Thad's eyes flashed. "Move!"

"But let's see, Thad! Let's make you walk. I know we can do it! Let's not waste time sitting around in that dumb old church with all the old geezers."

"Do you mean not go to church?" Max asked. "Not at all?"

"Yeah. We could be making Thad walk instead."

"Well, when would we go?" Max asked. Thad stared up at Eli, who still blocked his way.

"Never!" Eli said, nearly shouting. "Do you want to?"

"Well, no, I guess not. I never thought about it," Max said. "But I guess I'd rather go to church now than to hell later on." Max tried to laugh.

"Get out of my way, Eli," Thad said.

"But, Thad . . ."

"Get out of my way!" he yelled. "I hate this! I'd pound you to nothing if I wasn't in *here*." He gripped the arms of his chair and rocked it impotently.

Eli stepped back but still had Thad cornered against the sidewalk edge. The lawn had been trenched back and Thad's wheel caught in it as he tried to throw himself past his brother.

"Damn you!" Thad screamed. Eli stood dazed, watching Thad's face, twisted and red. "Get out of my way! You couldn't even do this if I wasn't smashed up!"

Eli bent forward to wrench Thad's wheel from the

ditch and Thad took a wild swing at him. Eli jumped back and Max moved in from behind, freeing Thad's wheel. "Hey, Thad," he murmured. "You're out. He didn't mean for you to get stuck."

Thad trembled in his chair. "I can't stand being so trapped in this stinking chair," he said.

"OK," Eli said, growing angry himself. "We'll go to church and smell the purple lady for an hour."

"Of course I'm going to church. I never wasn't going. But don't ever do that again, Eli, never. Or I swear I'll pound you."

"I want you to, you idiot. I want to get you walking just so you can pound me. I just thought we could skip that stupid hour to do it." He jerked his thumb toward the church. "All you had to do is say no. You didn't have to go crazy."

"I didn't even have to say no. You knew I wouldn't skip it. You're so dumb, Eli! I could care less about church. But don't ever get in my way again. I can't stand that."

They were walking again, faster now. No one talked. Finally, when the church was in sight, its steeple gilded on the east side by the sun rising over the lake, Eli whispered, "Sorry, Thad, I didn't mean to get in your way." It was the first time he could remember saying he was sorry to Thad, except when he was forced to by his parents.

Thad wheeled on without looking up. "OK," he mumbled. "It's just that it makes me feel so help-less."

Thad kept pushing the chair to the side door. "What about the ramp?" Max asked.

"I'll use my crutches," Thad said. "We'll just leave my chair out here. Leave the towels on it, too, Eli. Nobody's gonna steal some gimp's chair."

An elderly woman walked into the church. Max whispered, "I wouldn't be too sure about that, Thad. Lot a people here could use a nice chair like that."

They all grinned a little. Thad stood up on his crutches and Eli pulled the chair against the side of the church and set the brake. When he turned, Thad was already up on the first step. Eli jumped to the step above him and got ready to catch him should he pitch forward. Max was behind him.

"This isn't working," Thad said after the first two steps. "At therapy they act like there aren't any steps anywhere in the world." Before Eli or Max could answer, he said, "Here, take this." He pulled out the crutch nearest the railing and clutched at the railing instead. The boys missed the crutch and it clattered down until Max snagged it with his foot.

With one crutch and the railing, Thad pulled and pushed himself up the stairs. Sweat had just begun to glisten on his forehead when he reached the top. "They're already starting," Max said, in the instinctive church hush.

Thad panted and smiled at Max. "Those are the first steps I made it up."

"Really? Wow. That's pretty good."

"Yeah," Eli said sarcastically. "You could practically see God helping."

Thad smiled. "You see, Max," he said, not bothering to whisper although they crossed the threshold to the rows of dark, nearly empty pews, "Eli's got it all figured out: There's no such thing as God."

Heads turned and Eli hissed, "Thad!" Thad smiled back. They shuffled into the nearest pew. Eli and Max knelt like everybody else. Thad sat, his braces booming against the hard, wooden seats.

Max stared at Eli until Eli was forced to make faces at him to get him to quit. It was the longest hour Eli had ever spent, interrupted only by the shifting from standing, to sitting, to kneeling, and back to standing again. He kept his head down, avoiding the glaring eyes of the saints on the ceiling, letting the priest's voice drone on and on, and on.

Max startled Eli with a tap on the shoulder. The priest's monotonous murmur had nearly settled Eli into sleep. He blinked several times and saw that it was time for communion.

Still holding onto the pew in front of him, Eli lowered himself until his butt rested on the edge of the pew seat. He looked at Max and at Thad, but Thad was already up and getting his crutches set in the aisle.

Taking a deep breath Eli decided to skip communion. He just couldn't pretend the flat, dry bread was somebody's body. He pushed off the kneeler and sat on the pew seat, tucking his legs under the wooden bench. When Max didn't pass by, Eli gestured for him to go ahead. With his head down, he saw Max shuffle by, brushing lightly against Eli's knees.

When Max was past, Eli lifted his head. He watched the thin gray line break up and drift into gaps at the communion rail. The priest and the altar boy went back and forth along the line with the gold chalice and plate. Eli could tell by the tilt of the heads which were the early birds — the women who knelt with mouths gaping, tongue out, eyes closed, waiting for their host, with the priest still two or even three people away.

He watched Thad's progress and was oddly proud to see him march up to the rail. Max knelt beside him, but Thad stood, tall on his crutches. The priest reached Max and stuck a host on his tongue. Then the priest stood up straight, surprised out of his crouch by Thad's position. Eli saw the priest smile and mumble the words and watched Thad's head tilt at the very last second. Thad made the sign of the cross then and got his crutches going again. At least he's not an early bird, Eli thought.

The mass wound up quickly, and the boys raced to the side door with the last reedy, quavering replies of the elderly still drifting in their ears. Eli and Max took their positions and Thad lowered himself slowly down the stairs with his backwards gait.

Thad told them he wanted to use his crutches, since he'd rested for an hour. "You see?" he told Eli. "Wasn't a total waste of time."

Eli released the wheelchair's brake and didn't answer. Max looked at both of them and said, "He's not kidding, Eli? You really don't even believe in *God*?"

Eli glanced at a woman coming down the steps and whispered for Max to shut up. He spun the chair around and pushed it at Max, saying, "Do you want to drive down to the beach?"

The woman hesitated at the bottom of the steps. There was no way she could've heard Max, Eli thought. He snuck a glance at her. She wasn't even old. She had wavy, blonde hair and looked vaguely familiar. He looked away again and they started off.

Something was really familiar about the lady. Eli hadn't noticed her in the church, even though she must've been the only one except for them without gray hair. Eli peeked over his shoulder. The lady was still watching them. She looked sad, Eli thought. Then Eli remembered a field of snow outside the back door of the school, and a nun with sad eyes, saying how she liked the snow before the children trampled it, and asking Eli to pray for her.

Eli stopped in his tracks. He turned around, squinting at the woman. They were the same sad eyes. Eli took a step toward her, taking in her plain gray dress and white blouse. She smiled and he knew, despite her normal clothes, that it was her. "Sister Mirin?"

"Hello, Eli," she said in the same smooth voice that he'd remembered. "I thought you boys were going to pretend I wasn't here."

Max and Thad stopped, too. They came in closer. "Hello," Eli said, dropping the "Sister," but not sure that he should.

"Hello, Max, and Thad. I was so happy to see you in church today. And proud of you, Thad. Walking up to Communion."

"I'm getting better," he said as Max scrambled out of the wheelchair saying, "Hello, Sister."

"I'm sure you boys can see it's not Sister anymore," she said very quietly.

The three boys stood in front of her, dumbfounded.

"I asked to be released from my vows after the school year. I thought you might have heard about it."

They shook their heads. "So you aren't going to be teaching there anymore?" Max asked.

"I'm trying to stay on. But nothing is easy now."

They nodded and Eli smiled. He said he knew what she meant.

"You do?"

Eli shrugged. "Maybe."

She searched his face but said nothing. To Thad she said, "How long have you been on crutches?"

"Too long. But it beats the wheelchair."

"And how much longer before you can go without the crutches?" she asked, then stammered, "You will be able to, won't you?"

"Oh, yeah!" Eli blurted.

"I'm already doing a little without crutches," Thad added.

"We were just going to the beach to practice," Max explained. "Because of the sand."

"Where do you live?" Thad asked. The idea of a nun living outside a convent was too strange not to investigate.

"I have an apartment on Murray."

They started walking and when they reached the corner Eli asked, "So you're not Sister Mirin anymore?"

"Same person, different name."

"What's your name now?"

"The same as it was before. Katherine Duvall."

"So we should call you Miss Duvall now?"

She smiled her smile. "You three can even call me Katherine. Or Kathy, if that would be easier."

"OK," Eli said. They began to separate, she going west, the boys east, toward the lake.

"Good luck, Thad," she called after them.

They chimed, "Good-bye, Miss Duvall," in unison. She called, "Good-bye," back, laughing as she turned around.

"Wow! Not a nun anymore. Why, do you suppose?" Max asked.

"Yeah? Why?" Eli wondered.

"Weird," Max said. "She was always nice though, even though she was a nun."

"She laughed a lot. More than any nun I ever saw."

"S'pose they kicked her out for being too nice?" Max asked.

"No." Thad laughed. "They wouldn't do that."

"She said she *asked* to be released, or something." Eli said.

"Why do you suppose she'd've done that? She had heaven in the bag."

The boys walked several blocks without speaking. "Maybe it was 'cause she was too nice," Max said at last. "Not many people could stand living with Sister Dorine."

"No kidding," Thad said. "That'd do it for me."

They walked to the top of the bluff above the beach, Thad and Max kidding all the way about why Sister Mirin had quit the nuns. It was all friendly and funny but Eli didn't join in. When they arrived at the bluff he was surprised. He'd been thinking so hard he'd forgotten where they were going.

He knew why she'd quit. He'd seen it in her face, that day outside the school door. That's why she looked so sad. Eli was sorry he hadn't figured out about God by then. Maybe he could've helped her. She'd always helped him.

But deep down Eli knew he wouldn't have said anything about it then, even if he'd known everything he did now. Because she was a nun and an adult and . . . Eli shook his head. He didn't want to talk about it anymore. Even Thad couldn't understand.

Eli was afraid the whole time they'd talked to Sister Mirin that she would say something about his skipping communion. Thad was acting so weird about it Eli figured he could've blurted out the whole thing, like he did to Max, right before they went inside the church. He took a peevish, sidelong glance at his brother. You didn't have to go crazy on me, just because your stupid chair got stuck in the crack, he thought.

Then it began to dawn on Eli. He'd watched the whole communion process. He never saw Sister Mirin at the communion rail. Eli stopped with the shock of it.

"Hey, you guys?" Eli said haltingly. "You don't suppose they kick you out of church for not being a nun anymore, do you?"

Thad guffawed. "Where do you think we saw Sister Mirin?"

Eli waved his hand. "I *know* that," he said. "But she didn't go to communion. That's pretty weird for a nun. Maybe she was like sneaking in or something."

Max and Thad both laughed and Eli cursed himself for saying anything. There was one thing he'd learned since all of this started. It was always better to be quiet and figure things out for yourself.

"I don't think you do," Max said. "You know, get thrown out. You've got to do something really bad before they do that to you. Like kill somebody or something."

"Yeah," Thad agreed. "Maybe she went yesterday and got communion. You know nuns go about a hundred times." He tried to laugh, but Eli didn't respond.

"Maybe she did go to communion. Maybe you just didn't see her. They couldn't've kicked her out just for quitting the nuns."

"Yeah," Eli grunted.

He stumbled to the gate behind Max and Thad. He had never felt sorrier for a person than he did for Sister Mirin right then. He'd never really even thought about God until after Thad got hurt. But when he did, it all fell apart pretty fast and he knew what he had to believe. But Sister Mirin was an adult — a nun even, and she'd just started to figure out that she'd been fooled her whole life.

No wonder she asked me to pray for her, he thought, furious at whatever he'd once thought was God.

CHAPTER
TWENTY-ONE

The boys stood at the beach entrance. "It's locked," Thad said. They stared at the chain across the fence. Just behind it sat the little toll booth and the machinery for the tram that the old and the lazy rode up and down the bluff.

"When's it open?"

Max pressed his face against the fence, trying to read the hours. "Nine o'clock, I think it says, on Sundays."

"Jeez, it's only eight now."

"There's the hole at the other end."

"How're we going to get Thad through there?"

"He can crawl under. He did it at the old depot."

"You guys were there?"

"Yeah," Thad said. "But we didn't have any BBs."

He began crutching across the bluff top toward the hole. "Come on. I can go anywhere you guys can."

"It's awful steep there and there's no room for crutches."

"I can walk skinny with them."

"What about your chair?"

"Fold it up and stick it under the tree."

Eli caught himself smiling at Thad. "You're not even going to take your chair down the walk?"

There was a pause as they all pictured the poorly paved trail that switchbacked down the bluff in six hairpin turns. Then Thad laughed. "It'd be fun," he said, "But I don't think we could get the chair through the fence. We'd kill ourselves on the corners anyway. Maybe not Max though, he's getting pretty good in that chair."

When they were a few feet from the hole Eli folded the chair and pushed it under the giant spruce. The chair disappeared and Eli ran back to the fence, picking at a gob of sap caught in his hair.

Thad was already through the hole and the others followed quickly. Once on the other side, the slope looked more serious, the weeds along the path thicker and more tangled.

"You sure, Thad?"

"Jeez, Max, lay off."

Eli got in front of Thad and they started down the dirt path. The weeds grabbed at Thad's crutches until he had to move them one at a time. "I forgot there were so many vines," he said.

"We're practically to the ramp now."

Thad tripped once, a creeper catching his crutch just as he thought it was free. Eli caught him before he toppled over and Max pulled from behind. He stood shakily and smiled. "Thanks, you guys," he said. "That one snuck up on me."

When they finally broke onto the crumbling pavement, Thad started into a run on his crutches. He slowed in time for the corner and they all walked the next straightaway. Thad said, "I think if I walk one, run one, my hands'll be able to take it." But as they neared the second corner, he said, "Holy cow, it's going to be harder to walk than it is to run, it's so steep."

"Yeah. But if you wiped out . . ."

"I'd be a tangled ball of metal." He laughed, slapping his braces with a crutch and breaking into a run.

Thad ran the last two sections, slowing only when he reached the bottom, feeling his way as the walkway disappeared in the sand. When his crutch tips disappeared completely he let himself go, turning to land on his side. Max and Eli threw themselves down beside him. "You OK?"

"Sure. I did that on purpose."

"Don't those braces dig in a lot?" Max asked.

"They sure do. I can't wait to get rid of them. I don't even mind the wheelchair as much as these."

"It's nice here with nobody else," Eli said. The sun was still low, only a few inches above the razor straight line of the water. The lake glinted, glassy flat. "It's gonna be a scorcher."

Thad laughed. "Our dad says that every time he comes here."

Eli peeled off his shirt and Thad struggled out of his pants and started undoing his braces. "Are you guys going to change right here?" Max asked.

Eli was already wriggling out of his pants. "Where else?" he asked. "Changing rooms'll all be locked."

Eli was in his suit before Max started to undress. Thad sat in the bright sand, naked and scarred, tugging his suit over his thin ankles. "Boy, it's nice to be able to dress yourself," he said, catching Max and Eli watching him. They lifted him enough to allow him to brush the sand off his rear before pulling his suit up. Eli stared down at the cruel red dents the braces left on Thad's naked legs.

When his suit was on, instead of lowering him again, Eli gave Max a signal and they stood him upright.

Thad stood biting his lip and gripping their arms. "How does it feel?" Eli asked.

"Great," Thad said. "Shaky as anything though."

"Want to try a step?"

Thad ducked his head and thought a long time. He finally started to lift one foot and the boys tightened their grip. But Thad put the foot down immediately. He shook his head and let his breath out in a long, long sigh. "They're used to the braces holding most of the weight," he said. "I could feel that one start to buckle as soon as I lifted the other one."

"Maybe if we held you up a little."

"No. That'd be the same as walking between the bars."

They lowered him back to the ground. "Maybe when you walk around some with the braces," Eli said, "maybe you'll be warmed up enough."

"Sure, Eli. We'll see then." He was buckling his braces back into their dents on his legs and Eli turned his head away. Suddenly the jingle of the buckles was too much. Eli let out a whoop and ran across the beach, kicking up spurts of sand with each step. Max started to follow but hesitated until Thad said he could get there by himself.

The first splash into the water was shocking, but Eli charged into the lake until the water was pulling at his legs. With one more yell he plunged in and under.

He tried to stay under as long as he could, down where those buckles could not follow him, but his forehead was tingling and he knew he'd have to go up or get a cold headache. Surfacing, he yelled again, spluttering and dancing on the bottom, his arms clasped around his chest. The beach looked very different from the water. Now the sun was at Eli's back, and the sand sparkled instead of the water. The beach house always looked brightest early, when the sun hit it dead on, covering the peeling whitewash with glare. The big, black hands of the clock showed eight o'clock. They had an hour to themselves.

Max reached the lake and Eli watched the water shatter around him. His war whoop sounded small and tinny with nothing but the lake behind Eli.

Then Eli saw Thad push up from the sand at the end of the walkway, all braced up, crutching down to the water. Max hit Eli in the legs underwater, but Eli stood hard, staring at his brother. After a moment of wrestling Max surfaced, complaining about Eli not playing the game.

"Jeez, Max. We could've carried him down. Now he'll have to take the stupid braces off again to come in the water."

"I forgot."

Eli started back to shore, leaning forward against the water. "Maybe he wants to walk first, while nobody's here. Then he could swim later."

Max was walking beside Eli, clutching his skinny arms around his body. "Kind of cold," he said. Eli didn't answer.

When the water was only knee-deep, Eli said, "Hey, Thad? Do you want to walk around some before we go swimming?"

"Looks like it's too late for that." He was in the water up to his ankles, with his braces still on.

Eli and Max passed him and sat down on the just-warming sand. "Won't they rust?" Eli asked.

"Yeah, I guess. It'd mess up the leather, too."

"Let's walk then. You can take them off for swimming."

"OK. I don't think this sand'll be as bad as I thought. It doesn't grab my feet much now. So, here goes. No crutches."

Eli was up, brushing nervously at the sheet of sand that clung to his leg and side. Thad already had his face set into his concentrated stare. He said, "Here," and held out a crutch to Eli and the other to Max.

Eli let the crutch drop and had his hands halfway to his brother's arm. "Don't touch," Thad warned.

Without the usual gathering of himself, Thad lurched forward. The gait was jerky at first, walking with his hips more than his legs, but it began to smooth out.

Eli leapt after him and saw Thad's face set harder than ever. "Don't touch," he hissed. "I'm going to the breakwater."

Eli and Max stayed on each side of Thad. The breakwater was still twenty yards away, but Thad's steps were improving. His upper leg swung from the hip, and his knees bent. His trail in the sand looked less and less snakish.

As he got closer, Thad began to lean forward. Eli closed in, but with an audible grunt, Thad pulled himself back and walked more slowly, more under control. And then he was there. He stopped, still on his feet, and grinned, his breath coming hard and fast now that he remembered not to hold it. He looked at Eli and laughed. "How come *your* tongue is sticking out?"

Eli pulled it in and laughed, too. Then Thad let out a whoop like Eli's, but containing more triumph than Eli'd ever heard. "I've never done that, Max!" he yelled. "Didn't even fall over at the end!"

But he did fall when he tried to turn around. Eli and Max weren't expecting it and Thad went all the way down. He laughed and struggled up by himself. "You were right about the sand," he said to Max. "See? I can even get up by myself!"

"Yeah. That was a long walk, too. Ready?" But Thad was already on the march.

They followed Thad around, catching him sometimes when he fell, missing others. But the falls were infrequent, usually coming during a turn or at the end or start of a walk. Thad practiced turning by walking in a circle, then the other way, until he had a figure eight carved in the sand.

Eli was beside himself. He kept glancing back to the pair of crutches lying just beyond the reach of the lapping waves, as if they had just washed up. Thad was walking now without the desperate concentration, his mouth curved into an unbelieving smile. Then he would laugh, for no reason at all.

Thad tried to bend over to pick up a rock in front of the beach store and toppled over. Eli sat beside him when he didn't get up immediately and said, "This is great, Thad!"

279

"You're telling me. I'm walking, Eli!"

"Yeah. You look like you never stopped," Max said.

Eli glanced at the clock in the center of the beach house. "It's ten to, you guys. We better go through the fence to the private side until the guards come down and let more people in."

"Think they'll mind?" Thad asked, too happy to care.

"Yeah. They wouldn't like it if we were here before them."

Eli went to the stretch of wet sand and picked up Thad's crutches. When he looked back, Thad was walking toward the dilapidated fence at the end of the public beach. He and Max reached him at the same time.

"You're walking great," Eli said. "Your legs are moving the right way."

"Yep." Thad kept laughing.

They heard the motor kick in at the top of the hill and knew the guards were on their way down. Without speaking, Eli handed Thad the crutches and they ran the rest of the way to the gap in the fence. They were all laughing uncontrollably by the time they were on the other side. "This is great!" Thad said. "Why don't we do this all the time?"

"We should," Max said. But Eli remembered how they'd argued on the way to church and he already knew that they wouldn't be doing this all the time. It seemed hardly anything came this easily anymore. Not since the fall.

CHAPTER
TWENTY-TWO

The private beach was rockier, with tangled shrubs and scrubby maple saplings growing close to the water. "If we stop here, we can still see the beach," Eli said. "Then we could slip back in when the lifeguards aren't looking."

"Let's keep going a little more," Thad said. "I haven't been down here in a long time."

The cobbles crunched and clacked beneath their feet. The stones glistened black or tan, some almost blue where the waves had washed over them; dry, they were pale and gray.

Eli'd been to this beach before on one of his stupid trips with Roger and Sonny. They had a kind of cave down here. Not a real cave, but a hollow under a matted pile of brush. The walls were tight and hard to see through except on the lakeside, but even there it was impossible to see into if you were outside. Eli had only been there at night and he wasn't sure if he could find it now. He'd just begun to look when he heard Sonny call, "Hey, Eli!"

They all stopped. Thad said, "Was that Sonny?"

"Yeah," Eli said. "What're you doing down here, Sonny?" he asked. He hadn't seen him yet.

The bushes rattled and parted. Sonny crawled out grinning. "Hey, you guys. Hey, Thad. Hey, Max."

"Is that a fort or something?" Thad asked.

"Yeah. Me and Roger were just sitting around."

"Roger's here?"

They heard Roger giggle and he squeezed out, too. "I knew you guys didn't know I was here."

"Hey, Roger," the boys said quietly.

"What're you guys doing?" Sonny asked.

"We were over at the beach but had to leave 'cause the lifeguards were coming," Eli said.

"We hardly go over there anymore," Roger said.

Thad inspected the entrance to the hideout. "This is pretty neat, Sonny. I never even saw you."

"I found it," Roger said. "You can go in if you want."

Max knelt down and looked. Roger pushed by him. "Come on. Let's all go in. I think we'll fit."

Eli went last, following Thad in case he needed help. It was dim in the shelter, and too close with five bodies, the air thick with a pungently sweet smell. Roger threw a couple of well-worn *Playboys* into the small center of the ring. "You guys want to look at these? They're my dad's," he said, his voice affectedly nonchalant.

They were the same issues that'd been in the cave the last time Eli had been there, their address labels peeled off. Eli wondered if they were really his dad's. He giggled, picturing an adult version of Roger.

Thad pulled at a magazine and it fell open to the centerfold. He turned it to Max. Eli could hear Max swallow. Thad turned the picture to Eli and Eli shook his head. "I saw it last time." He was thankful for the dimness. He knew the guilty excitement on Thad's face would be the same as his had been. He didn't want to see that.

The thrill of the pictures wore out fast, despite Roger's bragging that he could get as many as he wanted. When no one seemed interested anymore, Roger stashed the magazines behind his back.

Thad's braces creaked in the ensuing silence. His legs stuck straight before him. "You all right?" Eli asked.

"Just a little stiff."

Eli nodded and stared through the tangle of ropey branches to the waves pushing against the shore. The wind was up a little. The waves were slow and slick, their bulging surfaces collapsing just before the shore and tumbling in unevenly. A breeze touched his face and Eli turned back to the ring of faces.

Roger dug behind himself again. "Any of you want a beer?"

Instantly Eli recognized the smell that had taunted him since they'd entered. It was his father's breath when he'd wrestle with them after lunch on Saturdays, after the beer. Roger pulled out several loose cans. "There's enough for each of us. Sonny doesn't need one. He's already drunk."

"I am not!"

Roger waved the cans around, but no one reached. He shrugged and set them down. He took one himself, saying "What a bunch of girls." He popped the top and the warm beer bubbled out, filling the room with its pungent smell.

Eli smiled at Thad's look of complete contempt.

"There's a lot more, so you guys can have as many as you want. This is my third." Roger took a long pull, sighing deeply afterwards.

"You can have another, Sonny," he said when no one followed him. "I suppose you won't barf yet."

"Naw," Sonny said.

Eli watched for a moment as Sonny squirmed and Roger laughed at him. "I'm leaving," he said. "It stinks in here."

"Yeah," Thad said. Eli scrambled out and helped pull Thad after him. Max was right behind them. Sonny crept out a moment later. Roger came last, gripping his can and sneering at the others. "What's the matter, Sonny? You don't want the sissy-boy Martins to know you drink beer?"

Thad said, "Shut up, Roger."

Roger laughed. "What're you going to do about it?" he said, turning red with laughter, "Hit me with a crutch?"

Thad dropped his crutches. "Uh-uh," he said.

"Oh shit," Roger giggled. "You can't hardly stand up." But his laughter faded and he backed away from Eli.

"I'm gonna kill you, Roger. You're the biggest creep in the world." Eli lashed out, knocking the beer from Roger's hand. "You gross tub-o'-lard!"

"Don't, Eli," Thad said. "I don't want you fighting him for me. I could take the lard bucket right now. No problem."

Eli looked at Thad, then back at Roger. "Anybody could kill you, you slob. Why don't you go crawl away?"

"Jeez, you guys," Roger said, "I was just kidding."

Eli spit on the ground. He, Max, and Thad turned back toward the beach. Sonny followed and Roger tagged several yards back. "You guys aren't sissy-boys. I was just kidding."

Soon Roger's whining began to grate on everyone. Thad finally said, "Shut up, Roger. Nobody cares what you said."

The stones and sand crunched beneath their feet and no one looked up until they could see the public beach. The tram was trundling up and down the bluff and a few people were on the path, but there wasn't enough of a crowd to mingle into yet.

Thad sat down. "We could swim here, I guess."

"It's always weedy here," Max said.

"It isn't so bad this year," Sonny said.

"We might as well. We can't get on the public beach," Thad said, and, started to unbuckle his braces.

"Do you have a suit?" Eli asked Sonny.

"We just go in our underwear," Roger said. He peeled off his shirt. Sonny started out of his pants.

Max and Eli stayed to see if Thad would need help getting in, but Sonny leapt in and Roger wallowed in after him, flabby and white, yelling, "Last one in's a rotten egg!"

Max and Eli laughed as they helped Thad up. Roger looked so funny in his wet jockey shorts. "He wouldn't be bad if he wasn't such a jerk," Max said. Just then, Roger surfaced, spitting an enormous spout as he rolled onto his back. "Hey, I'm a whale!" he yelled. Thad laughed and shouted back, "You sure are."

Roger rolled and grinned. "Are you guys coming in or not?"

Eli looked at Thad who said, "Don't hold me up, all right?"

Eli and Max held him tightly, but didn't support his weight. Thad took two steps and was in the water. A wave swept almost to his knees and he tottered but stayed up. "It's cold," he giggled. "You guys are holding me up. I can tell."

Eli released his grip slightly. "That better?"

Thad walked until the water was at his knees. He took several breaths. "All right. Now let go. Completely." Eli hesitated and Thad said, "All the way. Don't even touch."

As soon as he was free, Thad took a step. A wave swelled around him and he tumbled forward. He bobbed up and started stroking out, keeping his head above the water. When he rolled onto his back, Eli and Max were swimming alongside him.

"I almost took a step," he said. "Without braces even."

"You probably would have except for that wave," Max said.

"How do you feel?"

"Great. This is great. It's like floating. My legs don't have to do anything." Thad rolled over and dove. Eli dove after him and came up a long distance away.

"You always fall for that one," Thad cackled. "You got to swim with your eyes open."

"They were. You can't see anything though."

Eli hung back from Thad as they swam. His arms had grown bigger than anyone else's from using the chair and the crutches, and he pulled himself around easily. When Eli asked if he could kick, Thad said he was having too much fun to worry about it.

Roger imitated the whale again and again and, with his fingers held at his mouth for tusks, he was a walrus. When they had a splash fight he got wiped out, diving under water to escape, his huge white rear disappearing last.

Max swam into a pile of seaweed and had a fit, shrilling, "Weed-goo!" While everyone was laughing he snared a handful and landed it on top of Thad's head. Thad dove down to wash it off and swam beneath Sonny, pulling him under.

Sonny came up coughing and wound up laughing before he could get his breath back. Everyone else was laughing so hard he couldn't help it.

Then Thad announced he was getting out. They crawled on their hands into the shallow water, dragging their legs behind, beached until a wave would lift them closer to shore. When they could get no further, they got to their feet and trudged in. Eli and Max carried Thad to the hot sand beside his crutches and braces.

They lay flat in the sand, the sun warming them quickly. Eli let the red-black spots dance under his closed eyes and felt the tickling run the sand made as it dried on his skin.

"This is great," Eli said. "Why didn't we do this before? We always used to go swimming. Summer's practically over already," he added, but no one bothered answering.

When they were dry on one side they rolled over. The wet sand on their backs took longer to dry. Eli listened to the others scratching at the drying, tightening sand layer. He bit his lip, refusing to scratch as the sand tickled him. Finally, when he thought he would burst if he didn't, Eli leaped from the ground, yelling and pawing frantically at the crust of sand.

Thad sat up and carefully wiped every last grain from his legs. He buckled his braces on and sat sleepily on the shore. "That sun makes you tired," he said.

"Especially after swimming in the cold." Max eyed the public beach. "There's a guard at the fence picking up trash."

Thad crutched around in a circle. "Well, now what?"

Roger looked up. "I know where a wasp's nest is," he said.

"Down here?"

"Right by the cave."

"One of them got me the last time I was here," Roger said. He twisted his biceps around until they could all see the last trace of the welt left by the sting.

They started back toward the cave, their hearts quickening. Since they could remember, a wasp's nest was something to be destroyed. Wasps stung — hard.

But wasps hardly ever stung if you left them alone, Eli thought. He remembered sprinting away from a nest split open by a rock; he remembered the nights kicking grass-filled bags; the man chasing him. The wasps were like that man. They made it dangerous.

The butterflies began to dance in his stomach.

"There it is," Roger said. He stopped and pointed.

The nest was a large one, gray and papery. It hung, half hidden, in the branches of a dogwood.

"It's so big it's bending those branches."

"I know," Sonny whispered. All their voices were hushed now. There were several wasps crawling around the entrance hole and a few in the air around them. The nest hummed.

"How come you haven't busted it yet?" Eli asked.

Roger shrugged and Sonny mumbled, "I don't know."

"This is perfect." Eli pointed to the lake. "We could run right into the water. They couldn't get us there."

"What about our heads?" Thad said. "We'd have to breathe."

"We could splash so much they couldn't get close."

"How long do you suppose they'd try?"

"If they were getting blasted by water, I bet not long," Eli said. "They hate water."

A wasp landed on Thad's elbow and he brushed it away. "Suppose it might be better to just swim away underwater?"

No one answered for a moment. "You'd have to come up though. You wouldn't know if they were waiting for you or not."

"Yeah. They could sting you all over your head."

"Or right in your eyes, maybe," Roger said, shivering.

"What if you sucked one in when you were taking a breath?"

"It'd bite you on your tongue. Maybe it'd get all the way to your lungs!" Eli giggled at the squeamish looks around him.

"Are we going to or not?" Thad asked.

Roger pulled up a spear-shaped stick and broke off a few extra branches. "Ready?"

"You can't do it this close."

"I know. I'm just starting the spear."

Eli picked up a stone. He grinned, knowing he'd hit it long before Roger, and from farther away, too. He thought of Roger laughing at Thad standing without his crutches.

Eli motioned to the others and they started quietly toward the lake. Everyone except Roger. When he was far enough from the nest Eli stopped, twisting the stone between his thumb and first two fingers. He waved the others on toward the lake.

Roger stood facing the nest, twisting at a green fork on his spear. Eli could see the pale-green edge of the bark as it spiraled around its own stump. Roger'd be finished any second.

Glancing over his shoulder, Eli saw Thad and Max and Sonny. They were halfway to the lake but they could still see the nest.

Eli looked back at Roger and the nest. The stone

would have to go just over Roger's shoulder. Eli couldn't believe Roger still hadn't caught on to the joke. The branch he was twisting snapped off and Eli heard Roger laugh and toss the branch aside. Roger asked, "Ready?" again. Eli was surprised by how far away he sounded.

As he started the throw Eli saw Roger turn. The sun dappled across his wide, placid back and the giggle Eli'd been fighting died. He saw Roger blink dumbly and he thought he heard Thad yell something. Then the stone was gone.

Roger's stick, with the frayed, pale scar in its side, fell from his hand. The stone cleared his shoulder by a bare inch.

The nest split open slowly. Eli saw one side dangle down, bounce lightly back up, then fall completely, leaving a wide strip of the gray paper hanging from the half in the tree. More wasps than he'd ever seen in the world hung in the air for an instant, then belched out, their hum turning to a roar.

Eli turned and ran.

Thad was much closer than he should have been. He stared at Eli in shock, then lurched into a turn. He ran hard, the stones squeezing away from the tips of his crutches. Max and Sonny hit the water and went under.

Eli caught up with Thad and began to draw by him. He ran even faster when he heard Roger's first shouts. He pictured him galloping away from the burst grass bags and remembered how slow and awkward he was. Thad would be all right, Eli realized. Thad would make it to the water long before Roger.

The water caught at Eli's feet and he took one more leap before diving. He shot to the bottom and hung there, stunned by the peaceful, cool silence. How could Roger not have seen them sneaking away! How could anybody be *that* dumb! He thought of the wasps on that wide, soft, jiggly back. Eli hadn't really meant for it to work.

Eli stayed under until his breath gave out. Then he surfaced, throwing up as much water as he could in case the wasps were there. Even Roger'd have to be here by now, he thought.

Eli was stung in the forehead immediately. He yelped in surprise, swatting hard, and splashing madly. He should have swum out deeper when he was underwater. But instead of diving and swimming out farther, Eli stayed where he was, unable to look away from shore.

Roger had just hit the water line. He dropped immediately, crawling out to deeper water. A cloud of wasps hung over him.

Eli watched Roger's bellying wake approach, then burst as Roger surfaced, gasping. A wasp came up with Roger, on his cheek, just below his eye. Its abdomen pumped and jerked and it pulled free just before Roger threw himself under again. The wasp fluttered lamely down and lay on its back, too wet to fly.

But still Eli didn't dive. He grabbed Roger as he swam by. The whole time, the shrieks filled his ears. Thad was calling for him. Over and over and over again. And Eli stood holding Roger, staring at Thad crumpled at the water's edge, rolled into a tight, fetal ball.

Roger surfaced, swatting at Eli's arm. They both splashed water into the air around them. The main body of wasps flew undecidedly over the water where Roger had disappeared. They began to move toward Roger and Eli. "We gotta get Thad!" Eli screamed as Roger begged to be let go. "We gotta get Thad!" he screamed again, directly into Roger's face.

Roger hit at Eli's arm, begging to be let go.

Eli lurched toward the beach, dragging Roger with him, but the furious insects were upon them. Eli let go of Roger and dove. He squashed two wasps on his shoulder. He thought they were supposed to let go underwater.

Eli held his breath as long as he could and swam toward shore. He was stung again when he surfaced, but the cloud had moved off. Roger was gone. Thad was still yelling for him. Eli watched him try to stand. "Crawl, Thad! Crawl into the water!"

Thad struggled with his crutches, trying to stand up, as if he didn't hear. The wasps were almost on him. "Crawl!" Eli shrieked so loud his voice cracked. Thad fell before he got halfway up and Eli dove again. He swam until his chest scraped the bottom then he jumped up, throwing a tremendous spray toward Thad, who rolled wildly back and forth, like a burning man.

"Roll into the lake!" Eli screamed.

A wasp stung Eli on the ear and he gasped at the sharp, clear pain of it. He glanced over his shoulder, seeing Max stroking in fast, but too late.

Then Eli finally burst out of the lake, throwing spray as far as he could. He reached Thad in a second and grabbed him by the arms, barely aware of the wasp stinging his palm. Thad kicked at the sand, trying to help, but his hands continued their frantic thrashing across his body.

The wasps molded into one hissing, painful blur and Eli pulled until he fell backwards, losing his grip on Thad. He was surprised to find himself already in a foot of water. He flailed insanely, covering Thad in a choking curtain of spray. He hardly noticed when the wasps retreated.

Eli tugged Thad out farther. Max bumped into them and helped. But Thad finally turned and panted, "Not any deeper."

"We got to!" Eli yelled.

Thad shook his head. Only a few welts showed on his face, but Eli cried at the sight of his back. "No deeper," he said. "My braces'll sink me."

They stopped dead. Eli and Max splashed water

into a protective shroud and Thad clung to their shoulders.

Eli splashed until he thought his arms were going to drop off. Leadenly he slapped against the surface until Max grabbed him, forcing him to stop. "They're gone," he said quietly.

Eli looked around and the wasps were gone. Then he closed his eyes and felt Thad's arm around the back of his neck. If it wasn't for Thad, Eli thought, he'd slip underwater and swim so far out no one would ever find him. Thad's wailing cries rang in his ears and he couldn't forget his hesitation. He should have run in the first time he saw him. Eli's knees went loose and he struggled to stand and not be sick.

"Where'd they go?" Thad croaked at last.

"I don't know," Max answered. "They're gone."

"I didn't know they could sting you so many times," Thad mumbled. Eli marveled that Thad's voice could sound so calm.

"Yeah," Max answered. "They're not like bees."

Eli kept his eyes closed and listened to someone paddle in. "Are you all right?" he heard Sonny ask.

Max said, "Yeah. I didn't even get stung till the end."

"They bit all over Roger's face. He looks fatter than ever."

"Where is he?"

"He's staying out there till he knows they're gone."

Max yelled, "Come on, Roger. They're gone."

Eli heard the splash and dribble as Max waved his arm.

"That was mean," Sonny said.

"Who'd've expected it to work?"

"He's just stung up," Max said.

"It's only Roger," Eli said, surprising himself.

"He deserves it," Thad said. He was gingerly rubbing his lip, toying with the hard lump of a sting.

"Hurt?" Max asked.

"Not as much anymore," Thad said. "It's kind of numb. Like when you go to the dentist. They didn't even get me that bad really. Most of them went after Roger."

Eli opened his eyes and squinted against the new brightness. He turned to Thad and told him he was sorry.

"I couldn't get up," Thad said. "Thanks for getting me."

Roger swam in slowly. "Why don't you get my shirt, Sonny?"

"No way! It's right next to the nest."

"They're gone now," Roger whined.

Eli saw the puffiness under his eye and hated Roger for everything. "Whyn't you shut up?" he said.

"Me?" Roger gasped. "Me? And you guys always call me a creep." Roger began to shuffle into shore. "I've never done anything that lousy in my life."

"Oh, huh!" Eli barked after him. He wished Roger

would fight. He turned around so he wouldn't have to watch him. How could he *ever* say he was sorry to Roger?

No one said anything until Roger was near the fence. "I better go," Sonny said. "He didn't even get his shirt."

They began to shuffle into shore, carrying Thad. They angled away from the nest. "How do you feel?" Eli asked his brother.

"They got my back," Thad said. "The water feels good."

Setting Thad on the beach, Sonny and Eli walked toward the nest site. Dead and crippled wasps spotted the ground around Thad's crutches. "Wow," Sonny said. "He got a bunch of them."

Carefully Eli recovered the crutches. Sonny dashed in for the shirt and leapt back down the trail, shaking it at his side. "I never even got stung," he said, watching Eli touching gingerly at his forehead. Eli tucked the crutches more securely under his arm and said nothing.

"That was pretty neat, how you got Thad," Sonny said. "Like the guy in that one war movie."

Eli shuddered. "Hey, Sonny," he whispered, "Tell Roger I didn't mean it. I never thought it'd work. Tell him I didn't mean it." He ran away from Sonny as Sonny stared at him, then hurried to follow Roger. "See you guys," Sonny called.

Eli sat down next to Thad. "Here're your

crutches." He touched a welt on Thad's thigh. "Hurt pretty bad?"

"Kind of stings now. They hurt worst right at first. I'm so used to this kind of hurting . . ." He shrugged. "How're you?"

"Me? Fine."

"They really hurt right when they get you," Thad repeated. "Thanks for getting me," he said again. "They just kept biting. I sort of forgot to get into the water."

"I kept telling you." Eli nearly cried as he remembered yelling to Thad.

"I guess I didn't hear."

"Well, why were you so close when I threw?" Eli asked. "Why weren't you way out with Max and Sonny?"

"I was trying to tell you not to."

"How couldn't he have seen us running away?"

"I don't know. But I wanted to tell you to stop because of my braces. They can't get wet. I forgot at first."

Eli stared at him, then at his braces. He had never done anything this wrong in his life. "Yeah. I forgot, too."

"Me too," Max admitted.

"Are they busted?"

"Naw. The leather's all wet though. I bet they'll rub like crazy on the way home."

"We brought your chair."

"Yeah." Thad smiled weakly. "That'll be all right."

The boys sat on the beach a long time. The sun warmed them and some of the burn faded from the stings. Eventually Thad decided their parents might have arrived at the public beach. Eli and Max stood slowly and lifted Thad. He hung loosely in his crutches. "How do we look?" he asked.

"Pretty bad," Max said. "You'll be all right though. Once you get your shirt on. Your lip looks almost regular again."

"That one on your forehead really shows," Thad told Eli.

Eli shrugged. "We'll just say we got stung some. We could tell them we stepped on a nest."

They stopped at their pile of clothes and started to dress. "Won't it look funny? You at the beach, all dressed?" Eli asked.

"I could say I got sunburned," Thad looked at Eli and grinned. "You too. They got you on the shoulders."

Eli pulled on his shirt. It rasped across the welts. He spun about at Thad's cursing.

"I hate these damn things!" Thad said, tugging at where his pants were snagged on the brace's knee joint.

Eli bent down and freed the material. "We're going to get you out of them, Thad," he said. "Remember? That's why we came here in the first place."

"That's right," Max said. "You did great walking."

But Thad refused to be placated. "I never would've got stung at all except for these stupid things." He stopped and smashed his crutch against his leg. It ricocheted off the metal.

Eli stared at his brother's legs. The wet padding and leather had soaked through his pants, outlining the braces. And I was too chicken to even pick him up, Eli told himself. Just because of some lousy wasps.

"Come on, Thad," he said, his voice quavering. "We'll get you out of those things real soon."

Eli thought of the day Thad had fallen, and the little cloud he'd kicked up, shaped like his body. He remembered wondering if that's what Thad's spirit looked like. "We'll get them off, Thad," he said. "I hate them as much as you do."

Eli stuck a crutch under each of Thad's arms and they walked to the hole in the fence. As he waited for Thad to go through, Eli hung on the fence, letting the wire dig into his fingers. He glared skyward and dared God to make his brother walk right there, right then. When Thad continued to crutch along the beach on the other side of the fence, Eli lowered his head. "God," he murmured so quietly no one could hear, "If you really were there, I'd hate you." He crawled through the hole last and walked behind Thad.

CHAPTER
TWENTY-THREE

When their parents discovered the stings, Eli told them they'd stepped on a nest. They didn't make a big deal out of it until Roger's dad called to see if everyone was all right. Roger's parents had taken Roger to the hospital claiming that you could die from too many stings — Eli wished that he had. Especially when he found out that Roger hadn't told on them. That made it worse.

Thad's screaming echoed in Eli's head and kept him awake at night. He squirmed deeper and deeper into his bed but his insides twisted with guilt and Thad's cries rang on, hurting his ears while he cowered in the lake, safe from the stinging horde.

Several times Thad asked what he was thinking about, but Eli only complained of the heat and tossed the sheet off. The yelling would continue until Eli finally dropped off.

The wasp stings healed quickly and the boys never slackened walking practices. If anything, they went out more often, any place they thought they could be alone and where the ground might be softer than other places. Thad began to walk fairly steadily without his crutches. Max always cheered then, but Eli couldn't. It wouldn't be real until the braces were gone.

He kept seeing Thad curled by the lake shore, crumpling under the wasps instead of taking a few small steps. He remembered the first time Thad brought the braces home, and the night they threw them in the closet. And by Thad's weak smiles at his new walking milestones, Eli knew Thad realized it, too. The braces hollowed everything. It wasn't real walking.

And summer was closing fast. They watched their vacation fade to two weeks. Then school would start and "the eighth grade" the nuns had talked about for seven years would swallow them. It couldn't be all they said though, not with Thad still broken.

Eli roamed the streets each night, seething with anger. He attacked the grass bags he found, but the wonderful, burning rush was gone. He almost wished he would get caught — then there'd at least be something to fight. But hoping to get caught killed the excitement of escape and Eli would return to his quiet, well-lit house, and his parents would be reading and Thad would be watching TV, too tired by his new therapy to go out at night anymore.

His parents would ask where he'd been and Eli would grunt something noncommittal, his throat tearing at the urge to scream. Everything had gone so wrong! He couldn't stand the peaceful evening-time home — Thad lying in front of the TV, lifting his foot absently in one of his useless exercises. Sometimes the braces would squeak.

Eli would flee up the stairs then, fearing he wouldn't reach the darkness of the second floor in time. Throwing himself on the bed, he'd stare at the ceiling. Simmering there, listening to the pounding of his heart and the surge of his blood in his ears, Eli would brood about how he had been fooled.

Everything downstairs was a façade. His parents read and smiled and asked the same inane questions when the real answers would only wound them deeper than Thad's back had.

"How was therapy today, Thad?" — Worthless! "Did you go to the early mass again today, Eli?" — Hell no! What for?

How could they just sit there? Even Thad. How could he lie around flexing the same worthless muscles? They couldn't even hold him up!

He pretended to read while his body trembled and he listened to them climb the steps for another night. It felt impossible, but Eli knew his head would have to clear sometime. He couldn't bear it otherwise.

As always, Thad and their parents came upstairs and the worst part of the day would follow. After listening to Thad's braces slide to the floor, Eli would turn off the lights and stare at the bathroom door, dreading the moment when the crack of light became a flood.

Eli fought hardest for the minute or two of those evening prayers. He loved his father. While the big voice rolled low over the words of the prayers, Eli would scream out all of the reasons for which he loved his father. Sometimes it would drown out the senseless droning, but other evenings, the words would burst through. '*Thy kingdom come, thy will be done . . . , Glory be to the Father and to the . . .*' And then the hatred welled in Eli. He struggled to point it at God, or whoever had made Him up, but it would lap over to the silhouetted figure in the door, so fervently spouting His words. Eli hated himself then.

When it was over, Eli's sweat soaked his sheets. His father asked him twice, and only then did Eli realize he hadn't recited the second half of the prayers.

"That's three nights in a row, Eli."

Eli swallowed, not trusting himself to speak.

"What is it, Eli? Why won't you pray with us?"

"I'm saying them to myself," he mumbled, despising himself. He turned away from the big, dark figure filling the door frame. For a long time his father was silent.

"Maybe you boys are getting too old to have me say your prayers with you." He hesitated in the doorway and then whispered good night.

When the door closed, despite the surrendering sorrow in his father's voice, Eli breathed a sigh of relief. If only it was true! If only his father wouldn't say the prayers he would never have to hate him for it again. Eli rolled over, rustling the sheets, pretending he didn't hear Thad. Although it made Eli miserable, he loved his father even more for the sadness in his voice. He scrunched his face deeper into the pillow. If only the prayers would stop torturing him every night.

He didn't want to do anything to hurt his family. When they found out about God though, it would be a hundred times worse than anything that had ever happened to them. Eli realized it would even be worse than Thad falling out of the bleachers and his hate surged back at God. He fought it down. There was no such thing, so how could he hate Him so much? But he did hate God, for the heartbreak He would eventually cause his mom and dad.

The next day Eli wandered through his route wondering why anyone would have made up something as cruel as God. And how in the world did so many people believe in Him? It was so obvious! He cast a glance to Thad, stumping along a few steps ahead of him. Boy, was it ever obvious. He shook his head.

If he had those braces he'd sure never wear shorts like Thad did.

"What're you thinking about?" Thad asked, talking loudly so he didn't have to turn around.

"Nothing."

"You've been kinda weird lately. What's the matter?"

"Nothing." Eli dropped a paper behind another screen door.

"You're always thinking about something."

"I think we got to get rid of those braces."

"Yeah. I know. What've you been doing out every night?"

"Nothing."

"Busting grass bags?"

"Yeah. But it's no fun anymore."

"Mom and Dad asked if I knew what was bothering you."

"What'd you tell them?"

"Nothing." When Eli didn't say anything else, Thad asked, "How come you stopped saying your prayers?"

"I couldn't do it anymore."

"Dad was kind of sad, I think. Couldn't you just pretend?"

"I hate it, Thad! I hate God, and there's no such thing."

Thad didn't answer and they walked a long time in silence.

"How come you don't come out at night anymore?" Eli asked. He wished he hadn't told Thad how he felt about God. All that talk only made Thad feel sorry for him.

"They're doing new stuff at therapy that kills my legs."

"Oh." Eli dropped a paper. "When's Max getting back?"

"Right before school. They went canoeing again."

"I've never been in a canoe."

"Me neither."

They looked at each other and slowly started to smile. They both knew the other had never been in a canoe. They knew everything about each other. Or they had, for a long, long time.

With the last paper gone, they stopped at the boulevard wall and Thad handed his crutches to Eli. His crutchless walk along the last block of the route had become a daily ritual.

At the end of their driveway Eli handed Thad's crutches back. "We gotta get rid of those braces."

"Yep." Thad fell into his swinging gait. "I'm going to do the route tomorrow without these," he said, indicating his crutches. "I really only use them because of therapy."

"What do you mean?" Eli asked. He couldn't believe how slow the therapists made everything.

"Just because I get so tired."

"What're you doing there anyway?" Eli asked. He'd ignored Thad's hints of a new therapy. Long ago, Eli had given up on anyone getting Thad out of his braces, beside Thad and himself.

"I'm still walking between the bars, and some new stuff. But," Thad paused and took a breath. "But I'm not wearing the braces, Eli. The whole time I'm there I don't."

Eli stopped and stared. "Why didn't you tell me?"

Thad looked away, then started moving again. "I don't know. You were weird. I didn't think you wanted to know."

"But, Thad," he said, "No braces? That's the best ever."

"I still gotta hold on to stuff, and I'm pretty shaky."

"But you were that way when you first used braces. You're walking, Thad! For real!"

Thad blushed a little. "Pretty soon."

"By school!" Eli insisted. "You gotta be walking by school!"

"That'd be great. Maybe . . ."

"Maybe, nothing!" Eli yelled. All kinds of plans burst out and they were still laughing when they went through the front door, Thad on his crutches and Eli following behind.

CHAPTER
TWENTY-FOUR

The next day Thad left his crutches at the first corner. "I'd've left them at home," he told Eli, "but Mom might've found out." He was exhausted by the end of the route but he refused Eli's halfhearted offer to retrieve the crutches early. From that day on he did the route without them. And his therapy was completely without the braces. At first he was nearly too tired to eat, but a new excitement began to grow. The change in Eli was so remarkable that their parents decided to ask no questions.

School loomed overhead, however, like a guillotine poised to cut their summer off. Eli suggested more and more daring practices until Thad finally had to back down. Then Eli fell silent, letting Thad dictate the course of their walks. Eli was working on his own confused skeleton of a plan.

On the last Friday of the summer they did the route slowly. Thad still wasn't walking — not really, and school started Monday. "You won't be able to do the route anymore, will you?" Eli asked.

"Nope. Therapy's going to move back to after school."

"That's pretty lousy."

"I know," Thad said. Then he whispered, "You know how it was when I got home today?"

"How what was?"

"You know. How Mom was always around?"

"Yeah, I guess." Eli dropped a paper behind a door.

"Well, this is the first time I could have told you."

"Told me what?"

"In therapy today," Thad said, stopping to wet his lips. "I, I didn't use the bars. I didn't use anything."

Eli stared a moment. "You mean you were walking? By yourself? No braces or bars or therapists?"

"Uh-huh." Thad's smile broke into an enormous grin.

"Without anything?"

"Nothing."

Eli whooped. "You're walking, Thad! For real walking!"

"It wasn't very steady," Thad said. "And only five steps."

"I told you, Thad! I told you we'd do it before school!"

"It's still real weak. I told them about the route though."

"You told them you weren't using crutches?" Eli interrupted. "Thad, you can't do that. You can't tell them anything."

"They thought it was great."

"But they told you not to do too much, didn't they?"

"Yeah, but they weren't mad or anything."

"Who cares?" Eli shouted, slapping Thad on the arm. "You're walking!" But when he delivered his last paper he said, "Don't tell them that stuff, Thad. They'll make you stop."

Thad shrugged and said he doubted it and Eli let it slide.

Eli could hardly sit still that night before dinner. He asked his mother twice when dinner would be ready. She smiled both times and said they'd wait for their dad to come home.

When Mr. Martin finally came home he announced that night as being the night of the traditional end-of-the-summer trip to the restaurant in the country. "The Fox and Hounds?" Thad asked excitedly and their father nodded. Then he asked, "Why what's the matter, Eli? You look like you just lost your best friend."

Eli fought down his disappointment and answered, "Nothing." He wouldn't ruin their surprise. He even managed to smile.

The drive through the rolling hills to the restaurant dragged for Eli. His father shot the car through a dip and he forced himself to laugh with Thad at the stomach-flying drop of the car. He caught his mother watching him in the mirror.

At the restaurant Eli ate handfuls of the popcorn from the big iron kettles as they waited for their table. It was dry and too salty but he knew they'd always loved the popcorn and it was what his parents wanted to see. Thad seemed to really like it. Eli was pretty sure he couldn't eat until tomorrow night was over.

During the drive home, Eli became more animated. As the moon came up, huge and orange over the farms and hills he pointed it out again and again.

"Yes," his mother said, "It's nice when it's full, Eli. Especially out in the country."

In bed, Eli waited for the bathroom door to open. It finally did, but as in the past two weeks, his father just poked his head through and said, "Say your prayers," and was gone.

When the bathroom light went out, Eli rolled over and said, "Hey, Thad, did you see that moon?"

"Uh-huh. You only talked about it a hundred times."

"Well, it's perfect. I didn't know it was full."

"Perfect for what?"

"I don't know. But it'll be neat tomorrow night. We can go out. It'll be the last time we can go out in the summer. The next night's a school night already. Do you want to go?" Eli barely got the words out he was talking so fast.

"Yeah. That'll be fun," Thad answered drowsily. He was asleep before Eli realized it. Eli rolled over and giggled. It didn't matter if Thad fell asleep on him. He was far too excited to sleep anyway. Thad had walked without his braces!

The family stayed together all day Saturday, getting several laughs out of Eli's effusive good humor. After dinner his father finally asked, "I haven't seen you this wound up in weeks, Eli. Are you really that excited to go back to school?"

Eli laughed so hard at that remark that he thought he would wet his pants. He said so. That set everyone off and Eli had to leave the room. His dad's deep, booming laugh was more than he could take. He lay on the base of the steps until his breathing was under control.

But when he returned his father was waiting for him with one of his famous faces and Eli couldn't stand it. He ran from the room, laughter pealing out of him as he shrieked, "Dad!"

When they finally settled down Eli looked at the clock and out the window, judging the amount of daylight left. He stood up slowly and asked, "Is it all right if me and Thad go out?"

"Thad and I," his mother corrected automatically. Then she smiled. "It's such a nice evening. We could all take a walk. Do you remember when we used to walk up to the drugstore, the four of us? We'd get animal crackers and you'd walk home carrying them by the string, like little lunch boxes."

Eli felt something crack inside him. They couldn't go with them. There was nothing he could say though. Not when she had that look.

"You always ate them piece by piece, Eli, identifying them first, then off with a leg or a head or something. Thad, you were a gulper." She imitated him. " 'Elephant,' you'd say, and pop, it was gone."

Thad giggled.

"But you were awfully young. I don't suppose you remember much of that."

She stood up and Eli broke into a sweat.

"Hold your horses, Mary," his father said. "This is their last night to be out painting the town. You and I'll run up to the drugstore some other time. I'm sure we wouldn't want to know half of what goes on during these nights of Eli's anyway."

His father looked at Eli and winked. Eli gaped. "Don't make it too late, Eli." He added, "Maybe we'll all walk to church in the morning."

"That would be nice," their mother said.

Eli smiled at her as he and Thad hustled from the room. "Thanks," he said, but he didn't know why.

Eli raced down the ramp outside, gulping in lungfuls of the sweet September air. He jumped around and watched Thad lurch down without his crutches. "Hills are tough," he said.

They walked down the street in the very last of the light filtering through the elms. The street lights were already on. "Where are we going?" Thad asked.

"I don't know, just out."

"You do too know," Thad said, but Eli didn't answer. "It would've been kinda nice to go out with Mom and Dad," he said, looking away. "It was fun with them today; last night, too."

"Yeah. I bet we go on a picnic tomorrow, if it doesn't rain." Eli glanced over his shoulder. "Here comes the moon."

Thad stopped and they watched the moon cresting the lake bluff. "How come it gets so small higher up?" Thad wondered out loud.

"Beats me. It'd be neat if it stayed big."

"Yeah," Thad started walking away again. "But maybe not. Then it wouldn't look so giant at first."

The darkness settled in by the time they reached Hubbard Park. They still had the old, dim lights there, spaced so far apart. In the darkness they marveled at their shadows in the moonlight. Eli threw some stones into the river and they grew quiet, watching the moon's reflection break and scatter only to come back together when the ripples flowed downstream.

"How're your legs?" Eli asked. He threw one more stone as hard as he could and turned away before it hit the black water.

"Fine. They're used to no crutches now."

Eli took a deep breath. "Do you want to go into

the old bus depot?" he asked, striving to sound nonchalant.

"The bus depot? At night?"

"It'd be neat with the moon and all."

"Yeah. OK." They started up the hill out of the park.

"It's right here," Eli said after fumbling through yards of brush looking for the trail. He held back a branch for Thad. "Are you going to be all right without your crutches in here?"

"Of course," Thad whispered. "I don't need them anymore."

When they reached the tunnel under the fence Eli pushed the plywood away carelessly. In the moonlight he could see the fresh row of splinters. It didn't matter, he thought. They wouldn't ever need this place again.

CHAPTER
TWENTY-FIVE

Eli slipped beneath the fence and helped Thad with a pull. "Hang on," Thad hissed. Eli saw him reach back and then he was through, pushing himself back up to his feet. "I tore my pants."

"Cut yourself?"

"No. It hit the brace."

"Well, you'll have to be more careful next time," Eli giggled. When Thad asked what was funny, Eli shook his head and started toward the gaping bay doors.

They stopped just inside, their feet crunching over the plaster and glass. "Wow," Thad murmured.

The moonlight streamed through the skylights in a silvery glow. Hard, black shadows crouched in every corner. The ladder shot up into the blackness beside the bright squares of light in the ceiling. "I knew it'd be like this," Eli whispered.

The moonlight was broken into individual beams by the framing in the glass. Even in the still of the night, the dust motes floated endlessly, trapped by the moonbeams. Thad stepped forward, trying to be quiet despite the crunching, gravely noise of each footstep. The echo was fearsome in the dark. "This really seems like church now."

"I knew it would," Eli said. He gazed at the silver light filtering down. He walked past Thad and stopped at the broken end of a wide piece of upright duct work. He dropped a rock into it. The hollow metallic boom was a long time in coming.

"Jeez. Where does that go?" Neither of them spoke above the slightest whisper.

"There must be some kind of super-deep basement."

"How do you get down there?"

"You can't. We looked all over." He pointed to where the ceiling had caved in. "It must've been over there."

Thad reached over and dropped a lump of debris down the duct. It clunked and echoed at the end of the fall.

"Hey, Thad," Eli whispered.

Thad turned to face him. "What?"

"We said you'd never go back to school in those braces."

"Yeah. That was right when we got out, in the spring."

"You've already walked without them at all."

"I know," he said.

Eli stayed silent.

"Do you want to do it here?" Thad asked, his whisper little more than a sigh.

Eli nodded. In the moonlight his forehead and cheeks were bright. His eyes were dark holes and his nose left a black gash of shadow across his mouth. "We've got to get rid of them forever, Thad. We've got to make it so they can never put them back on you. You got to start walking again."

"I know."

Their breathing became audible in the stillness of the depot. "But this isn't a very good place to try. There's so much junk and the light . . ."

"This is the best place! It's just like a church, you even said so. If there really is a God, we couldn't do any better. If He's there, He's got to help. There's no way anybody wouldn't." Eli spoke with such urgency that he ran out of breath.

Without saying another word, Thad sat down and slid out of his pants. He unbuckled the braces carefully, the clinking and creaking astounding in the echoing space. Eli watched the process as if he hadn't watched it hundreds of times before. He'd never have to watch it again.

Thad pushed the braces away with his feet and

pulled his pants back on. Eli knelt beside him. He reached his hand toward Thad. Thad jerked away. "If I'm going to walk by myself, I'm gonna have to get up by myself."

Eli bent down and picked up Thad's braces. They clanked against each other and Eli pressed them against his body to silence them. He took a step back, just touching the duct.

Thad clutched his fists and collected himself in a ball. His feet were flat on the ground beneath him, hidden in the shadow of his own body.

"I guess," Eli mumbled, "If you still pray like that, you know, the way you said — just talking to Him . . ."

"I already did." Thad pushed himself up and stood alone. He stared at Eli, his eyes bright in their darkened hollows.

"We got to get rid of the braces, Thad. Or else they'll just put them back on you."

"Throw them in, Eli. That's what we came here for."

Eli stood helpless a moment, stunned by the sudden force in Thad's voice. Then he lifted his eyes to the mote-filled rays of light. Trembling, he lifted his voice. "OK, God! Now prove it! Just prove it once!" He lifted the braces, daring God. "Prove it!" he yelled, hurling the braces into the hole.

His hand hit the edge of the duct but he didn't notice the pain. The braces rattled and banged on their way down. Eli didn't drop his eyes from the silvery hole in the ceiling until the noise had died. When he did, Thad was walking.

Eli left his arms at his sides, hardly daring to breathe. After the rattling crash of the braces, the silence of the room seemed magnified, cut only by Thad's heavy, controlled breathing.

Thad's back stayed straight and his legs moved like a walking person's should. Nothing like those first steps without the crutches. Eli shivered at the thought of those horrid, marionette-like lurches.

The triumphant smile that started across Eli's face collapsed. His gaze left Thad and crawled back through the shadows and floating dust to the sky-lights. If it was God, why did He wait so long? And why did He wreck Thad in the first place? Eli stared into the suddenly dazzling moonlight. *Why?*

Eli's thoughts were broken by the sound of Thad's yelp and crash. Eli leapt over to him. He could hardly believe how meager a distance Thad had traveled. He glanced upward for an instant. How could he have been fooled by a few steps?

Thad shouted Eli away. "I can do it myself!" he hissed. He crawled to his knees. In the moonlight Eli could see the plaster dust clinging to his brother's clothes. With a grunt Thad was back on his feet, swaying for a moment, then steady. His eyes were wild. "What do you expect?" he shouted, "Of course I'm going to fall! Look at this stupid place!"

His anger surprised Eli. Thad was walking again

before he could answer. "All right. So walk then," he said, but Thad tumbled and Eli bit his tongue, trying to stop the words.

He reached Thad in a single jump and was again shouted off. "I almost got it, Eli," Thad said, taking the edge off his voice. He crawled to his feet and started away again. "I just stepped on a rock is all."

But as soon as he spoke Thad fell again. Eli didn't even try to help him up. He stood where he was, at the site of the last failure.

Thad crawled in a little circle, catching his breath before he pushed his torso up and planted his legs beneath it. He was mottled everywhere with the dirty gray dust. He turned back to the duct and made four steps before stretching out headlong.

Eli bit his lip. Thad's crash sent up a small cloud of the dust, in the shape of his body. Like everything else it was silvered by the rays of light.

Thad stayed down a full minute before struggling back up. He collapsed at the first step and lay very still as the dust swirled around him.

Eli stood rooted, silently begging his brother to get up again. Thad's hoarse, ragged breathing eased slowly and even more slowly he sat up and started to stand. He fell before he was even up straight. The blood pounded in Eli's head. His face twisted with hate as he lifted his gaze to the skylight.

"I can't do it," Thad mumbled. His words cut the silence.

Eli glared at him. "Get up, Thad," he said.

Thad lifted himself onto an elbow, shaking his head wearily.

"Get up!" Eli commanded.

Thad didn't move. He didn't even turn to look when Eli ran to him.

"Get up!"

"I can't, Eli." Thad lifted his hands hopelessly. The knuckles were scraped, the blood dark against the plaster.

Eli's fists clenched and he dropped his head back and shouted. "Make him get up! Make him get up, damn You!" Eli danced in rage. "Make him get up!"

Eli crouched and looked furiously at Thad. He hadn't made the smallest effort to rise. "Get up!" Eli shrieked, inches from Thad's ear. "Walk, Thad!" He kicked Thad, hard. "Get up! You've got to walk!"

Thad let his head down till it rested on the gritty concrete floor. He pulled his knees up to his stomach in case Eli might hit him again.

But Eli sank onto his knees beside his brother. "God," he pleaded, "can't You make him walk? It's Your last chance." He lifted his face to the ceiling a final time. He squinted into the light and rested his hands on Thad.

When Thad didn't move Eli lowered his face. They stayed like that, in the moonlight, for a long time. Thad left his head on the cool concrete and Eli left his hands on Thad's side, his chin touching against his chest.

Eventually Thad lifted his head. Eli opened his

tear-filled eyes and touched Thad's face with his fingertips. "I didn't mean to kick you," he said. His voice broke.

"I know. It didn't even hurt." Thad sighed. "Nothing hurts anymore." He pushed himself into a sitting position. "This was just a bad place for it, Eli. I almost had it, but I couldn't see all the junk on the floor."

Eli sat back. They faced each other, careful not to let their eyes meet.

"It's late," Thad said. "We better go."

"Yeah."

Eli looked into Thad's eyes. They were so dull without the light in them. "How're we gonna do it?"

"I'll be OK if you help keep me steady."

"All right." Eli held his hand out for Thad and Thad pulled himself to his feet. "Couldn't you try once more, Thad?"

Thad had never looked so weary as when he shook his head. "They're just not ready."

"Couldn't you try? Maybe if you asked Him, like you do."

"He's not going to help. If He is there, that must not be what He's for, no matter what the priests say." Thad draped his right arm around Eli's shoulders. They began the long limp to the doors. Once there, they hesitated. The moonlight flooded the parking lot. Eli had forgotten how bright it was. "You didn't hurt yourself did you? Your legs?"

"No," Thad said. "They work as good as ever."

They walked through the unmercifully bright lot and crawled under the fence without bothering to replace the plywood. Eli piggybacked Thad down the trail. There wasn't enough room for them to go side by side.

Back on the streets, Thad limped beside Eli, his arm over his shoulders. As his legs grew more tired, Eli grasped him about the ribs and pulled more of his weight. Thad continued to stumble and Eli leaned farther away, his free arm swinging wide, the same way he carried heavy loads of papers.

They weren't quite halfway home when Thad asked for a rest. "Getting pretty bad?" Eli asked, lowering Thad to the grass.

"They're all trembly. Those braces held a lot of weight."

Eli stared at Thad's legs. They looked even skinnier without the braces helping to fill the pants.

Eventually Thad said, "We better go. We're already late. They're probably going to kill us."

Eli crawled up. "Probably? The only way we could've gotten away with this is if you walked home. We're dead right now. They won't even care about being late."

"Maybe we're so late they'll be in bed."

"No way," Eli grunted, pulling Thad up again.

They lurched along for a few more blocks, but Thad was fading. They started alternating blocks, one piggyback, one limping. With Thad on his back Eli asked, "Do you remember when you couldn't even wheelchair to school by yourself?"

"Yeah. That was a long time ago. We did this then. You'd push one block, I'd push the next."

"Yeah. Then you did it again when you started crutching." Eli didn't explain more. His breathing was too labored to talk.

Thad kept talking as Eli staggered along. His face was right next to Eli's ear and he whispered. "Yeah, you helped the whole time. Pushing me around and carrying my crutches before Dad made the rack. You even helped when I fell, getting me to the ambulance. You and Max. And you saved me from the wasps."

Eli only gasped, "Shut up."

"It's true," Thad said. "You did all that. I never had to ask. Never once had to ring that bell Dad got. Remember that?"

Eli chuckled and put Thad down. They waited at the corner until Eli's sweat dried. "Half that stuff was my fault, Thad," he said at last.

"Naw. The one thing I figured out is that nothing's anybody's fault." Thad crawled up, beginning to giggle. Eli helped him the rest of the way and they started walking again, pulling hard on one another.

"We did it this time, Eli," Thad said, laughing. "Threw the stupid things away!"

Eli didn't laugh. "We had to."

"I know. But nobody else is going to. I just wish we hadn't tried it there. That was impossible."

Eli knew that, too. "You said it was a good spot."

"I was wrong. It was good for you and your God stuff. But it was terrible for me. And you don't know anything more about God. Nobody'll ever know anything about that. That's the other thing I figured out. I wished we'd tried someplace else."

"I know about God. For sure now, Thad."

"Yeah, but we don't know if I can walk, do we?"

Eli carried Thad the last block and up to their front door. He tripped on the ramp and bit his lips at the pain in his knees. He could feel open skin under his pants. "You got to walk in, Thad," he said. "You can hang on to the railing going upstairs."

"There's only one light on. Maybe they went to bed."

Eli held his breath and opened the door.

Their parents weren't in the living room. Eli could hardly believe it. He crawled up the steps and peeked at their door. Then he hurried back for Thad. "Come on." He helped pull Thad upstairs. Surprisingly, with the railing, the steps were easier than walking. "The light's on, but their door's shut."

They made it up the stairs and past their parents' door. They slid into their room before they began to breathe again. Thad crawled quickly into his bed and Eli hustled to the hall bathroom. He brushed his teeth twice, once for Thad, in case his parents were listening.

On his way back, the light flicked off in his parents' room and the door opened. Eli jumped in surprise. "You two are late," his mother said. Eli couldn't see her in the darkness. "I know," he said dumbly.

"Get to bed now. You've got your route in the morning." He heard her door close and he went shakily back to his room.

"Mom's awake," he said after he got into bed.

"I heard."

"We're gonna get it tomorrow."

"I know," Thad sighed. Eli remembered Thad's raw, blistered hands and his pulled muscles and the wasps and the clouds of plaster dust he'd puffed into the moonlight.

When he did start walking again, Eli thought, he'd be surprised if Thad didn't just walk away from him.

CHAPTER
TWENTY-SIX

As Eli walked his route the next morning he knew he would never be lonelier. Thad had accompanied him almost every day during the summer, but he couldn't that morning, except in his wheelchair. And he'd refused to do that. Eli wondered what his parents would do to him. It probably wouldn't be bad enough.

During the long walk, Eli realized that his hate was gone. He had proof now that God didn't exist. Despite what he'd told himself earlier, he'd never been so positive. Eli found it impossible to hate Him now that he knew for sure He was something that had been made up. God hadn't abandoned Thad last night in the old depot. No real God would have done that.

As Eli pulled his wagon home he heard the mourning dove call. His throat tightened but he was able to call back. The dove answered and Eli shut his eyes for a moment. Thad had been right. It was the sad kind of mourning.

Eli parked the wagon in the garage and crept through the back door. He circuited the house once in its strange emptiness, then crawled over the couch and lay on the cool tiles of the radiator cover. He put his chin on his crossed forearms and tried to stop thinking once and for all.

He was still there when his mother came down to fix the coffee. He listened to her work and did not focus his eyes on anything. She surprised him when she said his name so close. He turned his face slowly and focused.

"You must be tired," she said.

Eli shrugged and followed her back into the kitchen. He heard his dad coming down the stairs.

"Didn't Thad help you this morning?"

Eli slid onto his bench. "Nope."

"Good morning," his father said. "You two were out late last night. What trouble did you get into?"

Eli shrugged again. He felt as if he might dry up and turn to dust right there.

"Is he still in bed, the lazybones?" his father said. "We got up early so we could all walk to church together."

"Thad can't walk to church," Eli said quietly. He

stared at what he figured was the absolute center of the table.

"Well, crutch, or whatever he calls it."

"He can't do that either," Eli said.

"Why not?" His father stopped and turned to look at him.

"Because we threw away his crummy braces."

"What do you mean?" his mother asked quietly.

"I mean he can't walk to church." Eli swallowed, still trying to find the exact center. "Neither can I."

"Why not?"

In the corner of his eye Eli saw his parents move together on the other side of the table — standing together, watching him. "'Cause it's too wrong." His voice trembled but he still had it under control.

"Church is?"

Eli nodded.

"Why is church wrong?"

"Because it's all lies." Eli gave up. He lowered his head to look at his hands. A tiny piece of skin hung from where he'd cut himself on the duct at the depot. He pulled it off and rolled it between his thumb and forefinger.

"Church is all lies?" his father whispered.

"Uh-huh." Eli drew in a breath that quavered audibly. "I didn't want to tell you. I knew it would hurt your feelings. But there's no such thing as God. You guys got fooled just like me." Eli ducked his head. "Sorry."

"How do you know?" his mother asked. Eli saw

that his parents were holding hands. They never did that.

"Because we threw Thad's braces down the hole. Thad even prayed. He still couldn't walk."

Eli flinched when his mother slid onto the bench next to him and put her arm around him. He heard his father pull out his chair and sit down across the table. He hadn't realized he was trembling until he felt his shoulders under his mother's touch.

"What hole?" his father asked.

"You can't get them," Eli said. "You can't ever put them back on him."

"But, Eli . . ."

Eli stiffened in his mother's embrace. "And I'm not going to church anymore. I can't."

"Now, Eli," his father started firmly, but his mother signaled for silence. She rocked gently with her son. "You're all confused, Eli."

"I am not!" Eli's voice rose. "It's so obvious!"

"Just because Thad couldn't walk when you wanted him to doesn't mean that there is no God, Eli."

"It's not just that. There isn't any God though," Eli said, shaking his head. "That just proves it."

"What else then, Eli?" his father asked. "Is this why you wouldn't say prayers?"

Eli nodded. "I can't anymore."

"But, Eli . . ."

"You guys!" he pleaded, his voice cracking. "It's all made up! You don't go to heaven. Nobody listens to your prayers. Nobody helps you when you need it. Nobody lives in church. Nobody does any of that! It just all got made up!" He ended breathlessly. "I'm sorry. I didn't want you to find out."

"Poor Eli," his mother started to soothe.

Eli sat straight. "There's nothing wrong with me! Thad proves it!" His voice rose uncontrollably. "He proves everything!"

"But he's going to be better, Eli. Don't you think we should thank God for that?"

"Who should we thank for making him fall? Or for making him hurt all the time? Should we thank God for that? How much sense would that make?"

"It is hard to understand," his father said.

Eli raised his head and glared at his father. "No it's not! Just say once that God's a fake! Then there isn't anything left to understand!"

"But that's the one thing we can't say, Eli," his father answered. His face twitched as he struggled to stay calm.

"You have to!" Eli yelled. He was losing it as he knew he would. Soon he'd be unable to speak at all.

"You can't! That's our faith!"

"Well, it doesn't make any sense then!" Eli hollered over his mother's warning to his father. "How are you supposed to believe in something so wrong? Something that's supposed to do good but only hurts everybody who believes in it? How are you supposed to believe in something you aren't even allowed to think about? Talk about *not* making sense!"

Eli couldn't say another word. His vision flashed black and red as the rage finally tumbled out. His mother reached across the table and put her hand over his father's forearm, but Eli didn't see it. He fought to get off the bench. His father hesitated and took a very narrow breath. "We can't explain what He does," he said, his own voice catching.

"Neither can I," Thad called.

His parents turned at the sound of Thad's voice. Eli let his head sink lower yet. He felt one of the tears of frustration he had held back so long roll down his cheek. It didn't make any difference anymore.

Thad walked through the doorway and into the kitchen. "Hey, Eli," he said, ignoring his parents' stares. "Look."

Eli lifted his eyes. Thad wasn't holding on to anything. His legs looked like toothpicks in the short, flimsy pajamas. Thad took two more steps.

Eli smiled cautiously and wiped at the tear. He saw the tense concentration in his brother's face. Thad walked behind his father, then turned, tottering for a second, and walked back. He licked his lips and stared at Eli. The concentration melted off his face and he grinned hugely. "It was just all that junk on the floor. I kept tripping."

Their father leapt out of his chair and swept Thad up in his arms, hugging him to his chest.

"I told you," Eli mumbled. He started to laugh,

but it came out strangely like a cry. "I told you!" he yelled triumphantly. He struggled away from his mother and stood on the bench. "I told you!"

Their mother eased off the bench and joined Thad and their father. "Thank God!" she said.

"That's not God!" Eli yelled, "That's Thad!" Thad twisted his head over his father's shoulder and grinned.

ABOUT THE AUTHOR

Pete Fromm grew up in Milwaukee, Wisconsin, before moving to Montana at the age of seventeen. His book, *Indian Creek Chronicles*, tells of the winter he spent alone in a tent in the Idaho wilderness, guarding two million salmon eggs. After that winter he worked as a lifeguard in the desert and a ranger on the Snake River before turning to writing full time. Mr. Fromm now lives in Great Falls, Montana. This is his first book for Scholastic Hardcover.